MURDER AT A COUNTRY HOUSE

A 1920s Cozy Mystery

A Lady Felicity Quick Mystery
Book 2

ROSIE HUNT

ISBN: 9789083290614

Editing by Effie Wilson

Cover art by DLR Cover Designs

For my father and his love of fiendish puzzles.

It's a love we share.

A Note on Language

This book is written in British English. There are two reasons for this:

- the story is set in England, and
- I, the author, am British.

Part of my British writing style is the use of s where z is used in American English. For example: agonise instead of agonize, and maximise instead of maximize.

However, you may have noticed that in the blurbs and marketing for this book, it's called a cozy mystery and not a cosy mystery.

This is because the American spelling is standard for the genre. Spelling it this way helps people (and algorithms) recognise my book more easily.

But outside of book genres, it's cosy all the way.

Cast of Characters

Quick family

Lady Felicity Quick, journalist

Lord Jasper Quick, Earl of Denbury, editor-in-chief of the Western Daily News and Felicity's brother

Lady Henrietta Quick, Dowager Countess of Denbury, grandmother to Felicity and Jasper

Pip, Felicity's Yorkshire Terrier

Langton household

Lord Edward Langton, Viscount of Exridge, businessman

Lord Derek Langton, son of Lord Edward Langton

The Honourable Miss Ursula Langton, daughter of Lord Edward Langton

The Honourable Mrs Clarissa Ridgeway, sister to Lord Edward Langton

Mr Oswald Ridgeway, son of Clarissa and nephew of Lord Edward Langton

Mrs Frida Ridgeway, wife to Oswald

Master James Ridgeway, son of Oswald and Frida

Mr Sebastian Ridgeway, brother to Oswald

Charlotte, Clarissa's Pomeranian

Mollie, Lord Edward Langton's mastiff

Staff

Miss Beatrice Pearce, secretary to Lord Jasper Quick

Mr Jacob Cherry, secretary to Lord Edward Langton

Miss Liliane Blanchard, companion to Clarissa

Miss Mabel Daniels, nursemaid to James

Mr Robert Crowther, butler at Langton Manor

Mr John Greenwood, valet to Lord Edward Langton

Mr Thomas Clegg, former valet to Lord Edward Langton

Mr Joseph Evans, footman at Langton Manor

Others

Miss Elodie Rossignol, singer

Mr Alexander Cooper, reporter for the Western Daily News

Mr George Palmer, solicitor

Chief Inspector Luscombe, police detective

Extract from the Western Daily News, 1921

Death and Deceit at Langton Manor

Eyewitness accounts and exclusive interviews from the scene of the crime!

NORTH EXRIDGE, September 29 — When thick fog hampered police attempts to attend a call for assistance at the home of Lord Edward Langton, Viscount of Exridge, the consequences were diabolical. In its seven-hundred years of history, the East Devon estate of Langton Manor has never witnessed as much intrigue and murderous mayhem as it did yesterday.

This newspaper's extensive account of the calamitous occurrences at Langton Manor is unique, because our own journalists were present and bore witness to the fateful events described in these pages.

Chapter One

OFFICES OF THE WESTERN DAILY NEWS, EXETER, EAST DEVON, 27 SEPTEMBER 1921

The high-ceilinged, smoke-fugged headquarters of southwest England's most-read newspaper contained a special sort of energy. The chatter of rows of reporters, typists, and clerks crammed behind a labyrinth of desks rose only slightly above the clatter of dozens of typewriters. Telephones rang. Messenger boys dashed about.

To the untrained eye, it was chaos.

But to a seasoned insider like Lady Felicity Quick, who surveyed the scene from a fine office chair upholstered in green leather, it was an efficient machine, every element of the tumult brimming with purpose.

Felicity joined the ranks of the Western Daily News two years ago as a writer for the society pages. Three months ago, she became a fully fledged news reporter.

Working for the paper founded by her grandfather in the Victorian era had been a childhood dream, and it thrilled her still. Most of the time.

"Cici?"

Lord Jasper Quick — Earl of Denbury, editor-in-chief of the Western Daily News, and Felicity's older brother — had risen, crossed the short distance between his desk and his office door, and yanked a dark yellow blind over the door's window, obscuring Felicity's view of the busy editorial office.

Felicity flicked her attention back to her brother.

Retaking his seat behind his oak desk with its red leather inlay, Jasper looked smart but not overly dapper in a finely tailored three-piece suit in dark blue flannel. Both his office and his desk at the newspaper were smaller than his facilities at Bradley Court, the historic family home nestled among East Devon's rolling green hills, where Felicity and Jasper lived with their grandmother.

But the Western Daily News was growing. Felicity and Jasper's late father, himself once also editor-in-chief of the title, would have been proud of Jasper's achievements, even if he would never have approved of Felicity becoming a reporter.

Jasper had refused to give up the red-brick Victorian building at the heart of the ancient city of Exeter. It had been the Western Daily News' headquarters since the newspaper's founding in 1858. But while he'd given up desk size and floor space, Jasper hadn't given up any of his commanding attitude, which befitted a busy and successful editor-in-chief who was not only Felicity's brother. He was also her boss.

Felicity held her brother's gaze as he attempted to suppress a scowl from the other side of the desk. Behind Jasper, a tall sash window framed the cathedral's stocky towers against a bright blue sky. Entering via an opening at the top of the window, a faintly cool autumnal breeze lifted the edge of some papers in a wire basket on Jasper's desk and played with the billowed sleeves of Felicity's smoky blue crepe de chine day dress.

Jasper twitched his chestnut-coloured moustache. "I asked you a question."

"I do realise that."

While Felicity's reply wasn't a lie, her brother having just informed her of the fact, she couldn't recall the question.

Jasper dipped his chin. "Is that a promise, then?"

Felicity hesitated. Crucial information was lacking, but she would take the plunge. It carried less risk than admitting she hadn't been listening.

"Yes," she said with a confident nod, her auburn curls bouncing at her cheeks.

Jasper's eyes narrowed. "And what, dear sister, have you just promised?"

Felicity's Yorkshire Terrier, Pip, was usually to be found on Felicity's lap, and that instance was no exception. The little dog shifted on Felicity's knees and lifted his tufted blue-and-tan head towards Jasper, preparing to act in his mistress's defence.

Employing irritation as a cover for the embarrassment at having been caught out, Felicity drew her eyebrows together. "Why shouldn't I promise to do whatever you, dear brother, ask of me?"

Jasper shook his head, a scowl now fully formed on his brow. "Oh, dash it all, Cici. I'm not sure why I even bother. You're thoroughly terrible at keeping your promises to me anyhow."

Felicity ran a hand over Pip's silky back to steady both the little Yorkie's nerves and her own. "You forbade me from reporting on crime and from getting myself into any kind of trouble. Haven't I done exactly that?"

Jasper shook his head again, slowly this time. "One doesn't easily forget one's own sister being in mortal danger. I came back from the Western Front imagining I'd put all that kind of thing behind me."

Felicity shifted uneasily in her chair, steadying Pip with both hands. She hated upsetting Jasper. She hated upsetting anyone dear to her, but she couldn't allow her actions to go undefended. "I was simply in the wrong place at the wrong time at Wolborne House. And as for the Reeves affair, I'd taken all the necessary precautions."

Jasper huffed, then went quiet. "I suppose you have been rather well-behaved since then."

Felicity smiled thinly. Her brother's concern for her was deeply touching. Not everyone was lucky enough to have a loving family. Defending oneself repeatedly was, however, tiring, especially when Felicity had no opportunity to be anything but well-behaved.

In recent months, Jasper had given her only the dullest of stories.

Once, she was sent to report on the opening of a shop dedicated to equipment for the maintenance of apple trees. Another time, she fell asleep in the middle of the day while proofreading a piece she'd written about a new museum dedicated to an extensive private collection of fishing weights.

Other reporters covered far more interesting stories. One journalist in particular got the best of the lot.

He'd been with the paper only a matter of months and while he had published nothing recently, he usually covered all the major crime stories. He also wrote splendidly well.

Felicity felt pangs of jealousy when reading his work, then grew angry at herself for her envy, because she had no right to bear any ill will towards Alex Cooper. He was the newspaper's star reporter for good reason, a close friend of Felicity's brother, and — most devastatingly of all — a thoroughly decent chap who had come to Felicity's rescue more than once.

Jasper sighed as he leaned forward and plucked an elegant pipe from the silver stand on his desk. "If only old Coop was being as well-behaved as you. I'm afraid he's been rather the opposite recently."

"Alex?" The mention of him took Felicity by surprise, as though her thoughts had been plucked from her mind. She frowned as she tried to imagine Alex being anything other than well-behaved. "What has he done?"

Jasper lit his pipe, silky white clouds lifting towards the open window. "Coop plays his cards close to his chest these days. Won't tell me what he's up to. I trust him, you understand, but I don't much like it. He's not been in Devon long. Hope he hasn't got mixed up in the wrong kind of business."

Felicity hid a smile as she stroked Pip. "Alex relocated to Devon from London. I rather doubt our local villains have much on the hardened criminals of the capital."

Jasper puffed rapidly on his pipe. "Doesn't take much to put a chap on the wrong track these days."

Felicity had met Alex for the first time three months ago, but she hadn't seen him in weeks. He was never about when Felicity came to the newspaper's offices. This left her both relieved and disappointed, because despite an inexplicable urge to speak to him, she had no clue what to say. They couldn't be classed as friends, and although they were colleagues, she and Alex didn't really work together. She certainly had no right to pry into his private life.

"Returning to that promise I made you," said Felicity, caressing Pip's tufted ears.

Jasper gnawed a little on his pipe. "You've confirmed your attendance at Langton Manor tomorrow, have you not?"

Felicity nodded without enthusiasm. The purpose of her meeting with Jasper was to collect information on the assignment, but it was clearly another duller-than-dull story saved just for her.

Jasper sighed deeply. "I asked you to promise me that should Lord Derek Langton be present, you'll keep a polite but definite distance from the chap."

Felicity considered the request. "Isn't he Lord Langton's son?"

"Indeed. He'll most likely be up in London mixing with his usual dubious crowd, but he's a bad lot these days, by all accounts."

"I shan't mix with any bad lots, whether sons of viscounts or otherwise. You can count on that." And Felicity meant it.

Despite life as a news reporter being so far less interesting than expected, Felicity remained determined to build her career. She was also keen not to disappoint Jasper. After all, he'd given her the chance to become a journalist.

"Glad to hear it," said Jasper, with a satisfied puff of pipe smoke. "You're to interview Lord Langton and his nephew, Oswald Ridgeway. Played golf with them before the summer. Both very sensible fellows. Very business-minded."

As her brother spoke, Felicity reached into her pocket for her trusty notebook. Without disturbing Pip, who preferred not to have his back used as a notepad rest, she jotted down the details Jasper shared with her. 'Sensible' and 'business-minded' typically meant boring, but Felicity didn't write that.

Jasper continued. "Oswald is Lord Langton's sister's boy. Complete opposite of Derek. That's why Lord Langton has him lined up as his successor for the business side of things. Had Teddy survived the war, I doubt any of it would have been necessary. He was a thoroughly capable sort, poor chap."

Felicity paused her note-taking. "Teddy?"

"Lord Langton's eldest son. Nothing to be done about the title and the estate, of course. That all goes to Derek. But Oswald will inherit the business portfolio Lord Langton's built up over the years. Transport, mining, heavy industry. You name it. All across the Empire. Lord Langton doesn't want it squandered on parties and gifts for female acquaintances when he passes on."

Felicity squinted at her notes. "And I'm to write about what, exactly?"

"The article should capture Lord Langton's explanation of the transition, which will no doubt skirt around his surviving son's capabilities, or lack thereof. The piece should also raise Oswald's profile, positioning him as a capable successor on the business front."

Felicity suppressed a yawn as she continued to take notes in brisk Pitman shorthand. If she could remain well-behaved for long enough, she would again approach Jasper about crime reporting. Just minor misdeeds at first. A snatched purse or a stolen motor—

"Questions, Cici?"

Felicity snapped out of her reverie. Before she could muster the wherewithal to bluff through her daydreaming and pose a question, there was a sharp tap at the office door.

"Who the deuce..." muttered Jasper between puffs on his pipe. "Come in."

A neat little freckle-nosed secretary in an emerald-green blouse and grey checked skirt stepped into the room, a pad and pencil in her hand. The clatter of typewriters and smell of cigarette smoke entered with her before she closed the door.

"You asked me to come at four o'clock, sir," she said, using Jasper's preferred form of address at the newspaper offices. 'Lord' created too much distance from his employees when Jasper himself was an experienced journalist. "You said you needed to dictate a letter, sir. It's four o'clock now."

Jasper tapped his pipe into a heavy crystal ashtray in a distinctly grumpy manner. "As you can see, Miss Pearce, my sister and I are not yet finished. Would you be kind enough to return in fifteen minutes?"

But Felicity was already tucking her notepad back into her pocket, unsure she'd be able to stay awake through a further fifteen minutes of discussing Lord Langton's business interests, only to hear it all again during the interview the next day.

She scooped Pip under her arm as she stood. "Oh, I believe we're finished. I have some other tasks to attend to here in town."

The tasks involved the trying on and possible purchase of shoes at a boutique overlooking the cathedral green. The boutique closed at five o'clock, but there was no need to alert either her brother or his secretary to that level of detail.

Miss Pearce appeared a little younger than Felicity, perhaps eighteen or nineteen. Her dark eyes sparkled. "Are you Lady Felicity Quick?"

"Please, Miss Pearce." Jasper drew his eyebrows together as he stood. "I'm really rather busy. You might find another time to—"

"I read all your articles," said the young secretary, who either had no fear of defying her boss or was so awestruck by Felicity she hadn't heard him. "You're a wonderful writer, your ladyship."

"Why, thank you, Miss Pearce." It never failed to delight Felicity when her writing brought pleasure to people. "How extremely kind of you to say."

Jasper rolled his eyes but offered no further protest.

"And you solved that murder case at Lower Diddleton, didn't you, your ladyship?"

Jasper's posture snapped taut. "Miss Pearce, really. I must insist—"

"I'm terribly sorry to disappoint you." Felicity spoke quickly and firmly, alert to her brother's sensitivities. "But that's simply not true. I got rather caught up in things, that's all. I didn't do any solving whatever."

Jasper pressed his hands into his waistcoat pockets. “My sister is a journalist, Miss Pearce, not a detective.”

“I do know that, sir.” Miss Pearce’s shining eyes switched between Felicity and Jasper. “But it’s what everyone around the office says, you see. That Lady Felicity and Mr Cooper solved the case.”

Thunder clouds gathered behind Jasper’s eyes. “They say that, do they?”

“It was awfully nice meeting you, Miss Pearce.” Felicity spoke with a lightness she hoped offset her brother’s deep scowl and distracted from the awkwardness she felt at Miss Pearce’s mention of Alex, for it had been in Lower Diddleton that they’d last seen one another.

“Likewise, your ladyship,” said the secretary with a little smile and a polite nod.

Felicity turned to her brother. “Will I see you at dinner?”

“No.” Jasper was still scowling. “I’m travelling to Bristol tonight, but I should be back tomorrow afternoon. The weather’s not looking too clever tomorrow morning, Cici. Have Finnegan run you over to Langton Manor.”

“Oh, I doubt that’ll be necessary.” With Pip firmly under her arm, Felicity opened the office door to the clatter of typewriters. “And please, Jasper, don’t worry yourself. I shan’t get myself mixed up in anything I shouldn’t.”

Chapter Two

THE ROAD BETWEEN BRADLEY COURT AND LANGTON MANOR, EAST DEVON, 28 SEPTEMBER 1921

Since Felicity had learned to drive a matter of weeks ago, spinning along Devon's country lanes in her two-seater Alvis saloon had become one of her favourite things. Her motor had sparkling cream coachwork and comfortable tan leather seats, and it was easy to lose oneself in one's thoughts while driving. The experience was especially glorious when the sun was shining, the thoroughfare was wide — she was still a new driver — and the road's surface was not too bumpy, which was better for both Felicity and Pip.

The little Yorkie sat on the passenger seat in a domed wicker basket furnished with a red velvet cushion. A stiff breeze tussled the fur on his ears and chest, and his little black nose twitched as he processed the scents whizzing past. Prior to introducing the travelling basket, a nasty bump in the road to Sweetbrooke nearly sent Pip flying out of the open window. Felicity shuddered to think of it.

"Do you remember that awful incident, Pip?" she said, raising her voice above the whirr of the Alvis's engine. "Quite the trauma, wasn't it?"

Pip yipped angrily, as if asking Felicity not to remind him.

She tapped the top of his basket reassuringly. "Don't worry. I'll not let anything similar happen again."

For so late in September, they were lucky with the weather, as yet another beautiful blue sky stretched across East Devon. Langton Manor was not a vast distance from Bradley Court, but it lay closer to Dartmoor, with North Exridge its nearest village. Despite the onset of autumn, the dense hedgerows lining the roads were still mostly green. The air smelt faintly of cut grass and had only a slight chill to it.

But while Jasper might have been wrong about the morning's weather, Felicity was determined to be mindful of the rest of his concerns. With her hands on the steering wheel and her eyes on the steeply climbing road ahead, she swore to herself that no matter how dull it was bound to be, Felicity would do her utmost when interviewing Lord Langton and his nephew. She would do so not just for Jasper, but for her career.

Reaching the top of the hill, a sweeping view of the countryside appeared like a sudden miracle. The River Exe sparkled silver in a softly undulating green valley. The rugged peaks of the moors rose in the distance, draped with a fluffy scarf of fog. Closer at hand was a huddle of roofs in blond wheat-reed thatch that made up the village of North Exridge. Beyond the village was Langton Manor, a historic country house, its tree-edged lake shimmering in the sunshine.

The beauty of her home county never ceased to move Felicity, but her heart fell a little when she remembered what lay ahead. Business-minded as he was, she doubted Lord Langton would be the kind of host to give her a tour of the estate's formal gardens or show her his family's collection of antique Chinese vases, of which his deceased wife had apparently been a collector.

But by the time Felicity reached Langton Manor's long, beech-lined driveway, she'd steeled herself. There was no point complaining, even inwardly. Her dissatisfaction with her current role wasn't the fault of Lord Langton, his nephew, or anyone else at Langton Manor. She was there to do a job, and that was that.

She was also precisely on time for her appointment, which meant there could be no dallying.

The tyres of Felicity's Alvis crunched on gold-coloured gravel as she drew up at the front of the great house. Langton Manor's facade was mainly red brick and of early Georgian design. Two sturdy wings, one on either side, had been covered with lime stucco then allowed to be blanketed in climbing plants, the dark green foliage of which rippled in the breeze.

Felicity took only the briefest of moments to check her appearance in her motor's mirror. Her dove-grey musketeer hat was still in place and her auburn ringlets didn't look too windswept, but the collar of her dove-grey top-coat and that of her peach blouse needed to be straightened, as was so often the case after a spin in the motor.

As she descended from her vehicle, she was met by a sharp-nosed, grey-haired butler and a young, thick-set footman. They were positioned in an orderly manner at the bottom of Langton Manor's front steps.

"Good morning, Lady Felicity." The butler spoke swiftly and confidently, as most butlers were wont. "His lordship apologises that he's unable to greet you directly. We're to bring you to his lordship's study, where he will join you presently."

Felicity had rounded her vehicle and was assisting Pip to the ground to stretch his legs. "Thank you," she said, smiling politely at the servant. "I've no objection to that."

She had to trust that a sensible businessman such as Lord Langton wouldn't leave her waiting for long. Without being rude about it, Felicity was rather keen to get the interview done and be on her way. She had no desire to hear a single word about investments in heavy industry than was strictly necessary for her article.

The butler glanced impassively downwards as Pip gave the man's shiny black shoes an intense sniffing. Felicity had tried leaving Pip at home while attending professional engagements. It had taught her that Pip's absence distracted her more than his presence. She could therefore tolerate a certain amount of awkwardly canine behaviour, and on the whole, there were more people passionate about dogs than unenthusiastic about them.

The butler returned his gaze to Felicity. “Might we assist you, your ladyship?”

“I’ve my photography equipment with me,” she replied, gesturing towards the rear of her motor as Pip trotted towards a narrow border of yellow-headed rudbeckia and honey-scented buddleja. Unlike her grandmother, Felicity wasn’t a keen gardener, but she knew enough to question the hydration value dogs brought to plants. Thankfully, Pip was only small.

The butler — who either didn’t notice or was unmoved by the business to which the little Yorkie was attending — gave a nod to the footman, and the younger man set about unstrapping the white leather camera case from the rear of the Alvis.

“If you’d be so kind as to please follow me, your ladyship,” said the butler, “I’ll accompany you to his lordship’s study.”

“By all means.”

Felicity began her ascent of Langton Manor’s lichen-splotched granite stairs. In doing so, she secretly admired her new grey one-strap shoes with their Spanish heel bought just the day before in Exeter. As they approached the manor’s main entrance, the butler ahead of Felicity and the footman carrying the camera equipment behind them, Pip came racing up the stairs. His little paws clattered on the stone steps as he sped in front of Felicity, which was always his preferred position.

But upon reaching the top of the stairs, the Yorkie stopped abruptly and yapped, his tail wagging hard.

“Pip, really.” Felicity scolded only lightly, for the little dog rarely barked without good reason. “What’s got into you?” But as she reached the top step, all became clear.

Before a pair of vast oak doors stood a black Pomeranian dog. It was approximately the size of Pip, although its true dimensions were obscured by a large amount of dense, fluffy fur, which fanned out in all directions. The Pom’s tail wagged vigorously, and its black eyes shone.

Pip ceased barking and advanced until he came nose-to-nose with the little black dog. There was sniffing, some footwork not unlike an old-fashioned Quadrille, and after a series of excited yips, the two little dogs entered a tumble of play together.

"Charlotte, please. That's no way to treat a guest."

The rich voice full of reproach belonged to a woman in her sixties who had emerged from the double doors. She had bright blonde hair arranged in curls at her temples and leaned on a black silver-topped cane. She was large, both in height and in girth, although a voluminous dress in black gauzy fabric embellished with tiny silver beads made it difficult to guess her exact size.

Her hand trembling a little as she pressed on her cane, the large blonde woman reached down and scooped Charlotte up, the stones of the woman's necklace and bracelets clacking as she did so. With the Pomeranian tucked safely under a fold of black fabric at her side, the blonde woman peered down at Pip with inquisitive, kohl-lined eyes.

"And who might this be?" she asked.

Pip continued to wag his tail and barked twice, disappointed that his new playmate had been snatched from him.

"Lady Felicity Quick, ma'am," said the butler. "Of the Western Daily News."

The blonde woman looked from Pip to Felicity, her face filling with delight. "Oh, of course. How simply wonderful. You must be here for the party. Sebastian is such a dear child. He thinks of absolutely everything."

Felicity smiled in a way she hoped communicated curiosity but also confusion. "The party?"

"Aren't you here to write a piece about it? It's going to be quite the event." The woman batted mascaraed eyelashes. "It's my party, you see."

Felicity continued to stare a little blankly at the woman. "And you are? If you don't mind me asking, of course."

"Oh, how frightfully, frightfully rude of me. I'm the Honourable Mrs Clarissa Ridgeway, sister to Lord Edward Langton, Viscount of Exridge. Today's my birthday. Surely, Sebastian told you?"

Pip let out another frustrated yap. In a bid to silence him, Felicity bent down and picked him up. The little Yorkie went quiet, but his tail continued to wag forcefully as he was again at eye level with his new friend. The sparkle of the Pom's eager gaze was only just distinguishable from the twinkle of the beads on her mistress's dress.

Felicity cleared her throat. "I'm awfully sorry, Mrs Ridgeway, but there seems to have been something of a mix-up." She was confident in saying this. A party sounded infinitely more interesting than a business interview, and Jasper had another writer for the newspaper's society pages.

The butler concurred, speaking in low tones to Clarissa Ridgeway. "Lady Felicity is to interview Lord Langton and your son, ma'am."

"Oswald is to be interviewed?" said Clarissa, the sparkle of excitement disappearing from her greyish hazel eyes with several blinks. "Quite. Well." She straightened a little and regarded Felicity with a businesslike air. "I suppose a woman can engage in whatever work she believes herself capable of these days. Although I must say, it's unlike Oswald or my brother to consider something as clever as contacting the papers. Do come with me, Lady Felicity."

The large blonde woman turned and tapped away with her cane, Charlotte's still-wagging tail sending ripples across the back of her beaded dress as she disappeared inside Langton Manor.

Felicity glanced at the butler. His eyebrows moved upwards almost imperceptibly, but it was enough for Felicity to understand that plans for her visit were becoming derailed. With any hope of getting things done quickly fading fast, Felicity followed Clarissa Ridgeway through Langton Manor's imposing oak doors.

Chapter Three

Langton Manor's entrance hall was larger and much grander than Bradley Court's.

Family forebears stared down from ornately framed portraits wherever one turned. There were two suits of armour, the obligatory grandfather clock, and an array of antique swords arranged in a fan above the front entrance. Four enormous flower displays featuring bright white roses and strong-smelling pink-tongued lilies stood on elegant wrought-iron stands beside the central stairway, hinting at the birthday celebrations already mentioned.

The stairway was carved in dark-stained wood and fitted with plush red carpet that led up to a central landing overseen by patterned glass in blue, yellow, and green. From there, the staircase split in two, its flights and landings framing the entrance hall with heavy wooden balustrades.

While the stairs were carpeted, the granite flagstones of the entrance hall floor were not. It gave the grand space a chilly feel, and Clarissa's cane tapped steadily as she crossed the room, as did the heels of Felicity's one-strap shoes. The butler and the footman moved silently.

"It would be best for you to wait with me in the morning room, Lady Felicity." Clarissa Ridgeway spoke without turning towards

Felicity. "It would be a great pity to have the dullness of my brother's business interests be your only lasting memory of Langton Manor." Out of respect for Lord Langton, Felicity could only silently concur, and her fondness for the large blonde woman grew. "Crowther, fetch my brother or my son, whichever you find first. It's not kind to leave Lady Felicity waiting."

"Very well, ma'am," replied the butler, but his departure was waylaid by the approach of rapid, purposeful footsteps.

A man of around thirty in a brown pinstriped suit with a two-button jacket appeared from a corridor tucked underneath the staircase. He had dark hair, tightly held broad shoulders, and darting eyes behind gold-framed spectacles. "Y-you must be Lady Felicity." It was immediately obvious he had something of a stammer. "Terribly sorry to have k-kept you waiting. Lord Langton should arrive in his study at any moment. Please, allow me to accompany you there d-directly."

Despite all hope of conducting the interview promptly having now disappeared, Felicity smiled politely, but she wasn't given time to reply.

"You'll do nothing of the sort, Mr Cherry." Clarissa's tone was that of the displeased school mistress. "Tell Edward and Oswald they can collect Lady Felicity from the morning room. She will remain in my company until they're ready to receive her."

The bespectacled man's jaw hung slack for a moment. "V-very well," he said, in no position to argue. "I'll inform his lordship. Mr Ridgeway is on an urgent t-telephone call and shall in any case be late to the appointment."

Clarissa shook her head dolefully, her beads clacking gently at her neck. "I don't know quite where I went wrong with Oswald. At least he and my brother understand one another. I'm certain I don't know what to do with either of them."

Felicity's fingers itched for her notepad. It was, as usual, in her dress pocket, along with her faithful mechanical pencil. She found Clarissa's frankness refreshing and was keen to flesh out the family tree she'd begun sketching in Jasper's office the day before, but it wasn't appropriate to take notes. She wasn't at Langton Manor to interview Clarissa. Felicity's memory would have to serve for now, although it was doubtful much if any of the more interesting family dynamics would make it into what was destined to be a rather dull article.

Felicity turned to the spectacled man. "I hope I'm not being indiscreet in asking, but you are...?"

"I-I—" began the man.

"This is Mr Jacob Cherry," said Clarissa, speaking over his stammer. "He's my brother's secretary. A proud war veteran, which I'm afraid explains his speech impediment. Not been with us long, but Edward wouldn't be without him."

Jacob looked from Clarissa to Felicity, nodding helplessly.

"Please, Lady Felicity," continued Clarissa. "Do come with me. Crowther, have extra refreshments sent to the morning room. We'll likely have guests arriving soon for my party."

"Very well, ma'am," said the butler as he withdrew towards the servants' door, while Jacob took the central stairs, turning right at the landing.

Clarissa looked from Felicity to the white case still in the footman's hand. "Are you staying with us long, Lady Felicity?"

"Oh, it's not a valise," said Felicity. "It's camera equipment. I take the portraits that appear alongside my interviews."

Since her last camera had been damaged by rain, Jasper had invested in a new kit that included a flash. It vastly improved the quality of her images, some of which had even graced the Western Daily News' front page.

Clarissa's eyes brightened. "How absolutely splendid." She set off walking again, and Felicity followed. "I do hope Sebastian's booked a photographer for my party. If he hasn't, perhaps you'd like to stay on for a while and take a few pictures of the fun and frolics?"

"Perhaps," said Felicity evasively. She was a news reporter now, no longer a society writer, and her career had to go forwards, not backwards. No matter how dull.

Felicity maintained an air of agreeableness, but her heart sank when she followed Clarissa into the morning room and found it quite full of people, none of whom were her intended interviewees.

Two sofas in pale blue damask faced one another beside a dusky marble fireplace. On the mantelpiece stood a collection of ornate vases decorated with Chinese designs.

Sitting on one of the sofas was a woman wearing a smoke-coloured Edwardian-style dress, which was belted at the waist and reached her ankles and wrists. Despite her old-fashioned clothes, she was perhaps in her twenties, and she looked up from needlework to meet Felicity's gaze for a moment. The woman's eyes were as hard as slate in a pale, doll-like face.

"My companion, Miss Blanchard," said Clarissa, gesturing towards the severe-looking needleworker. It wasn't appropriate to pry, but 'companion' was likely a paid position of some sort.

On the sofa opposite was a slightly younger woman with orange-gold hair, wide green eyes, and narrow shoulders. Her pretty features had been powdered to obscure still-visible freckles, and she wore a daffodil-yellow jacket, which both clashed with the woman's colouring and drew attention to her youthful allure.

Balanced awkwardly on the young woman's lap was a large, red-faced baby in a sailor-themed romper, complete with a navy blue square collar. He had the same heart-shaped mouth as the woman on whose knee he was seated, and his lower lip trembled.

Further along the same sofa, her eyes fixed on the child, was a serious-faced nursemaid of around Felicity's age. She wore a dark blue pinafore and striped blouse, her mousy-brown hair neatly pinned under a white cap.

Upon seeing Felicity, the young woman in yellow stood up, handing the child to the nurse.

"My daughter-in-law, Mrs Frida Ridgeway." Clarissa stood aside so the smiling Frida could approach Felicity. "Wife to my son, Oswald, and mother of my only grandchild, young Master James, who you can see with his nursemaid over there. Frida, this is Lady Felicity Quick."

"How wonderful." Frida's green eyes were as bright as emeralds, but her yellow brocade jacket and frock were ill-fitting, creating the impression of a child playing dress-up. "I was hoping it might be. It's perfectly splendid to meet you, Lady Felicity." Frida held out a hand.

Felicity shook it warmly. "How do you do?" She had no right to be frustrated with Frida, Clarissa, or anyone else she'd met so far. Everyone was being perfectly pleasant, and it wasn't their fault she wouldn't be breezing in and out of Langton Manor as she'd hoped.

Separated from his mother, James began a sorrowful wail, which quickly rose to the volume of a passing omnibus.

"I'm a devoted reader of your articles, Lady Felicity." Frida spoke as if there wasn't anyone screaming in the near vicinity. "It's perfectly splendid Oswald and his uncle will be in the newspaper."

The nursemaid tried to hush the child, to no avail. Next to start up was the Pomeranian under Clarissa's arm, who at first woofed gently, then steadily more loudly the longer the child continued crying.

Clarissa lowered her painted eyebrows. "Charlotte. Please."

Felicity smiled politely at Frida as Pip struggled under her arm. Usually, Felicity responded positively to anyone complimenting her work or her family's newspaper, but the surrounding cacophony made it a challenge to think.

"Quite," was all Felicity managed to say to Frida above the noise. So far, her time at Langton Manor was proving to be anything but dull.

Clarissa let out a deep sigh. "Well, that's it. You get it your way, Charlotte. You always do."

Pressing hard on her cane, Clarissa dipped forward and placed the yapping Pom on the ground. The little black dog ran straight over to Felicity, where she recommenced barking, this time combining it with jumps performed mostly on her hind legs.

Clarissa shook her head and looked dotingly at Charlotte. "I do realise I spoil her. She's a descendant of Queen Charlotte's own kennels, you see. Hence the name. She has me quite under her spell. Edward's no different, of course. That's his Mollie."

Clarissa pointed at a portrait beside the fireplace of a powerful fawn-coloured dog with a flat, dark muzzle. Felicity wasn't by any means an expert in dog breeds, but she fancied it to be some kind of mastiff. It was a beautifully observed painting.

She glanced down at the wriggling Pip, still in her arms. "We tend to indulge the ones we love, do we not?" Felicity had to force her voice to rise above the yapping and the crying, but the remark was well-received by Clarissa and Frida, who both nodded in agreement.

The nursemaid was now walking to and fro with James at her shoulder, but the baby was inconsolable. Miss Blanchard continued her needlework uninterrupted, although her eyes rose repeatedly towards Felicity, Clarissa, and Frida.

"If you wouldn't mind doing a little indulging of your own, Lady Felicity." Clarissa looked at Pip and raised her eyebrows. "Or I'm afraid Charlotte will never let us hear the end of it."

"Oh. I see what you mean." Two excitable little dogs running around a formal room full of priceless antiques wasn't what Felicity was used to, but as a guest in the house, she would follow Clarissa's lead.

As Felicity leaned forward to place the Yorkie down, Pip sprung from her grasp, landing almost on top of the Pomeranian, and the two little dogs went scrambling across a faded red Persian rug and under one of the sofas. Playful growling and the occasional excited yap added to the unhappy child's ceaseless crying.

"Miss Daniels." Clarissa approached the nursemaid and stroked the baby's head, which soothed the poor infant slightly. "Might it be time for Master James to return to the nursery?"

"It must be quite splendid to have a career." Frida's pale eyebrows were raised in wonderment. She spoke to Felicity as though she were the only other person in the room.

"It is, rather," said Felicity a little awkwardly. She wasn't used to such commotion. It made her almost hanker after the dullness of the business interview to come.

"I considered a career, you know," continued Frida. "I can't say what it would have been. But plenty of women have a career nowadays, don't they?"

Again, Felicity smiled politely. 'Plenty' was perhaps an overstatement. "There are an increasing number of us, yes."

As the nursemaid departed the room and the baby's cries receded, Felicity drew a deep breath of relief. Her moment of calm was disturbed when Clarissa let out a loud gasp.

"How dreadful," she said. "How absolutely frightful."

Felicity followed Clarissa's gaze. Tall windows with curtains in the same blue as the sofas provided a view of paths flanked with loose herbaceous borders still resplendent in late-summer colour. A thick but patchy mist was rolling through the garden like clouds of smoke, blotting out deep red dahlias and lime green nicotiana, then revealing them, before smothering them completely.

"Oh, dear." Felicity's dismay was perhaps a little too noticeable in her voice. She'd never driven in fog before, but she had no wish to stay at Langton Manor any longer than necessary.

The morning room door opened brusquely. A tanned man of around thirty in an elegant light-brown three-piece suit and shining Oxfords strode towards Clarissa. He wasn't especially tall, but his movements were fluid and self-assured, and the tailoring of his suit was subtle yet exquisite.

"Mother, please don't panic." His voice was deep and immediately comforting. "Everything's going to be absolutely fine. Trust me."

"Is that your husband?" Felicity spoke in low tones to Frida. She hadn't expected the sensible and business-minded Oswald to have instantly apparent charm.

Frida shook her head. "It's his brother, Sebastian."

Clarissa's face was a grimace. "But the boat ride on the lake. In this fog. How will we ever—"

"Hush, Mother. Leave it with me. I came as soon as I could to reassure you. I promised you a party, and a party you'll have. I'm sure this beastly fog will clear in no time. And even if it doesn't, we shan't let it spoil things. You deserve to be celebrated."

A smile full of relief and doting maternal love spread across Clarissa's face as she cupped a hand to Sebastian's cheek, bracelets clacking.

For the first time, emotion flickered across Miss Blanchard's face, her hard eyes fixed on Clarissa and Sebastian.

"Darling boy," said Clarissa. "You simply must meet Lady Felicity Quick."

Sebastian turned a sheepish smile on Felicity. "Please, do forgive me. I came marching in here without realising we had a guest. How do you do?"

As Sebastian held out his hand, Pip and Charlotte gambolled across his feet, their playful growls growing in volume, but Sebastian didn't seem phased in the slightest. His bright blue eyes remained fixed on Felicity.

"How do you do?" replied Felicity, but their handshake was cut short by a sharp knock at the morning room door and the entrance of Lord Langton's bespectacled secretary.

Jacob seemed highly agitated as he approached Clarissa. "I-I, um..."

Clarissa leaned on her cane and shook her head. "What is it, Mr Cherry? Out with it, if you please."

"Take your time, Cherry," urged Sebastian, concern creasing his tanned brow.

"There's, um..." Jacob fished a large paisley handkerchief from a pocket, took his spectacles off, and nervously rubbed at the lenses. "There's... Um." He was tongue-tied.

Miss Blanchard placed her needlework beside her and stood up.

"Come now," said Sebastian gently. "What is it, old boy?"

"There's been a-an accident."

"An accident? What sort of accident?" Clarissa brought a hand to the beads at her neck.

Miss Blanchard moved swiftly to Clarissa's side and put a

steadying hand on her elbow. Clarissa shrugged the touch away, but her companion remained close.

Jacob swallowed. His hands shook as he replaced his spectacles crookedly on his nose. "In his l-lordship's rooms. An accident."

"What sort of accident, old chap?" Fear tinged Sebastian's smooth voice, and it put Felicity on edge.

"The valet is..." Jacob took a deep breath. "Lord Langton's v-valet is dead."

"Dead?" Clarissa clutched at her chest, her eyes widening. "Greenwood, you mean?"

Jacob nodded, swallowing.

Felicity brought a hand to her mouth.

"How?" asked Sebastian.

Jacob screwed his eyes shut for a moment. "D-don't yet know."

"Oh," said Frida quietly, her heart-shaped mouth remaining open.

Clarissa had turned pale. "But Greenwood's only been with us a matter of months."

"And Lord Langton?" Sebastian spoke with calm seriousness.

Jacob's shoulders tightened towards his ears. "That's just it."

"What's just it?" Clarissa's eyes searched Jacob's with desperation. Again, she shrugged away Miss Blanchard's touch. "What's happened to my brother?"

"He's g-gone." Jacob blinked nervously. "Lord Langton is missing."

Chapter Four

Guilt was Felicity's strongest reaction to the announcement of the valet's death and Lord Langton's disappearance. Guilt at the relief she felt knowing that her interview with Lord Langton and Oswald would now unquestioningly be cancelled.

It wasn't anything she would admit to out loud, of course. Felicity truly hoped the valet's death had been peaceful and due to natural causes and that Lord Langton would quickly be found safe. She was curious to know if her hopes could be confirmed, but with the planned interview now cancelled, Felicity's course of action was clear. She would return home to Bradley Court without delay.

"My brother is missing, you say?" Clarissa's made-up features were pulled into a confused grimace. "A man can't go missing in his own home. Where's Mollie?"

Sebastian had put out a hand to support Clarissa's elbow. "Is anyone looking for him?"

Clarissa's companion, Miss Blanchard, stood behind her mistress, watching proceedings with a steely gaze. Frida had taken a couple of steps backwards, putting distance between herself and the developing incident.

Jacob pushed his spectacles with a clumsy finger, but they were already flat against the bridge of his nose. "I went in with the butler.

Into his lordship's rooms. That's where we found the, um... The b-body. Of the valet, Greenwood. Lying on the floor. No sign of his lordship. No sign of his d-dog. No sign at all. The s-servants are searching the house as we speak."

"But... This cannot be happening."

Clarissa lurched forward as she spoke, the point of her walking cane slipping on the carpet. Miss Blanchard moved quickly, but it was Sebastian's grasp on Clarissa's arm that saved her from stumbling.

"Everything's ready. Guests will start arriving. This really can't be happening." Clarissa addressed Jacob, but it was abundantly clear the secretary was powerless to change the facts.

"Mrs Ridgeway, please." Miss Blanchard's voice was low and as sombre as her appearance. "Come and sit down." Again, she touched a hand to Clarissa's arm, and again, it was shrugged away.

Felicity swung between choosing the right moment at which to announce her departure and the desire to continue to bear witness to the unfolding drama. She wished harm on no one, but the mystery of a missing lord was far more interesting than his business plans.

"I'm certain there's been some kind of mix-up," said Sebastian soothingly to Clarissa. "Do as Miss Blanchard says, Mother, and sit down. Mr Cherry and I will join the search for Lord Langton. I'm sure it's all a misunderstanding. We're bound to find him in no time."

Clarissa allowed Miss Blanchard to accompany her to a sofa as Sebastian and Jacob left the room. Pip and Charlotte, either sensing the change in tone or simply exhausted from playing, now sat together in the middle of the faded red Persian rug. Pip sniffed at the carpet while Charlotte scratched the back of her ear with her hind leg.

Frida raised her pale eyebrows at Felicity. "Oswald shan't be pleased."

The perfect moment at which to announce her departure had arrived.

Instead, Felicity found herself blinking at Frida. "Oh?" she said encouragingly.

There was the hint of a smile on Frida's lips. "Lord Langton can't change his will if he's missing, can he?"

Felicity paused and blinked again. The announcement of her departure still wasn't forthcoming. "Change his will?"

"Lord Langton was to sign the new one today, naming Oswald the inheritor of his business interests." Frida shrugged loosely. "But I suppose that will all have to be cancelled now."

Felicity nodded slowly. The timing of the will's signing added a nefarious dimension to the valet's death and the peer's disappearance. There was the distinct possibility of a misdeed at hand.

It was in Felicity's nature, in her blood, even — both her father and grandfather had been newspapermen — to get to the bottom of things.

But with a whiff of crime in the air, Jasper wouldn't want Felicity spending a moment longer at Langton Manor than was absolutely necessary, regardless of the powerful pull of her own curiosity.

Felicity smiled apologetically at Frida. "I'm terribly sorry about this awful situation. I'll be on my way. It would be wrong to impose any longer than I already have."

Frida's face fell. "What a tremendous pity."

Felicity made her way towards where Clarissa was now sitting, scooping Pip under her arm on the way, much to Charlotte's whining disappointment.

"Thank you for your hospitality, Mrs Ridgeway. If there were some way I could help, I would be glad to do so, but I believe it's best if I leave."

Clarissa didn't react to Felicity's words. She had her head in her hands and was sobbing, though whether for the dead valet and her missing brother or for the negative consequences for her party, it was impossible to say.

"I do hope everything turns out all right," added Felicity, for she really hoped so.

Miss Blanchard looked up from her seat next to Clarissa, her dark grey eyes fixing Felicity with a hard stare. "We hope so, too."

Felicity collected her camera case from the coatroom off the entrance hall where the footman had deposited it. It was heavy and rather an awkward thing to carry, especially with a Yorkshire Terrier under one arm. To call a servant away from searching for Lord Langton simply to carry something to her motor would have been boorish, so Felicity struggled along as best she could.

What urged Felicity towards her two-seater Alvis and away from Langton Manor wasn't discomfort with drama or even death, for she'd experienced both before. Felicity wanted to be able to tell her brother, hand on heart, that she'd done everything possible to keep herself safe and out of trouble. She owed him that. She'd caused Jasper enough concern.

But there was also her career to consider, which she was patiently developing under her brother's oversight. Jasper had been very insistent about Felicity not reporting on crime, at least not for now. Not that there was necessarily any criminal activity afoot at Langton Manor. It could all just be a misunderstanding.

Either way, Felicity would not wait to find out. Perhaps she'd return to Langton Manor on another occasion to complete the interview, but that day wasn't today.

Her heels tapped across the lily-scented hall, and she set the case on the granite floor as she wrestled with the large oak front doors, which were much heavier and stiffer than the front door at Bradley Court. She couldn't risk placing Pip on the ground. He couldn't be trusted not to run off to rejoin the little black Pomeranian.

After a struggle, the door gave way, and Felicity stepped outside.

Her beloved motor was still there, as were the lichen-covered stone stairs leading down to it. A patch of gold-coloured gravel surrounded the vehicle. Beyond that, the world had been blotted out by a cloud, a thick, greyish cloud that shifted and rolled before Felicity's eyes. The long driveway with its rows of beeches and tall gates had disappeared completely. Even the blue sky was gone, replaced by a thin milky veil that wafted about to reveal occasionally the dimly glowing orb of the sun.

Goosebumps prickled Felicity's shoulders. The outdoor

temperature was distinctly chillier than it had been when Felicity had arrived at Langton Manor, but her top coat was still under her arm. She hadn't yet had the chance to put Pip down and pull the garment on.

She swallowed as she began down the front steps. Felicity was a careful driver, but this would be her first time driving in fog.

"We'll just have to take things slowly," she said to Pip, speaking more for her own benefit than the little dog's, as he was most likely oblivious to the potential perils of driving in such conditions. "We shall proceed slowly and with care. It'll take a good deal longer, that's all. Perhaps the sun will burn it off before we get home."

Felicity tucked a shivering Pip — who quickly felt the cold — into his travelling basket and was about to wrap a tartan travel blanket around his shoulders when a metallic rattle made Felicity look up.

At first, there was nothing to see but cloud. Then a large box-like shadow appeared in the direction of the driveway. The metallic rattle developed into the sound of a motor engine, and a dark green Rolls-Royce emerged from the fog.

A woman's tinkling laughter rang out as the motor drew up to a gravel-crunching stop behind the Alvis. Felicity winced as she noticed the Rolls was missing a headlamp and that one of its front fenders was twisted upwards.

A rear door flew open, and a woman stepped out onto the gravel. The laughter had presumably been hers as the woman still wore a smile on her elfin face. Dark bobbed hair swung around her cheeks as she waved her head back and forth, as though dancing without music. A white fur stole hung errantly from one shoulder, and her dress sparkled with glass beads attached to wisps of chiffon in pale pink and blue. She was around Felicity's age or perhaps a little older, and the overall effect of her appearance was that of a mischievous fairy.

The woman's smile broadened as the driver's door opened. A tall, lithe man dressed in plus-fours and a garish jumper in yellow and brown with a wide flat cap in clashing green sprung eagerly from the driver's seat and towards the fairy woman. He was perhaps as old as thirty, and he stooped slightly to wrap his arms around the woman's waist and lift her onto her tiptoes.

"We made it," he said, burying his face in her neck. "Oh, darling. I don't know how the deuce we did it, but we made it."

Felicity had never seen the couple before. Considering the motor and the easy manner of the man's outlandish behaviour at the front of the house, it was possible this was Lord Derek Langton, the very person Jasper had warned about.

"Watch out," said the man in the plus-fours, peeking over the woman's shoulder, his deep brown eyes meeting Felicity's. "Someone's keeping watch over us."

The fairy woman took no heed and continued to melt into the arms of the golf-attired man.

Embarrassed, Felicity had luckily found somewhere else to look.

The front passenger door of the Rolls opened, and another person stepped out onto the gravel.

This time, Felicity knew exactly who it was. The broad shoulders and dark blond hair were unmistakable. He wore a dark grey three-piece suit and blue necktie, which were more dapper in style than Felicity was used to seeing him in, but his smile made her cheeks burn with a mix of emotions she couldn't quite identify.

It was fellow journalist, lifesaver, and former professional rival, Alex Cooper.

Chapter Five

"Hello, Felicity."

As Alex pushed the passenger door of the Rolls closed, he looked as confused as Felicity felt. Was that a blush on his cheeks?

"Hello, Alex. What are you doing here?"

Felicity knew her question sounded impertinent, but it was less offensive than the question that was really on her mind: *What are you doing with these people?*

Alex smiled. "I was wondering the same about you." It was as if he found something quite funny about the whole situation.

"You're already acquainted?" said the brown-eyed man in the plus-fours, looking from Felicity to Alex. He still had the fairy lady in his arms, swirls of mist flowing around their ankles.

"Indeed, we are," said Felicity somewhat tightly, her urge to escape growing.

Alex straightened. "I suppose I'm best placed to make the introductions. This is Lady Felicity Quick. Lady Felicity, this is Lord Derek Langton and Miss Elodie Rossignol."

So, this was Lord Langton's wayward son, the man Jasper had asked her to stay away from. Felicity would never have imagined

Derek's fast and glamorous set to have appealed to Alex, but she clearly knew Alex less well than she'd fancied.

She quickly decided she wouldn't report Alex's association with Derek to Jasper — it wasn't any of her business, after all — but she was determined not to get herself mixed up in it.

Felicity smiled awkwardly. "Pleased to meet you," she said, which was a perfectly acceptable gesture, given that Jasper had asked her to be polite with Derek.

Elodie twisted in Derek's arms. She had pale ice-blue eyes. "Enchantée." Her pronunciation of the word, combined with her very French-sounding name, led Felicity to the assumption that Elodie was a native French speaker.

"Quick?" said Derek, frowning a little under his cap. "As in the newspaper? Is this your boss, Coop?" He turned to Felicity. "Aren't you peeved he's not turned in any copy in a while?"

"I'm not Mr Cooper's boss, Lord Derek," said Felicity as kindly as possible. "I was here to interview your father, Lord Langton, but there's been a change of plans. I'm on my way home now."

Her evasion of the issue of Derek's father's whereabouts was deliberate. It wasn't right that someone he'd only just met break the news. Perhaps the search party had located Lord Langton already?

Alex raised a thick eyebrow. "You intend to drive in this? Surely, you're not serious."

Derek and Elodie, separated from their embrace but holding hands, advanced towards where Felicity still stood beside her motor. "Let's do away with Lord this and Lady that, shall we?" Derek held out a hand to Felicity, which she took and shook perfunctorily. "I'm Derek, and this is Elodie, and that rascal over there is — well, you already know all about him, I suppose."

"You have extremely beautiful eyes," said Elodie, whose handshake was limp, and whose accent was certainly French. She smiled languidly, long eyelashes batting her cheeks as she hung from Derek's arm.

Felicity nearly blushed at Elodie's unexpected and rather inappropriate compliment. She'd never understood her hazel eyes to be anything special. "Thank you, Miss Rossignol." Felicity glanced uneasily at Alex. The situation was anything but normal. She hardly knew how to address him. "Yes, I intend to drive through the fog."

"You can't. It's too dangerous." Alex's tone was serious. "We only just made it back in one piece from the golf course."

"Coop's right." Derek fished a dark red cigarette case out of the pocket of his voluminous plus-fours, his other hand now around Elodie's shoulder. "Look what I did on the way over here from the club." Derek gestured towards the battered front of the Rolls with the cigarette case. "If it weren't for Coop grabbing hold of the steering wheel, we'd have ended up in the Exe."

Alex shrugged. It was typical of him to dismiss any claim of heroism on his behalf, but Felicity could not, for the life of her, make sense of the company he was keeping.

With one hand, Derek put a cigarette in his mouth and lit it with a black-lacquer lighter. "And I'm not inexperienced, you know." The puff of his smoke swirled away and became one with the fog that drew closer around them. "Led cavalry into battle at Mons and again at Verdun. I know a thing or two about poor terrain."

Elodie was leaning into Derek, still gazing wide-eyed at Felicity in a way that made her feel rather uncomfortable. Pip was standing impatiently with his front paws on the passenger door. It was definitely time for Felicity to leave.

"Well, it's been splendid meeting you both—"

"Say," interrupted Derek. "Why's the interview been cancelled? I realise we Langtons aren't always the warmest of people, but it would be rather beastly, even by our standards, to invite you out here for nothing."

Alex watched Felicity, concern on his face.

Felicity looked from Alex to Derek. She opened her mouth, though she was not quite sure what to say.

Relief came in the form of a voice from the top of Langton Manor's front steps.

"Derek? Is that you?"

Wafts of white mist made the view of Langton Manor's front

door hazy, but it was still possible to see a portly man in a pale grey suit standing with his hands on his hips at the top of the lichen-spotted steps.

Derek rolled his eyes. “Blast it,” he breathed, which made Elodie smile. “Yes, Ossie,” called Derek. “It’s me. Who else is allowed to drive the Rolls?”

Ossie had to be short for Oswald. The nickname hinted at the kind of familiarity found between cousins, although there seemed to be no love lost on Derek’s side.

“I hate to be the one to tell you this, Derek, old chap,” continued the man at the front doors, “but we’ve got rather a serious problem on our hands.”

“Tell me what the problem is,” said Derek, sweeping a still-smiling Elodie towards the steps and beginning to climb, “and I’ll tell you if it’s on my hands.”

Felicity exhaled in a controlled manner. There was something uncomfortably fascinating about whatever was going on at Langton Manor, but it was truly time to leave.

Resettling Pip in his travelling basket, Felicity rounded the Alvis and opened the driver’s door, but another hand pushed the door gently closed.

Felicity looked up at Alex. His eyebrows were drawn low over dark blue eyes.

“I’m sorry. I can’t let you drive away in this. Your brother would never forgive me.”

Slowly, Felicity folded her arms over her chest. “And what do you suppose Jasper would say if he knew about the company you were keeping?” She wouldn’t have told her brother, of course, but Alex didn’t know that.

Confusion wrinkled Alex’s brow. He had a scar on his forehead that dipped to the corner of his eye, and it dented deeper when he frowned. “What’s that to do with anything?”

“Jasper said he has no clue what you’re up to these days.” Felicity hissed. She’d been so deeply grateful to Alex, so in awe of him, that the disappointment she now felt was like a pendulum swinging hard in the opposite direction. "I doubt he'd be pleased to know you're mixing with Derek Langton."

Alex watched Derek climbing the steps with an unsteady Elodie on his arm, then returned his serious gaze to Felicity. "You can't drive in this. Nobody can. Look at it."

The circle of golden gravel they stood in had shrunk further. The tops of the beeches lining the drive were now fully buried under thick cloud, and the dim disc of the sun had completely disappeared from the sky.

Even if she drove slowly, Felicity wouldn't be able to see much further than the end of the bonnet. It would be impossible to avoid dropping off the side of the road into a ditch at best, a rushing river at worst.

Frustration and a mild sense of panic rose in Felicity's chest.

Alex was right. She wasn't going anywhere.

Her legs heavy with reluctance, Pip under her arm, and with Alex carrying her camera case, Felicity again climbed the front steps of Langton Manor.

Would Jasper be disappointed in her? With no Lord Langton to interview and with his wayward son Derek in attendance, leaving — had it been possible — would have been the only correct course of action. Without being unkind, Felicity hoped the same fog was affecting her brother's journey from Bristol to Bradley Court. He might then understand the conditions she faced.

"I'm sure the Langtons will make you comfortable," said Alex, as though aware of the need to reassure Felicity without her having informed him of her concerns. "It shouldn't take long for this fog to clear. If the wind picks up, it'll be gone before anyone realises."

Felicity looked across at Alex. Apart from his dapper suit and him smelling a little different to how she remembered — he'd started using vetiver-scented pomade, perhaps — Alex was unchanged from how she'd last seen him back in July.

He smiled. "It's good to see you, by the way. Been wondering how you've been getting on."

Felicity was about to smile back, but she couldn't ignore Alex's association with Derek.

She nodded stiffly. "Very well, thank you," she said and turned her attention back to climbing the steps.

Derek and Elodie had already reached Langton Manor's oak front doors, and Derek was addressing the portly man, who had a dark, old-fashioned moustache and thinning hair. His pale grey suit had a large but subtle check, the stiff collar of his white shirt sat uncomfortably tight around his flushed neck, and he wore a worried expression.

"The valet's dead, and Father's missing? I don't believe it." Derek scratched his temple under his floppy cap. Elodie was still clamped on his arm, but her smile was gone, and her eyelids drooped.

"Wait a moment," said Alex, glancing between Derek and Felicity. "There's a man dead and Lord Langton's missing?"

Felicity nodded, mildly abashed at having kept the information to herself.

"Have you ever heard anything more ridiculous, Coop?" said Derek, before turning his incredulous frown back to the portly man. "Where's that blasted dog of Father's got to, then? I fancy he took her out for a walk and got stuck in the fog. Has anyone even tried looking for them?"

The portly man noticed Felicity, and his eyebrows shot up. "Ah, Lady Felicity. I was told you'd arrived. Oswald Ridgeway." He extended a hand, which Felicity shook. "Very pleased to meet you, although not under these circumstances."

"Likewise, and naturally," concurred Felicity, hiding her personal disappointment at still being at Langton Manor rather well. "May I say how sorry I am about what's happened?"

"Oh, it's not for you to be sorry, Lady Felicity. You're merely an innocent bystander." Oswald nodded towards Alex. "Mr Cooper," he said by way of greeting, which confirmed to Felicity that Alex, who nodded in acknowledgement, was no stranger at the great house.

Oswald then returned his attention to Derek. "There's a search party underway as we speak. And there indeed wouldn't be any reason for concern had your father been out with Mollie when the fog descended. Lord Langton can certainly look after himself on his own estate. But that's not how the thing played out."

"What the deuce happened then?" The relaxed aplomb with which Derek had presented himself at the bottom of the steps was quickly disappearing. "How can a valet die and no one knows what happened to him? Did the solicitor arrive yet?"

Alex spoke quietly to Felicity. "There's been a death as well?"

"Mm-hmm," she confirmed rather evasively, determined not to become mixed up in any of it.

"I can tell you what I know, Derek," said Oswald, doing his best to speak calmly despite the red of his neck now reaching his face. "Lord Langton wasn't out with his dog for a walk in the grounds. The last anyone saw of him, he was in his rooms, preparing to attend our interview with Lady Felicity."

"I'm sorry to interrupt," said Alex, addressing more than just Felicity now. "But who died?"

Elodie's eyes widened at Alex's rather unsubtle question.

Oswald cleared his throat. "A Mr John Greenwood. Uncle Edward's valet."

"Well," was all Alex could say in response. Understandably, he was rather taken aback.

"*Our* interview?" Derek drew back his chin and looked from Oswald to Felicity. Then he let out a high-strung laugh. "Were you planning on positioning yourself in the papers, Ossie? Oh, how splendid. How absolutely splendid. For once, Ossie's plans aren't going so swimmingly."

The comment was thoroughly mean-spirited, but Oswald was unruffled by it. Or, rather, no more ruffled than he already was. It was by now quite clear to Felicity what Jasper had meant by Derek being a bad lot, but at least she was now in the company of one of her two intended interviewees.

"I'm awfully sorry to impose on you." Felicity addressed mainly Oswald as she spoke, but she couldn't fully ignore Derek. Langton

Manor was his family home, and it was his father who was missing. "If it weren't for this terrible fog, I'd have been on my way by now."

Oswald shook his jowls. "Not a problem. Not a problem at all. We'll handle things. We always do."

Derek grimaced. "Did the solicitor get here yet? Is the blasted thing signed over? Where's Ursula?" He was like a petulant child, with his cousin Oswald in the role of parent. "Don't tell me my sister's gone missing as well. Where is she? I want to talk to Ursula."

"Calm, darling," slurred Elodie, her lips near Derek's ear. "Calm." Clumsily, she stroked Derek's arm. It had an appeasing effect on him, and Derek gave his cousin the opportunity to respond.

Oswald spoke with control. "The solicitor didn't arrive yet. I doubt he will now with this fog. And your sister isn't missing in the slightest. I saw her in the morning room just now."

"I'm going to speak to Ursula," said Derek, and he pulled a compliant Elodie with him through the front doors of Langton Manor, where they nearly collided with the butler, who was on his way outside.

Felicity stood up taller. "Will you not be accompanying your friends, Mr Cooper?"

Alex looked from Felicity to the white leather camera case he was still holding.

Felicity held out a hand to take it from him. Alex kept hold of it and frowned at her.

It was a stalemate.

The butler approached Oswald. "You wanted a report on how the search is progressing, sir."

Oswald put a finger under his shirt collar and tugged at it. "Yes, Crowther. Tell me."

"I'm afraid it's disappointing news, sir. We've found nothing yet. There's no trace of either his lordship or his lordship's dog. Along with the footman, I attempted to venture into the gardens, but it was rather hopeless, as I'm sure you can appreciate, sir."

Oswald's face darkened as he looked out at the fog, which surged ever closer towards the big house. "Any indication of when the weather will change?"

"No, sir. I'm afraid not. There was light mist expected today. Not fog of this sort."

Oswald sighed. "Well, there's nothing for it. I suppose we'd better telephone the police." He turned to Felicity and Alex. "If you'd told me at breakfast that I'd be telephoning to the police before lunchtime." He shook his head. "Mr Cooper, naturally, you're a guest of my cousin Derek's and must by now know that you're always welcome at Langton Manor. Lady Felicity, I'd like to make it clear that you're welcome to remain here with us for as long as you need, and I can only apologise for the highly unusual situation in which we currently find ourselves. I'm certain that Lord Langton would be of the same opinion."

"That's very kind of you," said Felicity, "and please don't apologise. The situation is surely no one's fault." At least, she sincerely hoped that was the case, although with the police being telephoned, the circumstances were becoming increasingly questionable.

"Please," said Oswald, holding an arm out towards the open front doors. "Do go inside. We'll make sure you're taken care of."

Oswald taking charge was more than a little strange. Surely, in the absence of Lord Langton, that should have been Derek? The will was being changed to leave the business side of things to Oswald, not the house and family title.

"After you," said Alex, also gesturing for Felicity to go ahead through the doors.

"Thank you." Felicity said this more to Oswald than to Alex, and as she begrudgingly re-entered Langton Manor, Pip still tucked under her arm, she knew she would have to keep her wits about her. Otherwise, she risked getting tangled up in something she might live to regret.

Chapter Six

Oswald brought Felicity, Pip, and Alex to the morning room. The blue damask of the upholstery had taken on a silvery quality now that the windows were blanked out with fog. Frida stood by the window, looking out at the whiteness, a cigarette in a short but elegant holder clamped between her fingers.

Clarissa wrinkled her nose at the tobacco scent. "Must you, Frida, dear?" Clarissa was seated on a sofa, her elbow on the armrest. Stern-faced Miss Blanchard was at her side. "It's not very ladylike, is it?"

Frida paid Clarissa no mind and continued to look out at the fog, drawing on her cigarette.

Upon noticing Pip, the little black Pomeranian sprung from Clarissa's lap and dashed across to Felicity, where she danced on her hind legs and yapped. Pip squirmed hard under Felicity's arm and let out a few yips of his own. Felicity would have preferred to keep Pip close at hand, ready to leave as soon as the fog cleared, but she had little choice. To stop the little dogs barking, she had to put the Yorkie on the floor, and the two of them tumbled away in a flurry of fur and playful growling.

Alex placed the photography case next to a walnut side table and smiled at Pip and Charlotte's antics. Oswald paid no attention to the canine chaos.

"Frida?" Oswald raised his voice to attract the red-headed woman's attention.

There was a pause before she turned away from the window. "Yes, Oswald?"

"Please see that Lady Felicity is kept comfortable for the duration of her stay here with us. We don't want to cause her ladyship more inconvenience than has already been suffered."

Frida nodded earnestly, clumsily stubbing out her cigarette in a heavy glass ashtray. "Of course, Oswald. I can do that. I can certainly do that."

"I'll return when I've telephoned to the police," said Oswald, and he left the room.

"Shall I ring for a tray of tea?" said Frida, approaching Felicity. "Or mix you a cocktail?"

"Thank you, Mrs Ridgeway, but there's no need to ring for tea." The idea of a cocktail before lunch was too bizarre to be taken seriously.

Frida smiled and waved a hand in a carefree manner. "Please, do call me Frida."

"Thank you, Frida, but I hope to be on my way soon."

Clarissa had pulled herself to her feet and approached Felicity, Frida, and Alex, beads clacking at her chest, the tip of her walking cane burying itself in the carpet's deep pile. "I would suggest you make yourself comfortable, Lady Felicity. The Duchess of Moreton was to be in attendance at my party, but she has just telephoned with apologies due to this wretched fog, and she's north of the moors. Oh, to think. All that effort and expense. I haven't had a party in years, then the day I do..." She raised her kohl-lined eyes to the heavens, taking on the dramatic air of a martyr.

"Would you like something to eat, perhaps, Lady Felicity?" urged Frida. "A scone or a plate of biscuits?"

Felicity smiled in a way that communicated commiseration to Clarissa and polite abstention to Frida, but she was rather at a loss for what to say to either of them. With a man dead and another missing, Clarissa's preoccupation with her ruined birthday celebrations was, at best, misplaced, while Frida seemed to operate on another plane of existence altogether.

Then there was Felicity's own despair at the situation she was now faced with. How long would it take for the fog to clear? When would she be on her way? And how could she prevent herself from getting too caught up in things in the meantime?

"I'm sorry to be imposing on your hospitality given the current situation." Alex addressed Clarissa and Frida, his voice low and calming. "I can only imagine how worried you must all be about Lord Langton. If there's anything I can do to assist, please do tell me."

Clarissa sighed deeply. "Mr Cooper. You always know exactly what to say. Quite what Derek did to deserve a friend like you, I do not know, but I sincerely hope he counts his blessings."

Felicity glanced at Alex, wondering indeed what bonded Alex and Derek.

Miss Blanchard had risen from her seat and now stood beside Clarissa. "Please, Mrs Ridgeway," she said, putting a hand on Clarissa's elbow. "Come and sit down. Do not exhaust yourself."

Clarissa allowed Miss Blanchard to lead her back towards the sofa, but she continued to address Felicity and Alex. "Do you know one another?" she said, looking between them. "I rather fancy you didn't meet for the first time just today."

Instinctively, Felicity looked at Alex, as if to check with him what ought to be shared.

"I'm a friend of Lord Jasper Quick's," said Alex without missing a beat. "I work for his newspaper."

Clarissa lowered herself slowly back onto the sofa, her hand on her cane. "Oh, of course you do, Mr Cooper. How silly of me to forget. So, you and Lady Felicity work together."

Given Alex's association with Derek, Felicity didn't want to give the impression she and Alex were at all close. "We're colleagues," she said, attempting to distance herself from Alex without offending him. "But we don't work together. The Western Daily News employs a number of journalists."

"Are you sure there's nothing I can get you?" Frida's wide green eyes were fixed on Felicity. "A sandwich, perhaps?"

With the room's windows blanked out by fog, Clarissa and Frida's parallel discussions, Alex's status as neither ally nor enemy, and the growl and tumble of the dogs, Felicity felt peculiarly uncomfortable. Most uncomfortable of all was the absence of concern in the morning room for the whereabouts of Lord Langton and the unexplained death of his valet.

Felicity had begun pondering departing Langton Manor on foot when Jacob and Sebastian entered.

"Oh, Sebastian, darling," crooned Clarissa, perking up. "Where have you been? You look exhausted."

Sebastian collapsed onto the sofa opposite Clarissa and Miss Blanchard. "I've seen entire wings of this place I didn't even know existed. It felt rather like a game of hide and seek, only without all the fun."

Jacob stood at the side of the room, wiping at his spectacles with his paisley handkerchief. "We saw Mr Oswald Ridgeway on his way to telephone the p-police. He told us to wait here for him. He'll b-bring news."

"But Sebastian, darling," continued Clarissa, as Sebastian fished in his inside jacket pocket for a cigarette case. "All that work you did, all the trouble you went to, and now it's all going to count for nothing. How are you not devastated? It's such a frightful shame it's all going to waste."

Miss Blanchard stared coldly at Sebastian. She clearly didn't feel the sympathy for him Clarissa did.

"Oh, no need to feel sorry for me, Mother," replied Sebastian as he lit a cigarette, the smoke of which didn't irk Clarissa's nose in the slightest. "It's your party, after all, but we don't yet know what will happen. This ghastly fog might disappear at any moment, just as quickly as it came."

Clarissa shook her head mournfully. "If only, Sebastian, darling. If only."

"It doesn't sound like it." Oswald had reentered the morning room, his plump face grave, his shirt collar seemingly tighter than ever. With his hands on his hips, he positioned himself near to where Felicity and Alex were still standing, Frida's idea of hospitality having not involved the invitation to sit. "I just got off the line to the police station at Cheriton Ash. They've heard from police headquarters at Exeter. There's a thick blanket of fog stretching from the moors to the mouth of the Exe. It's causing havoc on the roads. They've even got a couple of their own vans stuck in ditches about the place."

Alex quirked an eyebrow at Felicity, and she looked away. It was never a pleasant experience to be on the receiving end of an I-told-you-so.

Oswald continued. "Needless to say, there'll be no one coming out to us as long as this fog is about."

"Oh," said Frida, as though none of what her husband had said was particularly interesting. She put another cigarette in her holder and lit it. A flicker of distaste passed over Oswald's features, but he said nothing to his wife about her smoking.

"Has a c-crime been committed, then?" asked Jacob from behind crooked spectacles.

Oswald let out a sigh heavy with weariness and worry. "That's just it. We don't yet know. But the police have asked for the scene surrounding the valet's body to be secured."

"The scene?" whelped Clarissa. "Secured? As though the man were murdered? My guests could have been arriving, and a man has been murdered?"

Oswald nodded solemnly. "The police believe it to be a possibility, Mama."

Felicity swallowed. This was exactly the kind of business Jasper would want her to stay very far away from. The idea of departing on foot crossed her mind again, but where would she go? Felicity knew it was hopeless, especially in her new shoes, which weren't at all practical for walking.

"I don't understand." Clarissa sat on the edge of the sofa, her hand gripping the top of her cane. "Are they suggesting Edward murdered Greenwood? Why would Edward do such a thing? It makes no sense whatever."

Miss Blanchard moved along the sofa towards Clarissa and put a calming hand on her shoulder, gently urging her to sit back in her chair.

"There's indeed very little about this whole situation that makes any sense," said Oswald. "But we at least have the advice of the police to follow now."

Frida blew a thin and remarkably perfect smoke ring.

Sebastian stubbed out his cigarette, his tanned brow creased with concern. "And what's the police's advice?"

Oswald tugged at his shirt collar. "We're to remain together in a single location until the police can arrive and assess the situation. They've also asked that we leave everything around the body of the valet exactly as it is."

"That's all very well for the police to say," said Clarissa, shaking off Miss Blanchard's hand and again leaning forward in her seat. "But if a crime has taken place, then there's a criminal here at Langton Manor, and it's certain to be someone from below stairs. Who's to say he's not up there, tampering with the crime scene as we speak?"

Clarissa's assumption was an ugly one, and Felicity was glad no servants were in attendance to hear it. She exchanged glances with Alex and could tell he felt the same.

"Or she," said Jacob.

"She?" asked Sebastian.

"M-murderers can also be women, you know," clarified Jacob.

Felicity was very much in favour of a woman's right to choose her own destiny, but insisting that murder was just as much a woman's domain as a man's was a queer take on emancipation.

Sebastian frowned at Jacob dismissively.

"I'm simply relaying the advice the police have given," said Oswald, displaying an ounce of impatience. "And we'd be well advised to follow it."

Clarissa straightened her back and cleared her throat. "Oswald is right. We'll gather everyone in the ballroom. Mr Cherry, fetch Derek and Ursula and whatever ragtag bunch of ne'er-do-wells that nephew of mine happens to have with him today." She flashed a glance at Alex. "No offence, Mr Cooper. You're quite the exception."

Alex accepted the oddly framed compliment gracefully, with just a subtle nod of his dark blond head.

"Frida," said Oswald. "Help Mama get the ballroom ready to accommodate everyone."

"Of course, Oswald." Frida smoothed down her yellow skirt and headed towards the morning room door, where she stopped and turned back to put out her cigarette. "Of course," she muttered.

Clarissa pressed hard on her stick and lifted herself from the sofa. Miss Blanchard remained close at hand as Clarissa hobbled towards Oswald. "We'll have Crowther lock up Edward's suite, but not before it's been photographed."

Oswald scratched the thin covering of hair on the top of his head. "Photographed?"

"Lady Felicity has with her the necessary equipment," said Clarissa confidently.

Felicity had, until that moment, felt rather invisible, content to listen and absorb, rather like a member of the audience at a play. The mention of her name was like a splash of cold water on her face, and she had to react quickly to stop her mouth from falling open with surprise at being summoned to become involved.

"For making photos of a crime scene?" Oswald seemed perplexed.

"A camera is a camera, isn't it?" Clarissa looked at Felicity.

"Well," began Felicity, but she hesitated.

She wasn't at all squeamish about dead bodies, not even murdered ones — as she'd discovered quite by accident over the past few months — but becoming a crime scene photographer was rather a wild idea. Felicity was also certain it was the opposite of what Jasper had had in mind when he'd told her to stay away from trouble.

On the other hand, wasn't it right that she assist the inhabitants of Langton Manor in their hour of need? Wasn't helping people always the right thing to do?

Faced with this conundrum, Felicity looked at Alex. Her own

reflex surprised her. Was she looking to him for support? In any case, Alex's standpoint on the matter was clear. He looked more disapproving of Clarissa's proposal than Felicity imagined Jasper would have.

"I'm not sure—" began Alex.

"I'd be happy to help in any way I can," said Felicity, cutting him off. Alex had already scuppered her attempt to leave Langton Manor. She'd not have him making all her decisions for her.

"Oh, splendid," said Clarissa. "I knew you were the outgoing type the moment I met you, Lady Felicity."

"And I'd be happy to assist," said Alex quickly.

Felicity arched an eyebrow in his direction, but before she could inform Alex she didn't need an assistant, Clarissa said, "Of course you will, Mr Cooper. You can work together. You'll make quite the team, I'm sure."

Chapter Seven

Paff!

As the dazzling whiteness of the magnesium flash receded, Felicity slid the shutter on her camera closed, and the interior of Lord Langton's dressing room returned to view.

It was a narrow room panelled from floor to ceiling in dark oak with reddish undertones. The wood carried the sweet smell of polish, and its surface shone dully in the foggy light coming from a single tall window draped with pale, thin curtains, which faced the door to the hall.

Built-in cupboards with delicate handles and hinges in brass covered one side of the room. Against the opposite wall stood a large chest of drawers with gilded handles. Atop it, a selection of bottles and tubs in silver and crystal had been neatly arranged. A single Georgian-style wooden chair with a cushion upholstered in a pale golden-cream fabric was positioned in one corner, close to a tall, oval mirror, which had been tilted on its stand so that a person before it might view their entire outfit. On the floor was a thick, dark-red rug.

Towards the window, a further two doors faced one another, one leading to Lord Langton's bedroom, the other to his private bathroom, which was apparently where the body of the valet still lay.

The door to the bathroom lay ajar. Felicity shivered at the idea of what lay beyond it, even though she'd been reassured the dead man looked as though he were sleeping.

"It seems rather too peaceful for a murder scene."

Alex was frowning thoughtfully, a corded button in his hand. He'd offered to operate the flash, which happened to be Felicity's least favourite photography-related activity, as flash powder could be dangerous. When Jasper purchased her new equipment, she'd insisted on a tripod for the T-shaped flash lamp, the ignition of which was operated via a rather lengthy cord, meaning she could stand well away from the contraption. However, standing well away from anything in the narrow dressing room was rather a challenge.

Felicity said nothing in response to Alex's comment. She still wasn't quite comfortable with his presence, although she was now grateful for his offer of help. Pip was an unsuitable companion in such situations, as past behaviour attested, so he'd been left downstairs with his new Pomeranian friend. Felicity wasn't particularly delicate, but she would have found it eerie to photograph a dead body alone. Like most of the journalists at the Western Daily News, Alex was familiar with camera equipment — images rather than headlines sold newspapers these days — so he was also proving useful.

"I think we're ready to proceed to the bathroom," said Felicity, picking up her camera tripod and moving it across the rug.

Alex didn't follow. "Felicity."

She stopped.

Concern tinged Alex's dark blue eyes. "What have I done to vex you?"

Felicity blinked. "Am I vexed?" She knew she was, but she was aghast he could tell.

Alex smiled apologetically. "I realise we don't know one another particularly well, but you've been annoyed at me before, and I recognise it. If you tell me what it is I've done to offend you, I might rectify the situation. It looks like we're trapped here at Langton for the foreseeable, so we may as well stick together. Wouldn't you say?"

"Are you not here to stick with Derek Langton?" Felicity was relieved to discharge what had been on her mind, but the words came out quicker than she would have liked.

Alex winced a little and leaned some of his weight on the flash's folded tripod. "You do realise you're not the first to disapprove of Derek."

Felicity raised an eyebrow. "Jasper certainly does."

"Which is why I haven't told him I've been keeping Derek's company."

"May I ask just why you are in Derek's company?" Heat rose in Felicity's cheeks. She wouldn't tell Jasper about Alex's indiscretion, but she could be indignant on her brother's behalf.

Alex sighed deeply. "Can you keep a secret? Even from Jasper?"

Felicity rested the feet of the folded camera tripod on the carpet. "It depends what it is."

"Ah."

Alex's utterance was small, but its note of disappointment went like a dart into Felicity's chest. She owed Alex a tremendous amount, so much that she never imagined she'd be able to repay him. And now she was being churlish over a matter of personal trust when Felicity prided herself on her ability to be discreet, even when faced with less worthy souls than Alex.

"I spoke too quickly," corrected Felicity. "I'd be honoured to keep your confidences." She added a dusting of sarcasm to 'honoured', so as not to come across as too cloying.

Excitement glinted in Alex's eye. "Good, because I've been dying to tell someone. I'm undercover. For a story I'm working on." His excitement waned a little. "Well, a story I was working on. I seem to have hit something of a dead end."

Felicity frowned. "But Jasper said he didn't know what you were up to these days."

"Probably better that way." Alex glanced behind him to ensure that the door to the hall was closed. He spoke in lowered tones. "I've been investigating the trafficking of cocaine and other similar drugs into the region."

"Drugs?" Felicity couldn't hide her surprise. "In Devon?"

Despair flashed across Alex's face as he signalled for her to lower her voice.

Felicity switched to a whisper. "No wonder you've hit a dead end. This is a rural county. You're not in London anymore."

Alex kept his voice low. "Trust me. The Dangerous Drugs Act has them all crawling out of the woodwork now. You'd be surprised at who's using the stuff."

"Derek?" blurted Felicity, doing her best to conceal her disgust at the idea of Alex mixing with drug fiends.

Alex sighed. "You know, I feel rather bad about it all, really. He's a pal, and a jolly good one. I know him from the war. I'd heard he had links to the whole racket, but I've not been able to find anything."

"Is Derek using illicit drugs?"

Alex smiled knowingly. "I believe I've offended your sensibilities quite enough already."

Felicity raised her eyebrows. "We're about to photograph a dead body, and you're worried about my sensibilities?"

"Touché," said Alex, and he lifted the flash on its tripod. "I suppose we better get it over and done with before anyone thinks we've been tampering."

Though Felicity wasn't quite done with the conversation about Derek's potential drug use, Alex had a point. She picked up the camera and moved towards the bathroom door, but what Alex had just told her was set to play on her mind.

"I'm not quite sure there's a point to any of this," said Felicity, in an attempt to distract herself. "If someone had wanted to tamper with the crime scene, they'd have done so already. I'm also sure photographing crime scenes requires more expertise than simply possessing functional photography equipment."

Alex followed with the flash leaning on his shoulder. "Could Clarissa have had some other motive for sending us up here?"

Felicity reached the bathroom door, set the camera down, and looked at Alex. "Have your suspicions, do you?"

Alex's scarred forehead creased. "Don't you?"

Felicity said nothing. The talk of drugs had indeed rattled her, but an undercover investigation for her brother's newspaper was better than Alex spending time with Derek because he delighted in the wayward son's outlandish behaviour. Felicity also felt very certain Alex wasn't the sort to use cocaine or anything similar.

But while Felicity had in the past enjoyed puzzling over mysterious circumstances with Alex, she had decided to photograph the scene of the valet's death as a favour to the family at Langton Manor. Nothing more. Felicity wanted to walk away from the situation and tell Jasper she'd done everything she could to not become mixed up in things. Indulging her curiosity and developing theories were steps towards precisely the sort of further involvement she needed to avoid.

"I think one image per room will be quite enough," said Felicity as she pushed the bathroom door gently open.

The bathroom was larger than the dressing room and less traditional in decor. The wash basin and bath were jade green and surrounded by gleaming black tiling. In the middle of the floor, which was covered in tiny hexagonal cream tiles, lay a man with brilliantined hair in a black jacket with grey pinstriped trousers. His shiny black shoes had scuffed leather soles and were pointed towards the dressing room door. His head was towards the sink.

From the bathroom door, it wasn't possible to see the man's face, but Felicity noticed he had pale, elegant hands and a pocket watch on a silver chain. The angle of his limbs indeed made it appear that the man was asleep, as though he might wake and rise from the floor at any moment. The scene was lit by milky daylight filtered through fog and the thin net curtains draped over a single small window.

"Shall we set up here in the doorway?" asked Alex. Despite his questionable taste in friends, Alex's voice and presence were reassuring.

Felicity nodded and set to work, extending the legs of her tripod so that the camera had the best overall view of the bathroom. "I wonder what happened to him," she said somewhat absent-mindedly.

"I suppose a man dropping dead isn't the mysterious thing," said Alex, tapping flash powder into the T-shaped holder. "It's the combination of the valet's death and Lord Langton's disappearance that makes a mystery of it."

Felicity nodded, biting her tongue. Naturally, she had her views on the matter. Airing them simply wasn't an option.

After more fiddling with both the camera and the flash, Alex asked, "Ready?"

"The shutter's open."

Paff! There was another brilliant burst of pure white light.

"And it's closed."

"Did you see that?" asked Alex.

Felicity blinked, her eyes readjusting. "See what?"

"The light of the flash caught something shining on the floor. Over there—" Alex pointed towards the valet's head "—under the sink."

Felicity began removing her camera from the tripod. She ignored Alex's comment. She wouldn't get involved. "We need to get down to the ballroom," she said. "We should follow the police's advice."

Quite against anyone's better judgement, Alex stepped past Felicity and into the bathroom. He trod carefully past the dead man, and lifting his elegantly cut dark-grey trousers slightly at the knee, he crouched by the sink, peering past the corpse's head.

"Alex," hissed Felicity in a tone not too distant from the one she used for chastising Pip. "What on earth are you doing?"

He squinted at the bathroom floor. "I don't want to touch anything. Could you switch on the light? I say, the fellow's sleeve has been torn."

Felicity glanced at the black bakelite switches next to the door into the bathroom. "No, I certainly cannot."

Alex remained in a crouched position, squinting under the sink. "Use your elbow or something. You won't destroy any fingerprints that way."

Felicity huffed indignantly and folded her arms over her peach blouse. "I don't know what you're up to, but I certainly do not approve. We need to go downstairs."

Alex stood up and stepped back to the doorway. He used his

forearm to knock the light switch into the on position before fixing Felicity with a raised eyebrow. Under the warm glow of the electric lighting, he returned to the bathroom sink.

He didn't need to crouch back down.

"I see it now," said Alex. "It's a hypodermic syringe."

Chapter Eight

Felicity had to summon all her resolve to prevent herself from crossing the bathroom and joining Alex in examining the syringe.

It couldn't be denied. It was an enticing development, which lowered the chance of the valet's death being a natural one. Could there be a link with the story Alex had said he was undercover on?

Instead of allowing any of her questions or theories to form on her lips, Felicity folded her arms over her chest and glowered at Alex from the dressing room doorway.

"It appears to have been used," Alex said, crouching down. "The plunger has been depressed, and there's only a little clear liquid left in the barrel." He glanced at the corpse lying beside him. "Do you suppose it's how this fellow met his end?"

"I believe it's time for us to pack up and join everyone in the ballroom," said Felicity tightly, determined not to become mixed up in any kind of trouble, especially not a potential murder with possible links to illicit drugs.

Alex looked up at Felicity. He made no effort to hide his excitement at his discovery. "And we shall do just that. But have you any thoughts on what might be happening here?"

Felicity drew in a breath. "None that I care to share."

Alex grimaced. "Are you really Lady Felicity Quick?"

Felicity drew back her chin. "What's that supposed to mean?"

"I'm beginning to think—" Alex stood up "—that Lady Felicity Quick has an identical twin with the same splendid fashion sense, yet not an ounce of journalistic instinct. Or was the part you played in unravelling the mystery at Lower Diddleton indeed just a series of coincidences, as I've heard you rather too modestly telling people?"

Felicity opened her mouth, then closed it. After a brief pause, she spoke. "Naturally, I have my ideas. I just don't care to share them with you. That's all."

Alex sighed and stepped back across the bathroom, careful to avoid the valet's body. "It was perhaps foolish of me, but I was imagining we might somehow work together on this. It went rather well the last time, didn't it?"

As Alex came to stand beside Felicity in the narrow dressing room, his hands in his pockets, she could smell vetiver and the note of freshness he always had about him. It made Felicity think of early spring meadows, the dense grass spotted with daisies.

"Did it?" she pondered.

"I wouldn't want to drag you into anything you didn't feel comfortable with, of course. I know about the restrictions Jasper has put on your reporting, but I should like to hear your opinion on a few matters."

Felicity hesitated. Was there really any harm in discussing things with Alex? From experience, she knew him to be trustworthy.

She lifted her eyebrows. "Matters such as?"

Alex turned away and began folding the flash's tripod. "Well. We have a dead body and a missing man."

"And a missing dog," added Felicity, because just as she couldn't imagine life without a canine companion, she couldn't stand to leave such statements uncorrected.

A little smile appeared on Alex's lips as he dismantled the flash. "And a missing dog. A big one, if I'm not mistaken?"

"A mastiff, I believe. You've not met her?"

Alex shook his head. "The last anyone knows, the valet was with

Lord Langton — and his dog — helping him ready himself for the interview with you."

Felicity nodded.

"When the time came for his lordship to make his appearance, Lord Langton and his hound couldn't be located, and Mr Greenwood, the valet, was dead."

"That's also my understanding," confirmed Felicity.

"And we know the valet's death couldn't have been natural or accidental."

Felicity nodded. "Because otherwise Lord Langton would have reported the death to the rest of the household."

With the T-frame flash removed from its stand and the tripod folded and ready to be replaced in its case, Alex paused. "So, did Lord Langton kill his valet and flee?"

Felicity turned her attention to the camera and began removing it from its tripod. "There's another possibility."

"Which is?"

Felicity was quiet for a moment as she lifted the camera from its stand and carried it to the case near the door that connected the dressing room to the hall.

Again, she hesitated, considering whether to speak. Alex had kept her secrets from Jasper before, and expressing her ideas in a private conversation wasn't the same as actively becoming involved in the matter. If she was honest, it was also rather thrilling to be discussing her ideas with someone.

Felicity crouched to place the camera in its dedicated indent in the red felt lining of its case, tying it in place with the fastenings. "Lord Langton might have felt he was in danger."

There was a pause.

"Go on," said Alex.

Felicity re-crossed the thick rug to the camera's tripod and began dismantling its legs. "He was attacked, and he fled."

"Attacked by whom?"

"Perhaps he and his valet were set upon by someone, and Lord Langton and his dog escaped, while the valet did not. Or—" The camera's tripod now folded away, Felicity began carrying it back towards the case. "Perhaps Lord Langton was set upon by his valet."

Alex frowned. "And Lord Langton turned the tables?"

"The dead man's jacket sleeve is torn, is it not?"

Alex nodded.

"From a dog's bite, would you say?"

Alex glanced thoughtfully towards the bathroom where the dead man still lay. "Why flee if your would-be attacker had been overcome?"

Again, Felicity hesitated. As a precaution, she spoke barely above a whisper. "Because the valet wasn't working alone."

Alex's frown deepened. He matched Felicity's quiet tone. "You mean to say Lord Langton fled his own home for fear of an enemy — or enemies — within?"

A knock at the dressing room door made Felicity jump.

"Lady Felicity? Mr Cooper? May I c-come in?"

Felicity wasn't especially familiar with the voices of the male members of the household at Langton Manor, but it was clear from the stammer who had interrupted her discussion with Alex.

"Please do," called Felicity briskly and a little nervously.

The door opened to reveal the bespectacled Jacob standing in the hallway. "Mrs Ridgeway s-sent me. Lord Langton's sister, that is. Not Mr Oswald Ridgeway's wife." He cleared his throat. "Mrs Ridgeway w-wanted you to know that everyone is gathered in the ballroom and that she'd be most p-pleased if you were to join us. If you're finished here, that is."

"But of course," said Felicity, feeling more than a little flustered. Had the secretary been able to hear her and Alex through the door? She sincerely hoped not. "I believe we're quite finished in here. Isn't that so, Mr Cooper?"

"Well, yes," said Alex, bringing the flash and its tripod over to the carrying case. "I would say so. Except we didn't photograph the bedroom."

"N-no need for that," said Jacob, flapping a hand. "They wouldn't have been in there. Not after rising from bed. Here." He stepped past Felicity, then Alex, and went to the door to the bedroom. Grasping the round brass handle, he twisted it and flung open the door. Jacob's disregard for the matter of fingerprints at a crime scene shocked Felicity, but she supposed, from the ease with which the secretary moved through the space, that he was accustomed to being present in Lord Langton's rooms and that the police would find his fingerprints everywhere, anyway.

"See?" he said, gesturing to the bedroom beyond.

Alex went to Jacob's side and peered into Lord Langton's bedroom. As a journalist, Alex could be rather ruthless, and he was apparently unashamed of seeming at all curious about where the peer slept.

Felicity moved more hesitantly towards the end of the dressing room, unconvinced of the appropriateness of being invited to gaze unnecessarily into a man's bedroom. They at least had a purpose for being in Lord Langton's dressing room and bathroom.

Nevertheless, Felicity went and looked.

It seemed a perfectly normal bedroom, decorated mainly in rich blue with gold accents. The bed, which was large with a simple mahogany frame, had been neatly made, and even the pillow of the large dog bed at the side of the room had been plumped. Only the pale grey light from the foggy window made the scene at all unusual.

"We had a good rummage around when we were looking for his l-lordship," said Jacob, "but I gather the maid's been by since to straighten everything up."

Felicity sank a little with despair at the idea of the dressing room and adjoining bathroom having been rummaged through and tidied as well. Both spaces seemed suspiciously tidy given what had apparently transpired earlier that morning.

"I wonder how useful our photographs will be to the police if everything's already been tampered with," remarked Alex, as though speaking Felicity's thoughts.

The secretary's eyebrows shot up. "Oh, no. We all agreed n-not to come in here as the butler and footman had already looked earlier on. Nothing has been touched, at least not by any of the search p-party."

"Who was involved in the search party?" asked Felicity.

"Well, it was myself, Mr Sebastian Ridgeway, the b-butler, and the footman."

Felicity nodded, her fingers itching for her notepad. Alex glanced at her with a hint of amusement, as if aware of her frustration.

"So," said Jacob, pulling the bedroom door closed. "Shall I escort you to the b-ballroom, then?"

"Please," said Felicity with some relief, although she had enjoyed discussing her theories with Alex.

"Very well," said Jacob.

Felicity followed Jacob into the corridor, and Alex bent to pick up the camera case.

"Please, let me t-take it," said Jacob, and after collecting the case, he hurried ahead to where the footman was waiting at the top of the stairs.

"So, you're on the story as well now, are you?" whispered Alex as he walked alongside Felicity towards the portrait-lined staircase.

"It's only natural for one to be curious about what happened." While her tone was flat, her feelings about the situation were anything but. She felt as though she was being torn in a thousand directions at once.

"But you're more than casually curious, aren't you?"

Alex's blue eyes flashed with mischief. It was suddenly clear he'd been deliberately pricking Felicity towards taking a more active interest in the situation at Langton Manor. But seeing through the machinations of his efforts didn't lessen their effect.

To top it off, Felicity, a Devon native, still felt a faint sense of territorial rivalry towards Alex, a Londoner who'd been in the county merely months. He'd attempted to steal a story on home ground from under her nose before. She wouldn't allow him to do it again, and Felicity knew from experience the best way to achieve this was to work with him. Jasper wouldn't have to know. Alex had kept her secrets before. And it was enough for Felicity that she herself would know she'd had a hand in the story, even if it was Alex's name on the article when it appeared in the newspaper.

Felicity had to be patient for a real chance to be a crime reporter in a way that Alex — or any other male journalist, for that matter — didn't. But that didn't mean she had to miss out on all the fun while waiting.

She spoke quietly. "I thought you said you wanted us to work together on this?"

They began their descent down the stairs behind Jacob and the footman, who was now carrying the camera case.

"I did say that," whispered Alex, hope glinting in his eyes.

Felicity smiled. "Then it's agreed. We're a team."

Chapter Nine

Felicity's heels clicked across the granite flagstones of Langton Manor's entrance hall as she and Alex followed Jacob towards the ballroom.

"What did you make of the s-scene up there?" The secretary was doing his best to speak casually, but there was an undercurrent of nervousness about everything he did.

Alex glanced at Felicity. "Not much," he answered on both their behalves. If they were going to investigate the happenings at Langton Manor, a subtle approach would be needed. "Some poor fellow lying face-down on the bathroom tiles."

Jacob nodded. "Yes, I suppose you're right," he said, which prompted Felicity to wonder just how many members of the household had already tramped through the crime scene, and whether her and Alex's efforts to capture it on film had any merit at all. "I suppose we sh-shan't know for some time what exactly happened to him," continued the secretary. "Of course, it would change everything if anything were to h-happen to Lord Langton."

"Everything?" asked Felicity.

Jacob glanced at Felicity as they entered a carpeted corridor off the entrance hall. "It would mean leaving everything to his lordship's son, Derek." He threw a nervous look at Alex. "And th-that wasn't his lordship's intention at all, as I'm sure you're aware. The solicitor was supposed to come t-today to oversee the signing of the new will."

"Of course, and I understand the interview I was to carry out had been planned to coincide with the change." Felicity spoke as neutrally as possible, but the timing of the change to the will was too much of a coincidence to ignore. And if anything had happened to Lord Langton, then Felicity was now a guest in Derek's home.

Alex's blue eyes were dark with concern. "Would Derek be the only person to benefit if anything were to happen to Lord Langton? Ahead of the change to his will, I mean." Alex's mind had gone in the same direction as Felicity's, but with the added complication that he, for some inexplicable reason, considered Derek a pal.

The secretary's eyebrows drew together, creating a series of creases that extended across his forehead. "I hadn't thought of it like th-that." His voice trembled a little. "But you have rather a point, I must say."

The conversation was cut short as they arrived at a set of panelled double doors. Jacob pushed them open, and the three of them entered Langton Manor's ballroom.

The ballroom was a vast space. Its high ceilings were decorated with ornate plaster moulds painted in cream, gold, and a delicate pale grey-green. Three enormous chandeliers dripping with crystal pendulums and lit with electric lights filled the room with a warm, sparkling glow, which was amplified by a wall of long mirrors in gilt frames separated by flat plaster columns decorated in the same ornate style as the ceiling.

A large marble fireplace — unlit because of the fog — occupied the centre of the mirrored wall. Gathered around the fireplace on chairs and sofas upholstered in a pale silvery green were Clarissa, Miss Blanchard, Oswald, Frida, the nursemaid with the thankfully now-content baby on her lap, and a tall blonde woman in her mid-thirties whom Felicity didn't recognise.

A short distance away, towards tall windows white with fog, was a round table at which Derek, Elodie, and Sebastian were seated. A game of mah jong appeared to be in progress.

In the room's corner was an elaborate buffet. The racks of hors d'oeuvres, towers of translucent jelly, and canisters of hot drinks had doubtlessly been prepared for Clarissa's now-cancelled party. The butler stood impassively beside the buffet table, as did two extravagant arrangements of the same flowers that adorned the entrance hall. The lilies sweetened the air.

Jacob left Felicity and Alex and made a beeline for the food.

Felicity shivered. The large room was chilly, but there was also the unappealing possibility that one — or more — of the people gathered had been involved in the valet's demise and the lord's disappearance.

Derek leaned back in his chair. "Coop, old chap." He was wincing against the smoke of a cigarette held in the corner of his mouth, his hands full of tiles and scoring sticks. "Know anything about this blasted game? Sebastian's got us cornered."

Alex lifted a subtle eyebrow towards Felicity and set off for the mah jong table. Although they'd agreed to work together, they hadn't yet agreed on how and to what end. That didn't prevent Felicity from being mildly offended by Alex's prompt departure from her side to join Derek, even though Felicity was alone for no longer than a moment.

Under the watchful eye of Miss Blanchard, Clarissa pressed herself to her feet from a chair beside the fireplace and approached.

"Did you manage to get the photographs, Lady Felicity?"

Felicity nodded. "I believe so. The Kodak is eminently reliable. I suspect police have their own methods of capturing such images, of which Mr Cooper and I are not aware. I hope our efforts will be of some help."

"Well, you've certainly put my mind at ease," said Clarissa with a heave of her large sparkling chest. "It'll discourage whichever other members of staff are involved in this whole mess from fiddling around with things up there, that's for certain. And I must commend your fortitude, Lady Felicity, taking a dead body in your stride like that."

Felicity didn't share Clarissa's outlook on servants being more criminally inclined than anyone else, but it was true that the valet could have played a nefarious role in whatever had happened that morning in Lord Langton's private chambers. It wasn't an idea to share with Clarissa, however. Felicity would limit discussion of her theories to Alex, but as laughter rose from the mah jong table, she wondered how far Alex's association with Derek would allow him to take a neutral position.

Clarissa leaned on her silver-topped cane, watching as the butler poured tea for Jacob. "It's not at all what I had in mind for my birthday. Such a frightful pity, all the preparations going to waste. To think of all the fabulous occasions that were once held here." Clarissa sighed, lifting kohl-lined eyes to the chandeliers. "It's been absolutely wasted on my brother."

With its carpets and furniture, the ballroom was no longer set up for dancing, but it was still possible to imagine the balls that might have been held there over the decades, with musicians in attendance and candle wax dripping into the early hours. Yet something about Clarissa's manner perturbed Felicity, and she supposed that if she and Alex were working together, then their split was so they could carry out their own lines of investigation.

"Are you not concerned for Lord Langton, Mrs Ridgeway?"

"Who, Edward? Gosh, no. He's as tough as old boots and can take care of himself. He'll show up eventually, I'm certain of it." Clarissa put a hand on Felicity's elbow and began walking her towards the buffet table. "It's practically lunchtime. Won't you take a plate? There are a few odd items you perhaps won't recognise. Sebastian insisted on an Italian theme, but I made sure there were at least some English options. Edward hated the whole party idea, of course. He can't stand people having fun if he isn't having any. And my brother is always very careful to ensure he has no fun at all."

Felicity gently halted the process of her being swept towards the buffet table and glanced around the room. "That's incredibly kind, Mrs Ridgeway, but I'm actually wondering where Pip might be."

"Pip?" Clarissa said the little dog's name as though it were not a word but an unfamiliar foreign sound.

"The Yorkshire Terrier I arrived with," said Felicity patiently, although she was beginning to feel rather impatient about the matter. "You said you'd look after him while I was upstairs taking the photographs."

"Oh, why, yes. Of course." Clarissa's face relaxed. "He's with Charlotte. They're still in the morning room."

"The dogs have been left alone?" It wasn't at all Felicity's idea of 'taking care' of anything.

"There's no need to worry, Lady Felicity. They have no access to the outdoors. And they were having such a lovely time together. I thought, why interrupt their play?"

Felicity's eyes widened a little, but she kept her reaction under control. If Pip were to cause damage to any antiques, furniture, or haberdashery — and the little dog had chewed on a curtain tassel or two in his time — Felicity would have been deeply embarrassed. Moreover, there was already a dog missing from Langton Manor. She didn't want Pip to be next.

"That's extremely considerate of you, Mrs Ridgeway, but if you don't mind, I'd like to fetch him." Felicity started for the door to the corridor, resolute that she'd keep Pip close at hand until the end of her stay at Langton Manor.

"Crowther," called Clarissa. "Bring Charlotte and her companion to the ballroom, would you? Lady Felicity, please. There's no need for you to go running around the manor by yourself. I'm sure Charlotte will be disappointed at having her playtime interrupted, but you'll have your little companion back at your side in no time at all."

Felicity smiled politely, not betraying her growing anxiousness to be reunited with Pip. "Thank you, Mrs Ridgeway."

"Will you take a bite to eat? I can highly recommend the, um. The..." Clarissa craned her neck, from which multiple ropes of beads hung. "What are they called, Sebastian?"

"Cannoli," replied Sebastian from the mah jong table without looking up from the game. Alex and Derek also had their eyes on the tiles. Elodie, on the other hand, stared dreamily at the foggy windows.

"Cannoli," said Clarissa with satisfaction. "That was it. Cook didn't have any of the special cream they use traditionally, so she employed our local clotted cream as a substitute. The effect, I'm told, is really very similar to how they're made in Italy. You wouldn't notice any difference."

Clarissa held a hand out towards the food. Felicity wasn't hungry in the slightest, but she cast an admiring eye over the buffet table.

There was a large platter of decoratively arranged cold meats, neat piles of cucumber sandwiches that had been cut into squares, a salmon terrine, something that looked like scotch eggs covered in orange breadcrumbs, and the cannoli highlighted by Clarissa, which to Felicity looked like pale brandy snaps stuffed with cream and decorated with chopped nuts.

"That's awfully kind of you, Mrs Ridgeway," said Felicity. "And it all looks tremendously delicious. Perhaps later."

Before Clarissa could press further, Felicity's attention was stolen by the young ungainly footman arriving in the ballroom, a small wriggling dog under each arm.

"There you are, Pip," said Felicity, approaching the footman to take the Yorkie and tucking the little dog firmly under her arm. "Thank you."

She stroked the familiar softness of the Yorkie's ears and head. Had she not been in company, she would have explained aloud to Pip that there would be no further gallivanting with Charlotte and that he would remain close at hand until they left Langton Manor. Hopefully, the firmness of her grip and caresses communicated this to the little dog.

Clarissa accompanied the footman as he brought the Pomeranian to the sullen-faced Miss Blanchard, who remained seated beside the unlit fireplace. Miss Blanchard pressed the little black dog onto her lap without a hint of friendliness. In contrast, Clarissa lavished affection on the canine, stroking her head, tugging on her ears, and tickling her under the chin. Having tired one another out, both dogs were now calm, although they still watched one another with interest.

"I'm not sure how you do it."

The voice belonged to the tall blonde woman to whom Felicity hadn't yet been introduced. She stood before Felicity, holding a plate containing a single cucumber sandwich. Despite a shapeless moss-green jumper and a similarly ill-fitting taupe skirt, the woman's natural handsomeness was undeniable. She had honey-gold hair in a practical bob, a noble nose, and rich brown eyes.

"Oh," said Felicity, a little taken aback, her hand still stroking Pip's head. "How I do what?"

"Make so many allowances for these creatures. Father's the same. I grew up under the impression he'd lay his life down for his dog sooner than for myself or either of my brothers."

Felicity hesitated before replying. It was a lot to take in on a first meeting. "I don't believe we've been introduced," she suggested gently, although Felicity suspected she'd already fathomed who the woman was.

"Ursula Langton," said the blonde woman, extending a hand. "And you're Lady Felicity Quick, are you not?"

"That's right," said Felicity as Ursula gave her hand a firm shake. "You're Lord Langton's daughter, are you not?"

Ursula nodded. "The eldest of three sibs. Although that doesn't count for much if you're unlucky enough to be born a girl."

Felicity smiled faintly. It was hard to tell if Ursula was attempting to be funny. Because of her sex, Felicity was accustomed to being underestimated and having to work harder to prove herself, but she was Jasper's younger sister and had therefore never been skipped over as Ursula must have been.

Ursula smiled sardonically. "You know, I sometimes wonder what life would have been like had I been born a boy."

The woman's frankness put Felicity a little on edge. She did her best to hide it. "I believe if we'd all been born boys, the world would be quite a different place."

Ursula sighed. "It would have been easier to build my career, that's for certain."

"What work are you in?"

"Scientific research, at the Sorbonne, in Paris."

"You live in Paris?" Felicity couldn't hide her enthusiasm for France's capital. "How absolutely lovely. I've always dreamed of visiting."

Ursula scoffed. "I don't live in France for the sight-seeing. I would have stayed in England, but a woman researcher was a step too far, and I hadn't the energy to fight the established way of things. All I wanted was to get on with my work. Had father been willing to support me, I might have set up my own facility."

There was a bitterness in Ursula's tone that Felicity couldn't fully relate to. Although her career in journalism wasn't without its setbacks, Jasper was broadly supportive of her, and even their grandmother had come around to the idea.

More striking than the obstacles Ursula had met because of her sex, however, was her lack of concern for her father.

"Still," probed Felicity, "you must be terribly worried about Lord Langton's whereabouts. Everything that's happened today is quite awful."

Ursula cocked her head incredulously, but before she could say anything, she jerked forward, the cucumber sandwich sliding off her plate and onto the floor before Felicity's feet.

As Pip extended his neck and sniffed with interest, Ursula twisted sharply to look behind her.

Elodie, her white fur wrap crooked around her shoulders, was sauntering by unsteadily, having bumped into Ursula without even noticing.

"What the…" muttered Ursula.

At the mah jong table, Derek sat up straight, his eyes following Elodie as she continued her languid approach towards a set of French doors at the centre of the ballroom's windows.

"I go outside," she said in her thick French accent. "If they can go outside, I can go outside. No?"

Chapter Ten

Ursula scowled at Elodie as the latter approached the French doors. Through the glass, there was nothing to see but white-grey fog. *If they can go outside, I can go outside.* That's what Elodie had said, but who had she meant by 'they'?

Ursula turned to her brother. "If you must insist on inflicting your friends upon us, Derek, the least you can do is keep them under control."

Derek rose to his feet from the mah jong table, where Alex and Sebastian had also ceased play. "Elodie, darling."

Elodie had reached the doors and was fumbling with the handle, her pretty face creased with unsuccessful concentration.

Felicity took a step towards her, Pip still craning his neck in the direction of the sandwich Ursula had let fall. "Who did you say was outside, Miss Rossignol?"

"Darling," Derek insisted. "Come back and sit down."

To Pip's disappointment, the footman swooped forward to collect Ursula's dropped sandwich as Clarissa and Oswald made their way over from the fireplace. With Charlotte tucked under her arm, Miss Blanchard followed Clarissa, her usually sullen face now a deep, resentful frown directed at the wayward Elodie.

Derek also began moving towards the French doors. Felicity met

Alex's eye briefly, but he remained seated at the mah jong table. Sebastian leaned back in his chair, as though enjoying a scene from a theatre play.

Elodie dropped her hands with a sigh, having met the limit of her patience trying to get the doors open.

"They," Elodie said, jabbing a finger towards the footman, who looked stunned by the gesture. "I see them outside. They are moving around all the time. I shall move around also."

Felicity peered outside, but all she could see was thick mist. Was Elodie imagining things?

"Let's go back and sit down, shall we, darling?" There was a hint of irritation in Derek's tone as he arrived alongside Elodie, his hands tucked into the pockets of his plus-fours.

Clarissa turned to the butler. "Crowther, is that correct? Are the staff moving around outside?"

The butler blinked inscrutably. "Besides the footman and myself, all staff are gathered in the servants' hall, ma'am, as per the police's instructions relayed to us by Mr Ridgeway."

Derek put a hand on Elodie's arm. "We agreed with Oswald to follow the advice of the police, didn't we, darling?"

Elodie turned towards him. In her wavering ice-blue eyes, there was defiance but also confusion and weariness. After a slight amount of resistance, she allowed Derek to lead her by the hand.

The butler gave a nod to the footman, who removed himself from the ballroom.

Oswald approached the French doors and touched the handle, ensuring they were still firmly closed. Then he turned to address the room, his hands behind his back. "I'm dreadfully sorry that we all need to stay cooped up in here. But as I'm sure you can appreciate, the conditions here at Langton Manor are quite out of the ordinary, and the measures we're taking must therefore also be so." He turned to Elodie, casting not even a hint of exasperation her way. "I'm sure we'll be back to normal as soon as Lord Langton is found safe and well."

Derek's only reaction to Oswald's brief speech was to give his cousin a cool glance. He seemed to have no desire to step up to take control of the situation in the absence of his father, and neither did he seem bothered that Oswald was taking on the role. Derek's passivity was perhaps one of the reasons why Lord Langton was changing his will.

"We're all trapped here," said Clarissa, clutching a length of beads at her neck, "while others are desperate to be here and cannot attend. It's a thoroughly twisted situation."

Oswald sighed from under his dark moustache. "I'm sure the solicitor will be here as soon as the fog is lifted, Mama."

"The solicitor?" Clarissa's powdered brow creased. "I wasn't talking about my brother's will, dear boy. I was talking about laughter. About celebration. About people enjoying themselves. That's what my party would have given to the world. But I don't expect you to understand. You and Edward are just the same. All you can think about is money."

A flush of pink appeared on Oswald's neck, but his manner remained calm. It was perhaps not the first time his mother had spoken to him in this way. "The will isn't only about money, Mama. In fact, Uncle Edward shall be leaving me hardly any cash at all."

"Derek should get everything." The outburst was Elodie's. She was nearly back at the mah jong table, her hand still in Derek's.

Felicity raised her eyebrows a little at Alex. The expression he responded with was rather stiff and serious.

"Elodie, darling. Please." Derek sounded vexed by his companion's outburst.

Oswald smiled and shook his head. His cheeks had become quite red. He was experiencing more emotion than he wished to let on. "Is no one here concerned about Uncle Edward's whereabouts?"

Felicity was delighted. The question she'd been wanting to ask had at last been aired. She would have loved to have taken out her notepad, but it would have been entirely inappropriate. A victorious glance at Alex had to suffice, but he was watching Derek and Elodie.

Ursula sighed rather loudly. "Oh, Oswald. Do you not believe Father can look after himself? And I'm sorry, but for once I must agree with one of Derek's companions. I'm a modern woman, but tradition still counts for something, particularly in a family like ours. I came all the way from Paris for Aunt Clarissa's birthday, yet no one had the decency to tell me about all this changing-of-the-will nonsense before my arrival. Probably because Father knew I'd be upset about it. It's nothing against you personally, Oswald. I'm sure you're a very fine businessman, whatever that means. But put simply, I don't see why anything should pass out of the direct family line. I really don't."

"What an absolute darling you are, Ursula," simpered Clarissa. "You make an excellent point." Clarissa's was an odd reaction, because Ursula's negativity was mainly aimed at Clarissa's own son. It was a great pity, but not all families held one another in such high esteem as Felicity's own family did.

"Perhaps if you'd found yourself a husband by now," said Oswald matter-of-factly to Ursula, "Uncle Edward wouldn't have seen any need to rewrite his will."

Felicity's heart sank a little. Oswald had been the voice of reason at Langton Manor up to now. She could tell from his tone and the plain manner in which he looked at Ursula that he meant no harm with the remark. He was simply stating what he believed to be a fact.

Ursula experienced the remark quite differently, however. Her eyebrows lowered.

"I don't believe that to be s-strictly true, Mr Ridgeway." Approaching briskly from the buffet table, Jacob spoke before Ursula had a chance to. "I mean to say, you've w-worked alongside his lordship for several years now. I don't see how a husband of the Honourable Miss Langton's would prove an a-automatic substitute —" Jacob broke off, his fingers nervously playing with the button on his brown pin-striped jacket. "If the Honourable Miss Langton were to m-marry, of course."

Ursula and Oswald looked equally baffled by Jacob's contribution to the discussion. Not quite a servant yet certainly not a family member, it was somewhat audacious of Lord Langton's secretary to share his opinion during a discussion among members of the family.

"Well," said Clarissa with a short huff, keen to usher the conversation onwards. "Besides Oswald and Edward, there's at least one other among us who's not displeased with the new will."

Everyone followed Clarissa's kohl-lined gaze towards the seating by the fireplace and the back of Frida's yellow brocade jacket.

As if able to feel the stares, Frida turned her attention away from the baby on the nursemaid's knee and looked over the back of the sofa at her mother-in-law.

"I'm sorry," she said in a thin, girlish voice. "Did I miss something?"

Clarissa rolled her eyes. "You'd be happy about Lord Langton's new will if it ever gets signed. Wouldn't you, Frida, dear?"

"Oh, of course." Frida's heart-shaped mouth drew into an obliging smile. "If Oswald is happy, then I'm happy. Isn't it just so, darling?"

Oswald tugged at his shirt collar and nodded distractedly. He had other things on his mind than his wife's or even his own happiness.

Stroking Pip's smooth head, Felicity fantasised about what she might write in her beloved notebook, which sat waiting for action in her pocket. In her expert-level Pitman shorthand, she would have divided a page into three columns. At the top of each column, she would have written three headings: *Gains from the new will*, *Loses from the new will*, and *Neutral*.

So far, Oswald and Frida were clearly under *Gains* and Derek under *Loses*. Elodie could be put under the same heading as Derek, as they were clearly close and extremely fond of one another, but not being married or even engaged — at least that was Felicity's summation from the way the rest of the household addressed Elodie — there would be no guarantee of benefits for her.

For the rest of the household, it wasn't yet clear in which column they belonged. The likes of Jacob and Miss Blanchard would most likely fall under *Neutral*, with nothing to gain or lose, but even a small bequest could be life-changing to a member of staff.

However, taking out her notebook wasn't any kind of option, and it would remain that way until Felicity was either alone or with only Alex. So the three-columned list had to remain in Felicity's mind, at least for the time being.

She looked over at Alex, but he was in a whispered discussion with Sebastian.

The footman had reentered the ballroom and approached the butler. The butler stepped forward and addressed Oswald.

"There's a telephone call, sir."

"Who is it?"

"Lord Dimbleby's secretary, sir."

"Did he say why he's telephoning?"

Jacob speedily finished a mouthful of jelly, replacing his plate on the buffet table. "I'll take it."

"Nonsense," said Clarissa, bustling towards the butler, beads clacking, Miss Blanchard and Charlotte in her wake. "This will be another apology for the party. Oh, I still can't quite believe it. The splendid time we would have had. With Italian sweets and boat rides out on the lake. And look at it now." She swept a dramatic arm towards the ballroom's windows. "One can't even see the water."

Sebastian got up from the mah jong table. "Shall I go for you, Mother?"

"Would you? Oh, Sebastian, you're such a darling."

"N-no need," said Jacob, who was already at the ballroom door. "We've been waiting for a call from Lord Dimbleby's office. It'll be b-business matters."

"Lord Dimbleby was on the invitation list, wasn't he?" asked Sebastian.

Clarissa placed a hand melodramatically on her chest. "And Lady Dimbleby."

"Please, Mr Cherry." Oswald made a shooing motion with his hand. He sounded exasperated. "You go."

Sebastian shrugged before returning to the mah jong table, where Derek and Elodie had also retaken their seats. The door to the ballroom closed with a gentle click after Jacob.

Clarissa started towards the seating area. She made a beckoning motion, bracelets rattling at her wrist. "Lady Felicity, come. Let us sit together. We Langtons and Ridgeways are awfully sick of one another's company, as I'm sure you've noticed by now. Perhaps you can avail us with a tale or two from your work for your brother's newspaper."

Again, a little shudder of surprise passed through Felicity as she moved from the status of observer to centre of attention in the blink of an eye. This time, she was better prepared.

Frida's eyes widened with girlish thrill at Felicity as she, Oswald, Ursula, and Miss Blanchard approached the seating area beside the fireplace at Clarissa's behest.

"Oh, yes," said Frida. "Please do share with us a story or two. Or better yet, give us your assessment of our own mystery. The one with the dead valet and the missing lord."

Oswald frowned at his wife as he landed heavily back in his seat. "Now, now, Frida. That's my uncle you're talking about."

Ursula found a place on the sofa next to Oswald. "Frida's right. We have the makings of a detective novel on our hands here." Her tone was one of dry amusement. "Perhaps you could tell us how the story might end, Lady Felicity?"

Lowering herself gingerly into a wingback chair opposite the sofa upon which Clarissa, Miss Blanchard, and Charlotte were now sitting, Felicity placed Pip on her lap and smiled nervously.

All eyes were upon her, yet Felicity could not be seen to take an active, journalistic interest in the affair unfolding at Langton Manor. At the same time, she was a fully capable news reporter and loath to give anyone the impression she was anything but.

In short, Felicity faced a conundrum.

Repositioning Pip on her lap, she took a deep breath.

Chapter Eleven

"It was my idea to invite you, you know."

Frida broke the silence around the ballroom's fireplace.

It was an enormous relief to Felicity when the gazes that had been awaiting a pronouncement from her on the valet's death and Lord Langton's disappearance switched to the red-headed woman.

Frida leaned forwards in her chair, her baby gurgling on his nursemaid's knee beside her. "I told Oswald that he and Lord Langton ought to ask for you in particular. You do write so exceedingly well."

Frida's eyes glittered, and she spoke as though sharing a confidence with Felicity, but there wasn't anyone gathered by the unlit fireplace who wouldn't have been able to hear her. James followed his mother's gaze so that the baby, too, stared in wonderment at Felicity with large, innocent eyes.

"Why, thank you, Frida," said Felicity. It was always a pleasure to meet a fan of one's work, but it was, in a sense, because of Frida that Felicity had become trapped at Langton Manor.

Oswald eyed his wife warningly. "I don't think Lady Felicity needs to be mobbed."

Frida drew back from Felicity and sat up stiffly. "You're right, Oswald. You're quite right."

From his vantage point on the nursemaid's knee, the chubby-cheeked James looked between Frida and Oswald, perhaps not too young to sense the tension in their interactions.

"But do tell us, Lady Felicity." Clarissa adjusted her position on the sofa, as though settling in to listen to a story, while Miss Blanchard remained unmoved beside her. "What are your thoughts about the situation we have here on our hands? Frida tells us you're not inexperienced when it comes to dealing with mysteries."

"Oh, not really," said Felicity a little sharply. She added a smile. "Not at all, actually."

It was painful to downplay the moments in her career that had so far brought her the most satisfaction as a journalist, but it would have been disastrous if Jasper heard Felicity had been bragging about her involvement in crime stories. All her good behaviour and boring assignments would have been for nothing.

She stroked Pip as she spoke. "I just found myself in the wrong place at the wrong time on a couple of occasions. Nothing more than that."

Ursula narrowed her eyes disbelievingly at Felicity.

Clarissa huffed and glanced at her wasted buffet. "Well, I'm very sorry to say it, but you can certainly add your visit to Langton Manor today to the list of such unfortunate occasions. Had my party gone ahead, I've no doubt you'd have wanted to write it up for your newspaper. No doubt at all."

"Will you write something about Lord Langton and his valet for the Western Daily News?" Frida kept her distance, but the sparkle in her eyes was back. Baby James swung his gaze to Felicity, long eyelashes blinking, as if to underline his mother's question.

It was Oswald's turn to lean forward in his chair, his dark moustache bristling. He turned to his wife. "Really, Frida. Our focus should be on a return to normality just as soon as Lord Langton is found. Not sensation in the newspapers."

Frida bit her cheek, and the nursemaid tried to comfort James as he grizzled unhappily.

At last, there was something Felicity felt comfortable stating, something she knew would meet Jasper's approval. "The Western Daily News isn't a sensational sort of paper."

"Oh no, I'm aware of that, Lady Felicity," said Oswald quickly. "It's a very fine publication. Your brother is undoubtedly one of the best editors there is. That wasn't at all the point I was trying to make. My apologies for giving the wrong impression."

"Crime reporting is more my area of expertise."

Somehow, Felicity hadn't noticed that Alex had left the mah jong table and come to stand by the seating area around the fireplace. He stood with his hands tucked into the pockets of his waistcoat, the front panels of his jacket pushed back, and his chest a little puffed out. His manner was uncharacteristically arrogant, but at least the attention was no longer fixed on Felicity.

Clarissa wrinkled her nose. "Your 'area of expertise', Mr Cooper?"

"Coop's a journo, all right." Derek called this out from the mah jong table, where Elodie rested her chin on her folded arms and Sebastian had his nose in the tiles. "And he's a jolly good one, too. Had a successful career on Fleet Street before coming down to these parts. He's just not very active these days. Prefers a more relaxed way of life. What, Coop?"

"That's right." Frida perked up again. "Alexander Cooper. I recognise the name from the newspaper." She twisted in her seat so that she was half-kneeling on the sofa, looking between Felicity and Alex. "Oh, how wonderful. Two journalists. Do tell us your theories. You simply must."

Oswald's cheeks grew pink. "Frida, darling, Lady Felicity and Mr Cooper are journalists. Not police investigators. And there's absolutely no point theorising. It's not going to help matters in the slightest. What we must do is wait."

Clarissa ignored her son. "You saw Greenwood's body yourself,

Mr Cooper. Based on your experience, how do you suppose the valet met his end?"

Felicity was in equal measures relieved and disappointed that the questions were now being put to Alex instead of herself, but she was still slightly nervous. What would he say?

"As I saw it, there was nothing about the scene to give any indication of the cause of death." Alex spoke with an unusual amount of swagger. It was striking that he didn't mention the syringe they'd found. "A police pathologist would need to carry out their work to determine how the man met his end."

"It can't have been natural, though, can it?" pressed Clarissa, tugging at one of her necklaces. "Otherwise Edward would have simply come downstairs and informed us that his valet had just dropped dead."

Ursula nodded. "Father is very matter-of-fact in that way."

"I must say," added Clarissa, playing thoughtfully with the beads at her neck. "If it had been Edward's old valet, Clegg, that dropped dead instead of this new one, then my brother would have run outside and drowned himself in the lake. Clegg had been with Edward for decades and was absolutely devoted."

Oswald grimaced. "I don't think this kind of supposition is helping matters at all."

Despite the nursemaid's soothing, James' grizzling intensified.

"I disagree." Derek had left the mah jong table with Elodie latched sleepily onto his arm. "Coop, please. Do go on. We're all desperate to know what's happening here. If you've any theories, it's time to spit them out."

Ursula swept at her golden-blonde bob. "I can't say I'm not curious."

Sebastian also approached the seating area beside the fireplace and took a seat on the arm of the sofa next to Clarissa, much to Miss Blanchard's visible displeasure.

The only person who had expressed resistance to hearing Alex's theories was Oswald, and he was clearly outnumbered.

Alex said nothing as he eyed the gathering, the faint hint of a smile on his face. Was he deliberately building up the tension in the room? Felicity wasn't enjoying it in the slightest.

"Do you think Lord Langton is still alive?" pressed Frida.

Oswald scoffed. "Frida, honestly. What kind of talk is that?"

"Now, I'm not an expert in anything but journalism," said Alex, without a shred of modesty. "But I've written my fair share of crime stories, and I would say this: if the valet either died of natural causes or was working alone to bring harm to Lord Langton, why should Lord Langton disappear?"

Clarissa squeezed a handful of beads at her neck. "But that's exactly what we were saying. You don't believe Edward's been kidnapped, Mr Cooper?"

"I wouldn't say anything for certain," replied Alex, "but if external forces were to blame for the valet's death and Lord Langton's disappearance, do you not think there are enough people in the household that such an incursion would have been noticed?"

Alex had the room transfixed. He'd always struck Felicity as a subtle person, but he'd transformed himself into a showman. While she was thankful Alex had taken the attention away from her, it hurt to hear the theories they'd discussed together put forward as though they were his alone. It was a side to Alex she hadn't seen before. Was it really possible for them to work together?

"There's Lord Langton's dog to consider as well," added Alex.

Frida nodded slowly. "Mollie wouldn't have allowed Lord Langton to be kidnapped."

Oswald's face darkened. "I'm confident Uncle Edward knows how to look after himself."

Clarissa batted a hand dismissively. "Oh, Oswald. You always—"

She broke off as the rattling of the ballroom's double doors caught everyone's attention.

Chapter Twelve

The doors flew open, and a rather flustered Jacob re-entered the ballroom, approaching the seating area with his swift, nervous gait.

"Ah, Mr Cherry." Oswald's tone was suddenly much brighter. "What did Lord Dimbleby's secretary have to say? Will the Alexandria deal be going through?"

Jacob cleared his throat and adjusted his spectacles. "He said Lord Dimbleby will come b-back to us on the deal next week, Mr Ridgeway. He was telephoning to, um... To wish Mrs Clarissa Ridgeway happy birthday on behalf of L-Lord and Lady Dimbleby. He also asked me to offer heartfelt apologies for their not being able to attend the party due to the f-fog."

Oswald sank dejectedly into his chair, as baby James increased his grizzling into a sorrowful, red-cheeked wail. The nursemaid bounced him on her knee.

Clarissa straightened in her seat. "Is Lord Dimbleby's secretary still on the line, Mr Cherry?"

Jacob shook his head. "No, Mrs Ridgeway. But I c-can telephone him back if you'd like?"

Quick to take the hint, Sebastian sprung to his feet. "Don't worry, Mother. I'll take care of it."

"Oh, Sebastian. What a darling boy you are. Please, ask for a message of thanks to be passed to Lord and Lady Dimbleby, and congratulate them on their youngest daughter's coming out. Let them know I intend to be present at Lord and Lady Inglewood's grouse shoot, health conditions permitting. Let them know my disappointment at the cancellation of my birthday celebrations has been almost too much to bear. You might also mention the gondola, so they at least know the trouble we went to."

As Felicity stroked Pip's silky back, she exchanged looks of subtle amusement at Clarissa's effortless melodrama with Alex. He'd positioned himself by the fireplace, an elbow on the mantelpiece, his showman's swagger now gone. They weren't getting any closer to piecing together their story, but it wasn't the right moment to ask questions. For now, they had to be patient and listen.

Sebastian gave Jacob a stiff little smile as he passed him on his way out of the room. "Don't worry, Mother. I'll do exactly that."

Clarissa sank back into her seat, almost delirious with satisfaction. "That darling boy reminds me so much of my late Gerald."

Miss Blanchard looked even more unimpressed than usual. Oswald, though still gloomy in countenance, seemed unaffected by his mother's obvious preference for his brother. At a glance, Oswald appeared to be the eldest of the two siblings, but on closer inspection, there was a freshness to Oswald's complexion that Sebastian had lost, perhaps because of his time in sunnier climates than East Devon.

The butler was busy assisting Jacob with yet another plate from the buffet, and the ballroom door was rather clumsily allowed to bang closed after Sebastian. The noise prompted James to increase the volume of his crying.

"No. No, Derek." It was Elodie again. "I cannot. I will not." She stood up clumsily from the mah jong table and approached Oswald. "You want us to stay in here like prison." Elodie jabbed at Oswald with a finger as she stood before him. "Fine. We will stay. But not with that noise." She extended her arm sharply, pointing at the crying baby, her dark bob swishing at her ears and lengths of pale chiffon draped from her sleeve.

"Elodie, darling. Really." Derek was promptly at her side, but she shrugged his hand off her arm.

Elodie's interjection resulted in the volume of James' crying increasing even further. The nursemaid did her best to soothe him but to no avail. Frida made an awkward attempt at the same. Even the stroking of James' cheeks and sweet mumblings from Clarissa didn't help. The crying continued.

Miss Blanchard remained in her seat, a look of deep disapproval on her face and the Pomeranian still pressed into her lap.

"I cannot put up with this." Elodie folded her arms and jutted her delicate pointed chin towards Oswald. "Either he leaves, or I will leave. I give you the choice."

Felicity didn't know Elodie well, but the difference between the smiling rag doll of a woman Felicity had met at the front of the house and this outraged rebel was quite staggering. One thing was abundantly clear, however. Elodie was rather keen to leave the ballroom.

"Come now," said Derek softly. "Elodie, darling."

Elodie continued to stare at Oswald, nostrils flaring.

Oswald sighed as though exhausted by everything and turned to Frida.

Noticing the attention of her husband, Frida leaned away from her crying baby. She looked at Oswald, then back at James and his nursemaid.

"It's not my fault James is always crying, you know." Frida looked at Clarissa, who shook her head unsympathetically, then at the nursemaid. "Is it?"

"Some babes are like that, ma'am," said the white-capped nursemaid over the sound of the infant wailing on her lap. "'Tis no one's fault."

"You may take James upstairs, Miss Daniels," commanded Oswald.

Frida watched the nursemaid stand up. "Wait, Miss Daniels." She turned a look of desperation towards her husband. "Can I not keep him with me unless he's absolutely silent?"

Oswald didn't return his wife's gaze.

Frida laughed with disbelief and looked appealingly at Clarissa and Ursula. "It's not James' fault he can't be silent. It's no one's fault. Is it?"

Felicity felt a great deal of pity for Frida. Although she hadn't yet had an offer of marriage — eligible suitors sadly being in rather short supply since the Great War — Felicity expected to one day have a child of her own. She could only hope her baby wouldn't cry as much as poor little James, and for a better relationship with her future husband than Frida seemed to have with Oswald. Frida had said Oswald's happiness was her own. Was the reverse also true?

Elodie remained with her arms folded, her fingers tapping impatiently on her arm. Ursula and Clarissa both wore looks of concern, but neither of them interceded on Frida's behalf. The baby's face was turning bright red from crying.

After a last look in Oswald's direction, Frida stood up and tugged at her oversized jacket. "Fine. If James must go, I go, too," she told the room.

"No, no," said Elodie, making her way suddenly towards the ballroom's double doors. "You stay with the baby who cries. I go. Then we have no problem."

"Darling. Please." Derek caught Elodie by the arm, this time a little roughly. Elodie twisted towards him, her ice-blue eyes simmering with anger.

"Come, Miss Daniels." Frida sounded defiant, but her eyes shone, and her lower lip trembled.

Oswald didn't watch as his wife and their still-crying baby carried by his nursemaid left the ballroom. Sombre and exhausted, he was a different person to the commanding businessman Felicity had met on the front steps of Langton Manor.

Alex quirked his eyebrows at Felicity. She didn't quite know what gesture to use in response, so she stroked Pip instead, which was always reassuring.

In many ways, Langton Manor was an unhappy household, and as fascinating as the tangled web of relationships between the family members was, it was a rather sorry state of affairs that so far offered no real hints about Lord Langton's disappearance or the death of his valet. The police's advice for everyone to stay together had now also fallen by the wayside.

The sound of giggling caught Felicity's attention.

Derek had translated his grip on Elodie's arm into some kind of dance move, and he spun her around so that she landed in his arms. From there, they began a close tango together, moving without music in a hypnotic and beautiful yet quite scandalous way.

Miss Blanchard frowned and clutched at Charlotte as the Pomeranian attempted to jump from her lap and join the dance. Ursula sighed and sank further into her chair, as though inconvenienced by everything. Jacob paused his eating, his mouth hanging open. Alex smiled with amusement, but Felicity was almost too embarrassed to watch.

"Oh, how splendid," said Clarissa, clapping her hands together. "What a beautiful couple you are. Yet to watch you makes me quite melancholic. You do realise there was to be dancing at my party?"

Oswald rolled his eyes and put his head in his hands.

Clarissa's obsession with her cancelled festivities was so incongruous, it was becoming comical. Was it Clarissa's way of distracting herself from the seriousness of the situation of her missing brother and his dead valet?

Derek continued to move smoothly and rhythmically, Elodie moulding herself to him, wisps of chiffon wafting around her. Derek's golf-inspired outfit wasn't exactly suited to dancing, but it didn't deter him. "We can have music, Aunt Clarissa. Elodie's a singer. Didn't I tell you? She's on the stage in London."

Clarissa's kohl-lined eyes lit up. "Is she really? Upon my soul. I wish you'd told us earlier, Derek, dear. What can she sing?"

Elodie stopped twirling, clasped her hands before her chest, and raised her eyes to the ceiling.

The words she sang were mostly unintelligible, at least to Felicity, for Elodie was singing in French and Felicity knew only a few phrases in the language, but Elodie's voice was exquisitely beautiful and as effortless as a songbird's. Even Ursula was rapt, and Miss Blanchard, although still scowling, couldn't take her eyes off her.

Felicity and Alex exchanged glances. He was as moved as Felicity.

Suddenly, Oswald slapped his hands down on his knees. "Honestly, Mama. Are you completely incapable of taking anything seriously?"

Elodie stopped singing, her eyes wide with surprise, which quickly became indignation. Before she could mount a response to Oswald's interruption, Derek swept Elodie back into their dance, and they went whirling across the carpet.

Clarissa chuckled and tightened her grip on the top of her cane. "Oswald, my dear boy. If by 'anything' you mean the things you deem to be important in life, then no. I don't believe we share the same values."

"Don't be such a deuced hypocrite, Ossie," said Derek, without missing a move from the dance to which Elodie had given herself over, and which was, to Felicity's relief, less intimate than the earlier tango. "You care as little about Father as anyone else. What you care about is money. That's why you and Father get on so bally well." Derek continued to dance as he spoke, Elodie seemingly oblivious to the heated exchange going on above her head. "But please, Ossie. Do us all the decency of giving up the pretence of being genuinely worried about him. The only thing you're worried about is the new will and your share of the spoils."

"I-I must say," began Jacob, who was still somewhat transfixed by the dancing. "I am rather f-fond of Lord Langton, and I—" he looked from Derek to Ursula "—I wouldn't like anything to happen to him."

Ursula tutted at the secretary. "None of us wish Father any harm, Mr Cherry. There's no question of it. That's not the point Derek was making."

Oswald stood up, and with his hands in his pockets, he approached the fireplace. A faint smile spread under his dark moustache as he addressed his cousin. "Do you even know how many people are employed by the companies in which Uncle Edward is involved? How many families depend on the smooth running of those businesses for their weekly wage?"

Derek frowned and mis-stepped, jerking Elodie momentarily awake from her trance.

"Careful," she said crossly, continuing to dance.

"Boys, really," clucked Clarissa. "This is no time for squabbling."

"But is it any wonder you're so relaxed?" said Oswald, continuing to address Derek as he danced past. "Should anything happen to Uncle Edward before the new will is signed, you're the one that stands to gain, and I'm the one that loses."

Derek abruptly stopped moving, leaving Elodie a little stunned.

Felicity stroked Pip's silken back. The little dog shivered, and Felicity did her best to remain impassive, but the moment was rather exciting.

If anyone had wanted to stop the new will from being signed, surely it would have been Derek. The primary suspect at the top of Felicity's *Loses from the new will* column was at last being challenged. What would he say in his defence?

Chapter Thirteen

To Felicity's surprise, Derek wasn't the first to attempt a rebuttal of Oswald's claim that Lord Langton's disappearance was convenient for Derek.

"N-now," began Jacob, placing his plate back on the buffet table. "I wouldn't go that—"

Derek stepped towards Oswald, speaking over the secretary. "Just what the deuce are you trying to say? That I'd be happy if something happened to Father? Or that I'm somehow responsible for this whole blasted situation?"

Oswald looked satisfied to have roused his cousin. With a smile barely hidden under his moustache, he said nothing.

Felicity glanced at Alex, who was still standing by the mantelpiece, but he didn't meet her eye. He was watching Derek.

Clarissa leaned on her cane. "Boys, enough," she barked.

Her tone disturbed Charlotte, who was still under the care of stern-faced Miss Blanchard. The Pomeranian whimpered, which made Pip squirm on Felicity's lap. Felicity did her best to settle the Yorkie, but she was quite distracted by the tensions and revelations popping up like fireworks around the ballroom.

Elodie, now separated from Derek, waved her hands in front of her face. "No. It is finished. For me, it is finished. I don't stay here to listen to this."

Derek stepped even closer to Oswald, his short trousers and garish jumper diminishing the aggression in the gesture. "And how do you suppose I made my own Father disappear? I was at the golf course the whole bally morning. Dash it."

Felicity's heart beat faster. The gathering was on the brink of an altercation. Alex looked none too pleased about it, his forehead furrowed.

"Oh, I shouldn't think it takes much to bribe a servant these days," said Oswald. "Does it?"

The butler, who was still stationed at the buffet table, cleared his throat by way of reaction. Oswald's accusation of bribery was indeed blunt. However, it was not entirely unfounded, for if the now-dead valet had been involved in a plot to do Lord Langton harm, he would have needed motivation.

Ursula twisted in her seat, her nose wrinkled with disgust. "Really, Oswald. Now you're going too far."

Derek narrowed his eyes at his cousin, then shook his head. He had nothing to say in his defence.

"Come," said Elodie, taking Derek by the arm. "We leave. We don't stay to listen to this. It is disrespectful. Extremely disrespectful."

Oswald made no objection as Elodie and Derek moved towards the ballroom door, Derek casting dark glances at his cousin.

Alex watched them leave but didn't follow. His face was serious. While Felicity had been fascinated by the exchange between Oswald and Derek, her hands desperate for her notepad and pencil, Alex seemed to have been deeply troubled by it.

As Derek and Elodie left the room, they pushed past the nursemaid, who approached Oswald with a sense of urgency. "Mr Ridgeway, sir. I'm sorry to bother you. Would you be able to come to the nursery, please?"

Oswald frowned. "What is there, Miss Daniels?"

"It's Mrs Ridgeway, sir."

Oswald sighed. "Is it really necessary?"

Clarissa squeezed the top of her cane. "Go. You are the poor girl's husband, after all. In sickness and in health."

Begrudgingly, Oswald got to his feet. "So much for following the police's advice," he muttered and accompanied the nurse from the ballroom. His departure was followed by an awkward silence, broken only by the rhythmic sound of Pip bringing up a hind leg to scratch his ear.

Clarissa smiled graciously at Felicity, Alex, Ursula, Jacob, and Miss Blanchard, the only people now left in the distinctly awkward atmosphere of the ballroom besides the butler, who remained stationed beside the buffet.

"Well. Here we all are," she said. "Would any of you perhaps like to try the cannoli? I do believe I'm saying that correctly. Sebastian will be back at any moment, I'm sure. Perhaps he can tell us about his travels to the region of Italy where they're made. That should help us pass the time."

Felicity's mind whirred. She wanted to follow up on the accusations Oswald made towards Derek, but how to build a bridge to such enquiries without coming across as snooping?

Before Felicity could formulate her first question, Ursula stood up and slapped down her thick, boxy skirt. "That's very kind of you, Aunt Clarissa," she said, "but if we're no longer prisoners here, then I'm going to my room where I'll prepare my things. As soon as this fog lifts, I'll be going back to Paris."

"Ursula, darling," said Clarissa forlornly as her niece strode towards the ballroom doors. "None of us are prisoners. Can we not sit as a family and enjoy one another's company?"

Jacob watched Ursula's departure with nervous, darting eyes.

As the butler closed the door behind Ursula, Clarissa shook her head. "There is no reasoning with that girl. Such a strong character. How they ever put up with her at university, I couldn't possibly know."

"I'm t-terribly sorry," began Jacob, "but if we're indeed no longer obliged to remain gathered here, it would probably be best if I, ah...

I've a tremendous amount of w-work to do, you see." As he spoke, he took a plate of food from the buffet and made his way to the exit.

Clarissa's smile turned weary as Jacob left the room. Miss Blanchard, with Charlotte still on her lap, continued to sit stoically beside her mistress. Felicity and Alex were the only other people left in the room.

"Lady Felicity, will you at least try the Italian sweets?"

Felicity felt a little sorry for the grand old woman with her thick make-up and sparkling clothes. In her queer way, Clarissa had done the most to be hospitable towards Felicity since her arrival at Langton Manor. She'd certainly been the most loquacious.

"That's awfully kind of you, Mrs Ridgeway," said Felicity, "but I've not any appetite at all. Perhaps later."

"Mr Cooper?" said Clarissa hopefully, turning towards the fireplace where Alex still stood.

He shook his head politely. "We had a cooked breakfast at the golf course."

Fearful of further interruptions, Felicity wasted no more time. "I'm terribly sorry to pry, but I couldn't help but notice the tension between your son, Mr Oswald Ridgeway, and your brother's son, Lord Derek Langton." She spoke carefully, her tone denoting both discretion and concern. "Is there usually such hostility between the two men? I ask because I don't want to have the wrong impression. The pressure of the situation must surely have a bearing on things."

Clarissa waved a hand dismissively. "Oswald and Derek have always been different. Too different to be friends, but they're not enemies. Even with Edward's ideas for his new will. Derek isn't a businessman, and he doesn't want to be one. And Oswald, well." Clarissa chuckled. "You heard the tone he took with me, his own mother. He has quite exacting standards, and it's easy for one to fall short of them. Oswald rather takes after his uncle in that respect, even to the point of disapproving of his own father. Not that my dear Gerald in any way deserves such reproach. May his soul rest in peace."

Felicity nodded. If she and Alex were to piece together a story, she would need to find a quiet moment to jot down what she could remember in her notebook. Naturally, Clarissa couldn't be quoted in the newspaper without being properly interviewed, but the information she shared helped build up a rounded picture of the situation at Langton Manor, so Felicity did her best to commit everything to memory.

The footman re-entered the ballroom and spoke with the butler.

Clarissa continued. "I doubt Derek begrudges Oswald his position in Edward's new will, not that Derek will be the only one to lose out."

To Felicity's distinct dismay, it was precisely at the point of this important revelation that the butler approached Clarissa.

"I'm sorry to interrupt, ma'am. There's a telephone call for you."

Clarissa huffed and looked towards the mah jong table, which had been completely abandoned. "Can Sebastian not take it for me?"

"The footman has tried to locate Mr Sebastian Ridgeway, ma'am, but without success. It's the Duchess of Melrose. Shall we ask the duchess to telephone again later?"

"No, no." With some effort, Clarissa pulled herself to her feet. "I'm coming right away."

Felicity did her best not to look utterly disappointed by the interruption. Clarissa was extremely forthcoming with information that may have proved relevant to the mystery at Langton Manor, but would Felicity get another chance to question her? If it wasn't only Derek who stood to lose from Lord Langton's new will, who else would be left at a disadvantage?

For the first time, Felicity glanced out at the fog in the hope it would take time to dissipate, time enough for Felicity to make sense of things.

Both Miss Blanchard and the butler accompanied Clarissa as she left the ballroom. Pip squiggled on Felicity's lap and whined as he watched Charlotte disappear from view, tucked under the arm of Clarissa's companion.

Felicity insisted that the Yorkie remain on her lap. "Hush," she told him in a rather sharp tone, which she regretted, because she wasn't frustrated at Pip. Felicity was cross about her attempt to unravel the story being scuppered.

She and Alex were now alone in the sparkling grandeur of Langton Manor's ballroom. Felicity looked up at him, certain he would understand her frustration. But Alex didn't meet her gaze with commiseration and understanding. His jaw was tight, and Felicity sensed immediately that Alex's irritation was directed at her.

Chapter Fourteen

"I know what you're thinking." Alex's tone was as serious as his gaze.

He'd already surprised Felicity several times since his arrival at Langton Manor, and it was unexpected to find herself now on the receiving end of his annoyance.

Felicity stroked Pip's ears to soothe the whimpering Yorkshire Terrier's dismay at his newfound Pomeranian companion having left the ballroom.

"Go on," said Felicity, lifting an eyebrow.

"You believe Derek's involved."

"I don't." Felicity did, however, suspect it, but there was no need to share that. It was clearly a sore point for Alex.

He frowned, taken aback. "Oh."

"And I suppose you're convinced he's completely uninvolved?"

"I actually happen to know Derek Langton very well. And I happen to know he's not capable of anything quite so evil."

It was unlike Alex to jump to conclusions about people. "What has you so convinced?"

Alex lowered his brow further, the scar on his forehead visible. "Derek saved my life."

Felicity blinked. She couldn't imagine it.

"Near Verdun," Alex added.

That it had been during the war made more sense. There were many ordinary men who had risen to the occasion to become heroes in the most extraordinary of circumstances. "What happened? If you don't mind telling me, of course."

"I was out cold." Alex's voice was tense, as though revisiting the dread of the situation. "Derek risked his own life to pull me back into the dug-out."

Felicity nodded thoughtfully. Alex's attachment to the 'bad lot' that was Derek Langton now made more sense. She wondered if the incident had given Alex the scar on his forehead, but she knew better than to pry too far into the memories of war veterans. If Alex wanted Felicity to know, he would tell her.

His hand balled into a fist on the marble fireplace. "Feel awfully dirty going undercover on him, as it is. Not that I'd have written Derek up, you understand. I was just looking for connections. But I won't have this mess with his father and the valet pinned on him. I simply won't."

Felicity was surprised by the depth of Alex's feelings. She'd only seen him as cool and under control until now.

"I quite understand," she said, and she did. One's feelings about a person weren't always straightforward, especially when you owed them a debt of gratitude. She supposed she was in the same situation with Alex.

He sighed, his fist relaxing. "I'm aware I must apologise to you," he said, his honest blue gaze reminding her of when they'd worked together at Lower Diddleton.

"Apologise?"

Looking around as though to check they were truly alone in the ballroom, Alex took a seat on the sofa next to Felicity's wingback chair, bringing with him a waft of vetiver pomade.

"I saw your reaction when I repeated what you told me," he said. "When I used your ideas about Lord Langton's disappearance. Can you trust me when I say I didn't do it to claim any glory? I did it because I was afraid you'd present your ideas yourself."

Felicity frowned, but she wanted to laugh. "Is that quite the worst thing that can happen? A woman expressing her own opinions on a matter?"

Alex's face fell with dismay. "Of course not. I did it because I didn't want anyone getting the impression you had a real interest in the valet's death and Lord Langton's disappearance. Like you said, what if there's an enemy within? What if he or she were here in the ballroom? And what if that person came to see you as a threat?"

Felicity drew her eyebrows together. The situation Alex was describing was a terrible prospect. It was also eminently possible.

She stroked Pip as her heart sank. "Now whoever it is will think you're interested. They'll think you're investigating. Why did you put yourself in danger?"

Alex looked at the carpet between them. "I imagined what your brother might say if you were to get caught up in anything again." He looked at her. There wasn't an ounce of fear in his eyes. "If they come for me, I can handle it."

While she believed him, the idea of Alex dealing with another murderer on Felicity's behalf wasn't particularly pleasing.

Felicity drew in a steadying breath. "Let's hope it doesn't come to that. They all seem quite preoccupied by their own concerns."

"No one's mourning the loss of the valet, that's for certain. Sadly, there's hardly much more concern for Lord Langton."

"We were all absolutely distraught when Father died two years ago," said Felicity, who would always be thankful for her own loving family, even if it meant infinitely more heartache when a member passed. "There seems to be more interest in Lord Langton's will than in the man himself."

A little smile broke over Alex's lips. "You Quicks tend to be the exception rather than the rule in most things. There aren't many families as close as yours, you know."

"I know," Felicity said, choosing her next words carefully. "The situation doesn't look good for Derek, though, does it? He stands to gain by preventing Lord Langton's will from being changed. Who else do we know to be in that position?"

Thankfully, Alex wasn't offended by the suggestion. "Derek mentioned it to me on a couple of occasions. He seemed only mildly bothered by it. Like Clarissa said, he's not a businessman. He likes an easy life, but he's not completely obsessed with money and fine things, and he still gets the title and the estate, remember."

Felicity took her notepad out of her pocket. Careful not to press too hard on Pip's back, she found a clean page and in Pitman shorthand — in which Alex was also fluent — she created the three columns that until that point had been only in her thoughts. Alex watched as she headed the columns *Gains from the new will*, *Loses from the new will*, and *Neutral*.

In the *Gains* column, she wrote Oswald's name and looked up at Alex. "Correct?"

Alex nodded. "Yes."

Felicity poised her pencil over the *Loses* column. "And Derek goes here?"

Alex flattened his lips. "I see him more between *Loses* and *Neutral*. On paper, yes, he loses. But he's not that bothered about it, so is that really a loss?"

Felicity nodded and put Derek's name between the two columns, as Alex suggested. However, had Derek been plotting to do away with his own father, he might have been clever enough to avoid highlighting his motive.

"And Elodie?" asked Felicity, poising her pencil above the *Loses* column.

Alex shook his head. "She and Derek aren't married. What would Elodie stand to lose if the new will comes into effect?"

"She's a passionate woman. Perhaps she'd do something to Derek's advantage in the name of love?"

"And put her own life in danger? Murder is a hangable offence."

Felicity swallowed. To put her life on the line for the man she loved was aligned with Felicity's idea of romance, but it seemed too intimate and fanciful to admit that to Alex.

"And even if she has a motive," he continued. "Would a woman like Elodie be capable?"

"Well, if the death of Lord Langton was the goal, then whoever's behind it is not looking very capable so far."

Alex looked at the page in Felicity's notebook for a moment and sighed. "I should go to Derek." He stood up. "I'm his guest here after all, and I've no doubt he's feeling absolutely rotten after everything Oswald said. Are you coming?"

Felicity was now beyond taking offence whenever anyone wanted to take care of her, but despite Derek's hero status, Alex's association with Derek still worried Felicity. Jasper surely hadn't warned her for nothing.

However, her options were limited. She could remain alone with Pip in an empty ballroom, in a house with a dead body lying upstairs and another man and his dog missing. Or she could stay close to someone she knew from experience to be extremely capable in difficult situations.

"Yes, I'll come with you."

But as Felicity stood up, tucked away her notepad, and smoothed down her skirt, she became aware of another option.

If either Derek or Elodie — or perhaps both — were in any way involved in Lord Langton's disappearance, then Felicity would do her best to awaken Alex to the real possibility of their guilt and prevent him from further exposing himself to danger.

Because although Clarissa had hinted there might be others to add to the *Loses* column, who else could possibly stand to lose as much as Derek?

As they followed Alex towards the ballroom's double doors, Pip squirmed under Felicity's arm, twisting himself towards the tall windows and whining. The little Yorkie hankered for another run around, but it wasn't the right moment to go gallivanting outside. Thick fog still swirled against the glass, as though the whole building were floating through clouds. There were also some rather serious matters to which to attend.

Chapter Fifteen

It didn't take long to locate Derek. Felicity, Pip, and Alex found him alone on a flight of stairs leading from the entrance hall to the first floor. He was leaning back on the thick oak balustrade in what, from a distance, looked like a relaxed manner, his long-socked and short-trousered legs crossed at the ankles. He no longer had on his floppy cap, and his straw-blond hair was tousled roguishly.

Ascending the plushly carpeted stairs, Felicity saw that Derek's arms were folded tightly over his chest, and his face was distinctly glum. He was staring up at a large, gilt-framed portrait of a monocled young man with a chiselled jaw in a green army officer's uniform, complete with shining brown leather boots and a sword hanging from his belt.

"What's the matter, old thing?" Alex attempted a cheerful tone, pushing back his jacket and putting his hands in his trouser pockets. "Where's Elodie?"

Derek dragged his eyes from the portrait and stared at Alex. He seemed in no mood to be cheered. "Attending to a spot of personal business. She'll be back any moment."

"You look awfully down in the mouth, old chap." Alex clearly cared about Derek, who was hopefully truly worthy of Alex's affection. "You haven't let it get to you, I hope. Everything that was said in the ballroom just now. I'm sure things were said that weren't meant."

Derek tightened the fold of his arms over his chest. "What Ossie was saying, you mean? Oh, I've never been in the least eager for his affection, and I'm not about to start now."

"I need help." The voice came from the first floor landing. Miss Blanchard appeared at the balustrade overlooking the stairs. "It's Mrs Ridgeway. She's on the floor and cannot get up."

A touch of mirth passed over Derek's sombre features. "I suppose Aunt Clarissa's had too many Italian sweets, what? Go on, Coop. I know you're always desperate to help when you can. You're much stronger than me, anyway."

Alex was indeed already ascending the stairs towards the first floor. "Will you wait here for me?" he asked Felicity, who stroked Pip under her arm as she almost blushed at the directness of Alex's question.

"Don't worry, Coop." Derek saluted mockingly. "I'll look after Felicity while you're gone. Shan't allow her to disappear or get herself murdered or whatever. You will come back though, won't you? I'm rather keen on getting your advice on a certain matter."

"Of course," said Alex as he bounded up the stairs like an eager Labrador to join Miss Blanchard.

While Felicity wasn't exactly pleased at being left alone with Derek, and she sincerely hoped Jasper wouldn't find out about it, it presented her with an opportunity.

She smiled politely at Derek and readjusted her hold on Pip. "Who is the man in the portrait?"

Derek looked confused for a beat, then up at the painted man in military uniform. "Teddy. My older brother. Dead now, of course. Battle of the Somme."

Derek turned a pained half-smile towards Felicity. It disarmed her unexpectedly.

"I'm so terribly sorry," she said, and she meant it.

Derek shook his head. "Deuced shame, of course. Ripping fellow. Nothing like me. Very much like Ursula, but without all the bitterness that comes with being a woman capable of more than what society allows her."

Felicity stroked Pip. She'd imagined she might press Derek further on losing out to Oswald in Lord Langton's as-yet unsigned new will, but the conversation had already taken an unexpected turn. She hadn't expected him to be so aware of women's struggles.

"Was Teddy older than Ursula?"

"Ursula's the eldest, but Teddy was Father's heir and favourite. And quite right, too." Derek looked up at the portrait again. "He was a far better man than I could ever be."

"I'm sure that's not true," said Felicity. She hadn't expected this level of candour from Derek, and she never liked to hear people put themselves down.

Derek looked at her. He had the same warm brown eyes as the man in the portrait, but where Derek's face was rounder and more boyish, Teddy's was angular and manly.

"Oh, it is. You don't have to be kind to me for the sake of it. Ossie's got it right. I don't understand a jot about father's business. I couldn't even if I wanted to." He gazed back up at the portrait. "I suppose I've made rather a pig's ear of it all, really. I mean, I never expected Father would go as far as changing his will."

Felicity knew it wasn't always possible to tell if a person was lying, but there was no need to allow Derek to suspect she was questioning whether he was misleading her.

"He hasn't changed it yet, though, has he?" she said gently.

Derek looked at her with a sad sort of smile. "No. You're quite right. But I'm sure he will, just as soon as he's back." He looked up at his brother. "Dash it all. I don't know why Teddy had to go and die. If anyone should have been killed in all that dreadful mayhem, it should have been me."

Derek's words saddened Felicity. The Great War damaged even those able to walk away physically unharmed.

"If Teddy were standing here today," she said carefully, "and it was your portrait on the wall instead of his, do you not think he'd be saying the same about you?"

Derek paused before returning his brown-eyed gaze to Felicity. "If Teddy were here now, I know exactly what he'd say to me. He'd say, Derek, you're acting like a perfect fool. And he'd be right. I shouldn't have pushed Father so hard. I shouldn't have done my best to defy him." He looked again at the painting of his brother. "I'm certain Father would have preferred that it was me who never came home and not Teddy."

While Felicity may not have agreed with every decision her late father had made upon her behalf, she'd never been given any reason to doubt, even for the briefest moment, how much her father loved her. And he had always made it clear that he'd loved each of his children equally.

"I'm very sorry to hear that." Felicity couldn't help but feel sympathy for Derek.

Derek pushed himself off the banister. "Oh, well," he said, the sadness quickly dissipating from his manner. "All water under the bridge now, I suppose. Aha, there's Coop. Was Aunt Clarissa sprawled out on the floor, bemoaning her cancelled party?"

Alex came down the stairs towards them. He had his jacket tucked under his arm and was rolling down his shirt sleeves. "It wouldn't be polite for me to comment."

"Aren't Coop's old-fashioned manners simply splendid?" Derek said to Felicity. "You don't find such gallantry very often these days. Say, Coop. I need your advice." Derek lowered his tone as Alex approached. "I'm being framed, aren't I?"

Alex pulled his jacket back on. "Framed for what?"

"You heard what was said in the ballroom. They think it was me, don't they?"

Guilt burned in Felicity's chest. She'd been thinking precisely along those lines. Derek had her sympathy for the loss of his sibling, but she still wasn't convinced of his innocence.

Alex gave a firm shake of his head. "You weren't here when the valet died. Elodie and I can attest to that. And while we don't know where Lord Langton is, that doesn't mean anything awful's happened to him. How could anyone frame you?"

Derek's face was tense. He leaned into Alex. "The valet, Greenwood," he whispered. "He was my recommendation to Father."

Alex's eyebrows lifted in surprise for a moment. "I see. Well. We don't yet know how the valet died." It reassured Felicity that the discovery of the syringe remained hers and Alex's secret.

"For a city man, your naivety sometimes astounds me, Coop. You can't deny how rum this whole situation is. You said so yourself in the ballroom. It looks like an inside job gone wrong. By Jove, I regret ever recommending the blighter, whoever he really was."

"How did you come to recommend him?" asked Felicity.

Derek rubbed the back of his neck. "He was Elodie's recommendation. Some down-on-his-luck waiter from a club she sings at. I actually didn't know the chap. I was simply the one to put him forward to Father."

Elodie.

It was starting to make sense, but Felicity didn't have long to ponder the development as the crash of Langton Manor's great front doors shook the walls of the entrance hall and the paintings hanging on them.

Pip yapped with surprise.

"Derek. Derek, darling." The front door wasn't visible from the stairs, but the voice with its thick French accent lifting from the entrance hall was unmistakably Elodie's. "Come, please. There is a visitor. There is someone here to see you."

A look of confusion or perhaps fear passed over Derek's face. Felicity and Alex frowned at one another.

Despite the impenetrable fog, someone had arrived at Langton Manor.

Chapter Sixteen

With Pip still firmly under her arm, Felicity followed Derek and Alex downstairs, the scent of the lilies in the floral arrangements below rising to meet them. As they reached the central landing overseen by the great window of stained glass, Elodie came into view. She stood beside Langton Manor's imposing front doors, her white fur wrap in the crooks of her elbows. Next to her stood an upright man in a brown overcoat. In his hands he held a grey homburg hat and a small leather briefcase.

"I thought you said Elodie was 'attending to personal business'," said Alex quietly.

Derek pouted. "She said nothing about going outside."

That Derek found Elodie unpredictable was an interesting point. Given her involvement in hiring the now-dead valet, Felicity was keen to understand more about Elodie's potential role in Lord Langton's disappearance.

As Derek approached, the newcomer offered him a buttery smile from under a thin moustache. "I'm awfully sorry to be so late."

"Late?" Derek peered at him. "I don't mean to be at all rude, my good man, but just who exactly are you? And how the blazes did you make it through this blasted fog?"

"Oh. Of course." The man with the hat and the briefcase looked between Derek and Elodie, and then at Felicity, Pip, and Alex. Lines of confusion appeared on his prominent forehead. "I was already on my way, you see, when the fog came down. I had the choice either to wait in my motor or to continue on foot. Mindful of my appointment and with no way of telephoning, I decided to continue to Langton Manor. It wasn't easy, but I found the place." The newcomer cast a glance upward, taking in the scale and decoration of the entrance hall. "And a very fine place it is, too." He brought his eyes back to Derek. "Once again, I am terribly sorry for my late arrival."

Derek's eyebrows drew together. "Late for what? Elodie, darling, do you know this man?"

Elodie shook her head and shrugged, her long dark lashes batting innocently. "I find him outside. That is all."

"What was that awful bang?" Ursula arrived in the entrance hall, her arms folded over her moss-green jumper. "And who is this?" she said, glaring at the man in the brown overcoat.

Jacob arrived on the scene directly after Ursula, albeit from a separate corridor.

"Oh, dear," said the man with the briefcase, smiling again. "I realise I'm being quite rude. I'm from Fenwick & Graham. George Palmer's the name."

"You're from the s-solicitor's office?" Jacob blinked nervously.

Secretly, Felicity was disappointed at this revelation. If Mr Palmer was from the solicitors' office Lord Langton used, there was unlikely to be a link to Elodie beyond her happening upon the man in the fog. What she'd been doing outside was another question, of course.

Felicity looked at Alex, but he didn't seem to share in her disappointment.

Footsteps on the stairs announced the arrival of Oswald from the first floor. "What's going on here?" His tone was both agitated and weary as he approached the group at the front door.

"Th-the solicitor's here, Mr Ridgeway," answered Jacob. "Mr G-George Palmer."

"What?" Oswald stopped. "You travelled in this fog? Mr Cherry, did you not think to call their office and inform them of our situation?"

"N-no, but I—" began Jacob.

Ursula spoke up. "We've all had rather a lot on our minds today, wouldn't you say, Oswald?"

"As I was explaining," said the solicitor. "I was already on my way over when the fog came down. I abandoned my motor and made the rest of the journey on foot. There was no way of telephoning or being reached by telephone, so I'm afraid a telephone call wouldn't have made any difference."

Oswald looked the new arrival up and down. "Well. Has anyone yet told you about the situation we've got on our hands?"

The solicitor blinked at the faces encircling him. "No. I mean, I just arrived."

Without making a sound, Sebastian had arrived in the entrance hall. He leaned against the wall close to a suit of armour and watched with calm amusement.

"Leaving the matter of the fog to one side, Mr Palmer, had someone had the sense to call your office—" Oswald glared briefly at Jacob, who was even more nervous than usual "—you'd have been informed that Lord Langton is indisposed and therefore unable to make the necessary arrangements for his new will. Your arduous journey has, I'm afraid, been for nothing."

Alarm flashed across the solicitor's face. "Indisposed?"

"My father is missing," said Derek. Elodie, who seemed to have gone rather limp, stood beside Derek, her arm looped through his.

"Missing?" Again, the new arrival glanced around the faces gathered in the entrance hall, but the solicitor received no further information. His gaze came back to rest on Derek. "You must be Lord Derek Langton, then."

Derek bowed mockingly. "The one and only."

Oswald clucked like a fussy hen. "I'm sure there'll be time for introductions later, when we've found Uncle Edward and when this wretched fog has lifted. Mr Cherry, take Mr Palmer to Lord Langton's offices and ensure he's made comfortable for the duration of his stay. I must say, I've not come across you before, Mr Palmer. Was Mr Graham not available?"

Felicity's ears pricked up.

Mr Palmer smiled apologetically. "I am rather new, I suppose. Mr Graham's youngest daughter is getting married up in Yorkshire this weekend. He and his family are travelling for the wedding."

Oswald shook his head. "Of course, of course. How could I forget?"

Felicity stroked Pip, slightly disappointed by the lack of developments relevant to the mystery at hand.

As Jacob led the solicitor briskly away from the entrance hall, Derek addressed those remaining. "Cards in the billiard room, anyone? I'm beginning to feel quite restless and simply desperate to take my mind off this whole horrible situation. Sebastian?"

Sebastian stepped away from the suit of armour with an easy shrug. "Why not?"

Derek turned to his sister. "Ursula?"

Ursula had been watching Sebastian. "Perhaps," she told her brother as she glanced again at Sebastian.

"Coop?"

Alex hesitated. He looked at Felicity.

They both knew she wouldn't attend Derek's card game, but would Alex remain with Felicity or continue to nourish his relationship with Derek?

There wasn't just the matter of what Derek had done for Alex in the war. There was also his undercover reporting. Might a link be found between the drugs trade Alex was investigating and the hypodermic syringe found next to the valet's body? Illegal drugs could be administered via injection, couldn't they?

If it was Felicity's story, she'd want to follow up.

Pip twisted a little in her arms, and she stroked him calmingly. It was unusual to hold on to him for so long, but Felicity couldn't risk the Yorkie scampering away to be reunited with Charlotte and getting lost.

"Is it happening or not, Oswald?"

Frida was on the first floor landing, leaning over the balustrade, her red hair undone from its fixings to create a frizzy copper halo around her head. She had dark circles around her eyes and looked older than before. She spoke rapidly, her voice tense.

"If the solicitor is here now," she continued, "can we not just get it over with?"

Oswald sighed wearily. While he had an incredible amount to deal with, Felicity no longer felt as much sympathy for him.

"Frida, darling." He spoke coldly. "Shouldn't you be resting?"

"Rest? How can I be expected to rest with everything hanging by a thread waiting to come crashing down all around me?"

Derek whistled quietly as Elodie smiled, both of them thoroughly amused by the open display of unrest in the Ridgeway family. Ursula still stood with her arms folded over her chest, watching the dramatics somewhat impatiently. Sebastian appeared uninterested.

"Wait right there, Frida," said Oswald, his cheeks growing pink as he re-climbed the stairs. "I'm coming to you, and we can discuss this in private."

"I'll wait here." Frida's voice was becoming shrill. She lifted her hands as she spoke. "Where else can I go? I'm trapped. Trapped, waiting for the world to come crashing down around me."

"This isn't the first time," said Ursula in low tones to Felicity. "In case you were wondering."

"Oh," said Felicity, who had indeed been wondering, but it wouldn't have been tactful to admit it. "An unhappy pairing?" she whispered in a way that she hoped was not too improper.

"Not at the beginning," said Ursula discreetly. "But since the baby came, Frida's not been herself."

Felicity wished she knew what Frida meant by 'the world crashing down'. Did she really belong alongside her husband Oswald in the *Gains from the new will* column in Felicity's notepad?

"Now, now. What's all this about?" Clarissa had joined Frida on the first floor landing, the cheerless Miss Blanchard in tow. "Frida, dear," Clarissa said as Oswald trudged upstairs towards them, past the stained glass made milky by the fog. "Don't upset yourself like this.

You're a mother now. You have responsibilities and an important role to play."

"Coop, are you coming for a game of cards or what?" Derek pressed. "Of course, your good friend and esteemed colleague Lady Felicity is welcome to join us, but I wonder very much if it's her scene."

As he said this, Derek raised an eyebrow in Felicity's direction. Felicity raised an eyebrow back at him. It seemed Derek had been considering what made Felicity tick in the same way she'd been considering him.

The neat little nursemaid had now also appeared on the first floor landing. She and Oswald brought Frida away from the balustrade.

"Aha." Clarissa had shifted her attention to the ground floor of the entrance hall, her melodious voice carrying with ease through the space. "Lady Felicity. How utterly rude of me to have abandoned you."

As Clarissa began down the stairs, Miss Blanchard offered her an arm. In Clarissa's other hand was Charlotte, who, at the sight of Pip, began wriggling and wagging her tail. Felicity had to do her best to hold on to Pip, who was no less enthusiastic about being reunited with the Pomeranian.

"Will you join me for tea in the drawing room?" asked Clarissa from the staircase. "Ursula, dear. Why don't you join us?"

"But I don't want another injection!" Frida's voice rang out throughout the hall.

Felicity looked at Alex. He met her gaze with widened eyes, although no one else seemed at all perturbed by Frida's outburst. Just how many hypodermic syringes might there have been in the house?

"Will you join the card game?" Alex asked Felicity. "There's no need to play. You can just watch."

As keen as Felicity was to stay close to Alex and to defy Derek's expectations of her, she couldn't ignore the opportunity to put questions to Clarissa and Ursula, both of whom had been so far quite open to answering Felicity's enquiries. By splitting up, she and Alex had a better chance of gathering more information.

"Please go ahead," Felicity said to Alex. "I'll take tea with Mrs Ridgeway, and Miss Langton, if she'll indeed join us?"

After a mildly regretful glance towards the card players, Ursula nodded. "I came all this way to see Aunt Clarissa for her birthday, after all."

"Splendid," said Clarissa, supporting herself with her walking cane as she took the last stair and arrived on the granite flagstone floor of the entrance hall. "Miss Blanchard, summon Crowther, please. It must be past lunchtime by now. Ask him to bring sandwiches and scones with a tray of tea to the drawing room."

Miss Blanchard nodded and moved silently towards the green baize door that separated the servants' stairs from the entrance hall.

"Oh," gasped Clarissa, "and some of those Italian things. The rolls. Oh, dear. I forget every time. What are they called?"

"Cannoli," called Sebastian with rather beautiful Italian pronunciation, as he, Alex, Derek, and Elodie moved towards one of the corridors off the entrance hall.

"Yes, that's it. Cannoli. I simply must insist you try them, Lady Felicity. You too, Ursula."

With the two little dogs' tails wagging enthusiastically from under their mistresses' arms, Felicity followed Clarissa and Ursula towards the drawing room.

Before disappearing down the corridor after Derek and the other card players, Alex turned to Felicity. The look he gave her seemed to say, *Be careful*.

Felicity answered with a confident nod. She was surely safe in Clarissa and Ursula's company. And while she didn't relish the idea of Alex spending more time than was necessary with Derek and Elodie, Felicity was certain Alex could look after himself.

Besides, conversation over tea and cake was where Felicity excelled. Her discussion with Clarissa and Ursula would help Felicity unpick what was really going on at Langton Manor, and Alex would be thankful and perhaps even impressed when she reported back to him.

Chapter Seventeen

Langton Manor's drawing room was distinctly more Victorian than the areas of the house Felicity had so far visited.

A large indigo rug covered most of the floor. Wallpaper patterned with dark green tropical ferns was crowded by paintings of different sizes in mismatched frames. Subjects ranged from Elizabethan portraits to bowls of apples. Swagged curtains were in heavy green velvet with gold trims, as was the upholstery on the room's seating. At the centre of the ceiling hung an oversized red-tasseled lantern in the Chinoiserie style, complete with scenes of drooping willows and vaulted bridges.

The overall effect was rather oppressive. Even without the fog blocking out most of the light from the windows, the room would still have been gloomy.

But gruesome decor wouldn't distract Felicity from her mission. She'd come to the drawing room for answers.

Before beginning with her questions, a relaxed and convivial atmosphere needed to be established. Keen hostess that she was, Clarissa took the lead in doing just that.

"Astonishing, isn't it?" Clarissa approached an armless chair embroidered with clumsy floral motifs and decorated with a line of ugly gold tassels, having just been informed by Ursula of the solicitor's arrival. "To have persevered through this ghastly fog like that. And I know exactly what you're thinking, Lady Felicity." She lowered herself slowly onto the cushions. "But you needn't worry. I have grand plans for this room. Edward is by nature rather sparing when it comes to home comforts. He doesn't consider them good investments. Dusty old antiques, yes, but a comfortable chair can't always be resold for a good price. Yet you've seen what I've been able to achieve in the morning room and ballroom. I wanted to bring you here to give you an idea of the work I do when I'm given *carte blanche* to redecorate."

Felicity did her best to settle into a high-back chair that was far too upright to be comfortable. "I hadn't realised you were behind the decor of the ballroom and morning room, Mrs Ridgeway. I'd assumed professionals had done the work. If this is what you started with, then I'm really rather impressed."

A satisfied yet deliberately modest smile spread over Clarissa's painted features. "That's extremely kind of you to say, Lady Felicity."

Felicity struggled to keep Pip on her lap as she looked around the room appraisingly. Clarissa had set Charlotte loose, and the Pomeranian was dancing and yapping in front of Pip, her pink tongue lolling out the side of her mouth.

Ursula, who was in a straight-backed chair next to Felicity, frowned at the little black dog. Miss Blanchard sat impassively in a chair to one side of Clarissa, concentrating on needlework. The footman poured tea under the oversight of the butler.

Felicity, keeping a firm hand on Pip, did her best to ignore Charlotte. It wasn't her place to chastise her.

Clarissa sighed, her eyes cast upwards towards the red-tasseled lantern. "If Marigold had still been here, she'd no doubt have allowed me to continue my work."

"Marigold?" enquired Felicity.

"My mother," said Ursula, gesturing to a portrait above the fireplace. It was of a slender, blonde-haired woman with kind eyes, wearing an old-fashioned ballgown in pale green silk and holding an ostrich feather fan. "She passed before the war. She'd been ill for some time. We were devastated, of course, but it put an end to her suffering. And if she'd lived longer, Mother would have been here when Teddy didn't come home. She was at least spared that."

"How terribly sad." The words on their own were perhaps trite, but Felicity filled them with heartfelt emotion. She'd lost her mother when she was barely more than a baby, and her father's more recent passing because of the Spanish influenza had been deeply painful.

"Edward wasn't the same after her passing," said Clarissa. "Marigold held him in balance, just like my dear Gerald did me. To this day, I miss him quite desperately." She looked at the portrait above the fireplace. "Marigold deserves a better place to hang. She was such a gentle soul. Edward ought to remember her more often."

Charlotte's constant yapping and the occasional woof or two from Pip, who wriggled in earnest on Felicity's lap, undermined the sombre mood that had descended on the three women, all of whom were unfortunately rather accustomed to grief.

Clarissa blinked and nodded towards Pip. "Do feel free to put that darling dog of yours down, Lady Felicity. As I told you, this room is ripe for redecoration. Charlotte and Pip are welcome to pull the curtains off the rails, should the mood take them. Edward never comes in here."

Although not fully comfortable with the idea, Felicity was growing tired of the Pomeranian's barking, so she acquiesced and lowered a gleeful Pip to the ground, and the two little dogs disappeared in a flurry of black, tan, and blue fur under a delicate-looking table. The picture frames and items in crystal and porcelain atop the table shuddered as they knocked into its legs, but they weren't Felicity's to worry about. As long as the doors to the drawing room remained closed and Felicity remained present, Pip was safe. That was her chief concern.

Clarissa accepted a cup of tea from the footman. "You know, I suspect it's the real reason Edward is reducing his bequest to me in his new will."

Felicity did her best to conceal her delight at the will being brought up without her having to ask. She wondered if Alex was having as much luck around the card table.

"I'm sorry," said Felicity innocently, glancing between Clarissa and Ursula to ensure that both women felt part of the conversation. "But I don't quite follow."

"The redecorating," clarified Clarissa. "Edward can't stand it. And my birthday party is the first proper gathering he's allowed in years, isn't it?"

Ursula nodded.

"My brother would never send me away," said Clarissa, "but I do believe he's trying to tell me something by reducing my inheritance. Not that I'll necessarily outlive him. I am his older sister, after all." Clarissa said this jokingly, and Felicity smiled politely. "Edward said it was to increase what he's leaving for the younger generation, for their futures and their families. But he has money enough for everyone. There's no genuine need to reduce my bequest. I'm quite aware it's his way of telling me something."

Felicity was quiet for a moment as she took a sip from her tea. It was a deliciously dark blend with just the right amount of milk, and it helped her focus her mind. She needed to keep the conversation on topic without being obvious or pushy.

"You've shocked our guest, Auntie." Ursula smiled playfully, having misinterpreted Felicity's moment of silence.

"Oh, no," said Felicity quickly. "I'm not shocked in the slightest. It's quite normal for family relations not to go as smoothly as one might hope. These days, it's also increasingly acceptable to voice such considerations."

Clarissa nodded with wholehearted approval. "You're a modern woman with modern sensibilities, Lady Felicity. Quite after my own heart. And it works both ways, of course. No one held back from disapproving of my choice of spouse, let me tell you."

"Oh?" said Felicity between sips of tea. Hadn't Clarissa said something earlier about Oswald disapproving of his own father?

Ursula let her teacup clatter into its saucer. "You do like to exaggerate, Aunt Clarissa."

Clarissa and Ursula were both tall, powerfully built women, and both were unafraid of sharing their opinions. They could have passed for mother and daughter.

"How would you know, my dear?" Clarissa spoke coolly to her niece. "You were too young to remember my Gerald."

Miss Blanchard looked up from her needlework.

Ursula frowned. "Yes, but Father told us what—"

"My brother's version of things isn't the only version." Clarissa sat up straight, her hand pressing on her cane. "You must know that."

Ursula said nothing further, her jaw tense.

"I'm very sorry about the loss of your husband, Mrs Ridgeway," said Felicity.

Clarissa turned to her, her kohl-lined eyes mournful. "Oh, it was an exceedingly long time ago, I suppose, yet I miss him every day. My brother rather disapproved of Gerald, you see. He believed it was an act of defiance that I ever married the man. Marigold, of course, was different. She was always very accepting. She was a wonderful wife to my brother, but I'm afraid Edward wouldn't know what love was if it slapped him in the face with a wet fish."

Felicity couldn't conceal a smile.

"Perhaps you haven't experienced it yet yourself," suggested Clarissa.

Felicity blinked. "Experienced what?"

"Love, my dear," said Clarissa, her voice taking on a warbly, operatic tone.

Felicity frowned. This wasn't where she wanted the conversation to be going.

Ursula leaned back in her chair. "Oh, I would say Lady Felicity has at least one admirer of which we can be certain. Whether the affection is mutual is another matter, of course."

Felicity's stomach squeezed with embarrassment. What was Ursula getting at?

Thankfully, Clarissa continued as though her niece hadn't spoken. "When you meet the love of your life, you'll know, for there's nothing anyone can say to put you off caring for him. I had that with my Gerald, of course, and I was lucky to have had it. We cherished only five short years together before the poor, sweet soul passed away. He died peacefully after a brief illness, but I've always taken it as a lesson, you see. We really must be grateful for every day."

"And you had two sons together?" asked Felicity, between sips of tea that helped her regain her composure.

Clarissa's painted eyebrows drew together. "Two?"

"Oswald and Sebastian," clarified Felicity.

"Oh, my dear." Clarissa brought a hand to her ample chest, her beaded necklaces rattling. "How I wish Sebastian were mine. He is a precious soul. Very artistic. He is, of course, Gerald's son, but by Gerald's previous wife. I never met the woman, but she was a source of such woe to my dear Gerald. She went missing one day and was found the next on the rocks at the bottom of one of those dreadfully steep cliffs on the French riviera. Sebastian was merely a babe. As luck would have it, the darling boy doesn't take after his mother at all, but he reminds me so much of Gerald. Such a dear, sweet child. So caring and attentive."

The story of Clarissa's dead husband's unfortunate late wife caught Miss Blanchard's attention, and she halted her needlework to listen. Ursula was also transfixed by the tragic story.

Felicity spared a thought for the poor woman whose life ended dashed onto rocks by the waves of the Mediterranean and the little boy left without a mother. She also made a mental note that Sebastian likely belonged in the *Neutral* column in her notebook, neither gaining nor losing from the change in the will as he wasn't a blood relation of Lord Langton's. The assumption would need verifying, but perhaps Alex was already busy with that over the card game.

"What an incredibly sad story," said Felicity. "Sebastian seems such a well-adjusted fellow."

"Oh, he is," said Clarissa. "Indeed, it's Frida who makes me think of Gerald's previous wife. There's no relation between them, as far as I'm aware, but there's something of the unstable about her, although she hasn't always been like that."

"May I ask—" Felicity spoke gently "—what led to Lord Langton disapproving of your late husband so much?"

Clarissa flapped a hand dismissively. "Gerald and Edward were like chalk and cheese. There was no footing on which they understood one another. Gerald had the soul of a poet, while all Edward can think about is money. It was misunderstanding after misunderstanding between the two of them."

The picture Clarissa painted wasn't wholly clear, but it would have been impertinent to enquire further.

"Sebastian is an artist, did you say?" asked Felicity. Even if he didn't have a stake in the will, Felicity was a little fascinated by Sebastian's easygoing charms. Ursula had also shown no objection to Clarissa's glowing praise of her stepson.

Clarissa hesitated. "Well, not exactly. Sebastian is a lover of art, that's for certain. His sensibilities are very finely tuned. He has tried his hand at painting. He's tried his hand at many things. He's inspired mainly by travel." Clarissa paused again. "What he experienced in the war set him back a great deal, you see."

"I'm awfully sorry to hear that," Felicity said. The chances of so many young men had been ruined by the Great War, even among those who came back. "What happened to him?"

"Well, he prefers not to talk about it, as you can imagine."

"He copes very well," said Ursula.

"He does," agreed Clarissa. "Unlike Frida, who has experienced none of the trauma my Sebastian has."

Given that Clarissa's own choice of husband had been judged harshly by family members, Clarissa's lack of empathy for her daughter-in-law surprised Felicity. But there were other matters she needed to explore.

"Does Frida receive treatment for her ailments?" Felicity asked.

"She takes injections for her nerves," said Clarissa. "That nursemaid of hers is a very skilful girl."

Felicity tried not to look too excited by the confirmation. "Injections of...?" She hoped it wasn't a question too far.

"Opioids," said Ursula, who'd taken a fruit scone with butter on a fine china side plate.

Felicity wasn't certain exactly what Ursula's response meant, but before she could request clarification, Clarissa ushered the conversation onwards.

"But who doesn't these days? I have Miss Blanchard give me my medicine whenever I need a pick-me-up. If it's in a syringe, so much the better. Gets into the system faster that way. And Ursula—" Clarissa nodded towards her niece, who was biting into the scone "—well, her whole business is injections and pills and goodness knows what."

Felicity's head span with dismay. If nearly everyone at Langton Manor had access to drugs and hypodermic syringes, how helpful a clue was the syringe found with the dead valet?

Ursula finished her mouthful of scone and dabbed daintily at the corners of her lips. "It's not a 'business', Auntie, and you know that very well."

Clarissa looked disappointed. "Ursula, dear. Will you really not try one of the Italian sweets?"

"You work in medicine, Miss Ridgeway?" asked Felicity.

"I'm a medical researcher at the Sorbonne," said Ursula matter-of-factly. "Specialising in analgesics."

Felicity blinked. "Ana—"

"Pain relievers, my dear," said Clarissa. "I don't know why my niece insists on using language none of us understand. I only know it because I've had to ask her so many times."

Pain relievers could be administered via needle, couldn't they? And an overdose of just about anything would surely prove fatal, but these weren't questions Felicity could ask. She couldn't reveal what she and Alex knew about the valet's possible cause of death, nor could she advertise her interest in investigating Lord Langton's disappearance. Aside from warranting Jasper's disapproval, it could be dangerous. The atmosphere with Clarissa and Ursula was comfortable, but Felicity couldn't forget that Alex was the only person she could trust.

"I enjoy my work," said Ursula, her tone businesslike. "To be frank, I can't wait to get back to it."

"Oh, Ursula, darling. Don't say that. You came here for my party. I admit I'm surprised you did, but I was absolutely thrilled when you joined us—"

"Please, Auntie. Don't gush. The truth is, as soon as the train left the Gare du Nord, I missed my laboratory. It might seem unfathomable to you, but there's not a lot I enjoy above my work."

Clarissa frowned with loving disapproval.

Felicity nodded. "I enjoy my work, too."

Ursula responded to Felicity's comment with a warm and satisfied smile.

A rather loud scratching caught everyone's attention.

Charlotte was on her hind legs, pawing enthusiastically and destructively at the woodwork of a set of French doors that opened out onto... Felicity didn't know what lay beyond the doors other than thick, swirling mist. She was unfamiliar with the layout of Langton Manor and had lost her bearings as they'd moved along corridors.

Pip stood beside the black Pomeranian. Both dogs' tails were wagging, and Pip gave Felicity an imploring look she knew meant only one thing.

"The puppies wish to go outside," said Clarissa, confirming the obvious. "Miss Blanchard, please recall one of the servants to take them on a walk through the garden."

Felicity stood up. "No need. I'll go. I should like to keep an eye on Pip." She smiled as though full of enthusiasm. Felicity had no desire to be swallowed into the fog, but a dog sometimes simply had to go outside, and, for the duration of their stay at Langton Manor, under no circumstances would Felicity allow Pip out of her sight again.

"Of course, Lady Felicity. You must do as you please. I will warn you, however, that Charlotte will only use grass."

Felicity approached the French doors and peered outside. The ground immediately in front of the doors was paved with smooth, pale-yellow sandstone. Beyond that, there was nothing to see but cloud.

"Where might I find grass?" Felicity asked as she bent down to pick up both dogs, one under each arm.

"Continue forward with the doors at your back," said Clarissa. "You'll reach gravel first. Then, after that, the lawn."

Felicity nodded. Upon reaching the grass, she would put the dogs down, allow them to attend to their business, then scoop them both up and get back inside as quickly as possible. But with her hands filled with dogs — the Pomeranian wriggling much more than expected — Felicity could not twist the clasp on the French doors.

"Miss Blanchard, would you assist Lady Felicity, please?"

Clarissa's sombre-faced companion dutifully went to the French doors and opened them, the thick, starched fabric of her old-fashioned grey dress crinkling as she moved. As cold damp air surged inside, Felicity shivered. Miss Blanchard looked at her with slight disdain.

"Would you like Miss Blanchard to accompany you outside?" asked Clarissa.

Miss Blanchard gave Felicity a flinty stare. What if she had one of Clarissa's pick-me-up injections in her pocket?

"Oh, no. Thank you, Mrs Ridgeway. Thank you, Miss Blanchard, but that won't be necessary."

And Felicity stepped outside.

Chapter Eighteen

Felicity's teeth chattered as she stepped slowly across the sandstone paving, keeping her back to the French doors as Clarissa had instructed. She should have perhaps fetched her top coat from the cloakroom before venturing outside, but it was too late for that now.

Pip and Charlotte both fidgeted impatiently in her grasp as Felicity's visibility shifted with the movements of the fog. Sometimes, she could see barely six feet ahead. At other moments, she saw the vague outlines of tall trees and other garden features. She did her best to continue in a straight line so she could easily make her way back to the drawing room, although by the time she reached the gravel, Langton Manor had all but disappeared behind her.

"Patience, please, dogs," said Felicity to Pip and Charlotte, who wriggled continuously. "I'm certain we'll find a patch of grass soon enough."

Venturing into the fog when there was already a man dead and another missing wasn't high on the list of sensible decisions Felicity could lay claim to, and she dearly hoped Jasper would never get to hear of it. It came, therefore, as an enormous relief when she finally reached a neatly mown lawn.

Stopping on the grass, Felicity's mind went to the painting of the powerful mastiff beside the fireplace in the morning room. It wasn't just Lord Langton that was missing, but his dog as well. Mollie was her name, wasn't it? Surely, if Mollie was any threat to little dogs like Pomeranians and Yorkshire Terriers, Clarissa would have warned her. As relaxed as Clarissa could be about certain things, she obviously cared deeply for her Charlotte.

Felicity set the Pomeranian down first, as she had been struggling the most. When the little black dog went immediately bounding into the mist, quickly disappearing from sight, Felicity almost uttered an oath, but she calmed herself. Charlotte was at home at Langton Manor and no doubt knew the gardens well. She wouldn't end up lost.

Pip, however, like Felicity, was a stranger to the surroundings.

Felicity had once considered a collar and lead for Pip, but he had always been very against the idea, and she couldn't blame him. The prospect of being led around by the neck was distinctly unappealing.

Taking the Yorkie in both hands, Felicity brought his little face before hers.

"Pip, listen to me."

Pip stopped squirming and looked at Felicity, his tufted ears twitching and his brown eyes shining.

"I'm going to put you on the ground, and you're going to attend to whatever business it is you need to attend to, and then I'm going to pick you up again, and we're going to go back inside. Is that understood?"

The Yorkie's black nose twitched.

"You must stay close. There are to be no silly games. We can't risk becoming separated or we'll never find one another again. Do you understand me?"

Pip twitched his tufted ears and licked his nose.

"Very good. Now, with the terms agreed, I'm going to put you down."

Slowly, Felicity lowered Pip until all four of his paws were in contact with the lawn. Gently, she released her grip. Pip remained close, sniffing the grass directly next to Felicity's left shoe before gingerly taking a few steps.

Felicity sighed with relief. "Oh, Pip. I knew I could count on you."

As Pip continued to sniff the nearby grass, Felicity rubbed the sleeves of her peach blouse against the chill in the damp air. As the fog moved, it revealed outlines before erasing them. A little way off was a row of either statues or topiary creatures, arranged along a wall. It was hard to tell which.

From somewhere in the mist came a high-pitched yap. This yap was followed by a series of yaps, and Pip's ears pricked up. The little barks were undoubtedly Charlotte's, and even though Felicity instantly realised what would happen, she was powerless to stop it, for Pip's reactions were far faster than her own. He shot off at full tilt, disappearing into the mist.

"Pip! Come back!"

Felicity's cries were answered by the yapping of the two little dogs, which grew fainter by the moment. In a fit of desperation, Felicity began after Pip, then she remembered that if she moved too far away from the line she'd traced away from Langton Manor, she might become disorientated and end up lost herself.

"Pip! Charlotte! Please, come back!"

The fog muffled Felicity's shouts. The yapping of the two little dogs had all but disappeared.

Helpless and utterly disappointed in herself for allowing Pip to run off, Felicity could find solace in only one thought: Alex. He'd know what to do. He'd helped Felicity out of tough spots before. He'd surely be able to do so again.

Convinced that finding Alex was the best course of action, Felicity turned and headed towards the house, moving as quickly as she could in her new shoes, which were more for fashion than for walking.

After crossing an eternity of gravel and entering the paved area at not quite the same angle she'd left it, her hopes rose as she saw the still-open French doors of the drawing room. As she stepped inside, her heart soared even further when she found not just Clarissa and Ursula standing in the centre of the room, but also Jacob and Alex.

"Cleared us all out, he did," said Alex, rocking on his heels, his hands in his trouser pockets. "Luckily, I didn't have much cash with me." Alex lifted his eyebrows. "But Derek did. He claims to be committed to winning it back, but I have my doubts."

"That's my Sebastian," said Clarissa rather proudly. "He takes after his father. Did you lose anything, Mr Cherry? Oh no, of course you didn't. You have more sense than to sit down at a card table with Sebastian Ridgeway."

Alex was the first to notice Felicity's return to the drawing room. He looked pleased to see her, but his expression darkened with concern as she made no effort to hide her distress.

Soon, all eyes were on her.

"Lady Felicity," said Clarissa, leaning on her walking cane. "My, you do look worried. And where are our little four-legged friends?"

"They, ah." Only with speaking did Felicity realise she'd become quite breathless. "They both ran off."

Clarissa chuckled. "I should have warned you. Charlotte can't go outside without wanting to examine every tree and every bush within a ten-mile radius. You wouldn't think it to look at her, but she's incredibly territorial."

Felicity did her best to remain as polite as possible, so she only silently agreed that yes, it would have been better had Clarissa warned her. "Pip's gone too."

"Oh, don't worry dear. I'm sure they'll be back soon enough. Charlotte's taking her new friend on a tour of the garden, no doubt."

"Would you like me to find Pip for you?" asked Alex.

Felicity could have melted into a puddle with relief. "Please," she said. "I'm aware I already owe you so much."

Ursula raised an eyebrow at this, but Felicity couldn't give two figs about what anyone else thought at that precise point in time.

"Lord Langton's dog is out there somewhere as well," added Felicity a little desperately.

"I'll be right back," said Alex reassuringly, and he headed out of the French doors and into the fog. It gave Felicity such a deep-seated feeling of reassurance, were she at home, she would have collapsed into the nearest chair.

"Mollie wouldn't hurt a fly," said Clarissa, lowering herself back into her seat. "She's a sweet girl."

Felicity was further relieved. Without collapsing, she retook her seat.

Ursula remained standing beside Jacob. "Unless you do anything to threaten Father, of course. Then there's no telling what she'll do."

Jacob nodded in concurrence. "Mollie is d-devoted to his lordship."

Felicity remembered the valet's torn sleeve. Had Mollie indeed defended her master from his valet? The thought of the mastiff's powerful jaws coming anywhere near Pip made Felicity's stomach tie into a knot, but she needn't worry. Alex was taking care of matters.

"I fancy I might telephone the station and book myself onto an earlier train," said Ursula. "I'll be leaving as soon as this fog is lifted."

Clarissa scoffed. "You can try, my dear, but when the fog will lift is really anyone's guess."

"I'd be happy to h-help make arrangements for you, Miss Ridgeway," said Jacob attentively. "Were you not planning to stay on until the day after tomorrow?"

Ursula eyed Jacob carefully. "I was, but I'm keen to get back to my work."

Jacob adjusted his spectacles. "Couldn't arrangements be m-made for a trip to the moors or some other, uh, *divertissement* for tomorrow? To make your presence more w-worthwhile?"

Ursula smiled patronisingly. "I grew up at Langton Manor, Mr Cherry. Do you not think I've seen the tors hundreds of times already?"

"Certainly, certainly. It was s-simply to say—"

Crack!

The sharp sound that rang out in the fog carried clearly into the drawing room.

Crack!

It came again.

"What was that?" asked Clarissa, wide-eyed.

Felicity recognised the sound, and the colour drained from her face.

"Gunshots." She and Jacob said the word simultaneously.

"I-I'll go." Jacob swallowed and stepped towards the French doors, his hand shaking as he yanked them open, Ursula watching him with a mix of anxiety and respect.

"I don't think anyone should—" began Clarissa.

"No," said Felicity firmly, her heart pounding hard in her chest. "I'll go."

Felicity had sent Alex into danger. It was her responsibility to make it right.

Without waiting for any further reaction from anyone in the drawing room, Felicity went back out into the fog.

Chapter Nineteen

Felicity moved swiftly across the sandstone paving, her pulse racing far quicker than she would have liked.

"Alex!"

Her voice was muffled by the dense fog. She tried to peer through it but to no avail. Venturing outside had seemed like the only honourable thing to do, but Felicity was quickly realising it wasn't the wisest of decisions. Or the safest. Jasper would be immensely disappointed in her, yet somehow that no longer mattered.

She had to find Alex and Pip. She had to make sure they were all right.

Reaching the gravel, there was still no sign of either of them, but there was something dark lying on the ground. Approaching through the mist, Felicity came upon a shining black revolver lying on the gold-coloured gravel.

Crouching, she gingerly picked up the weapon, touching it only lightly on the brown textured handle. It might be wanted for fingerprints, but there was no time to fetch a handkerchief with which to pick the gun up. Such a deadly weapon could not be allowed to remain in circulation.

Growling made Felicity look up.

A figure was coming towards her through the fog.

Instinctively, she adjusted her grip to be ready to fire the weapon if necessary. Not that Felicity had ever handled a revolver in her life. She didn't even know if it was loaded.

But to Felicity's immense relief, the figure in the fog was Alex, and the growling was Pip's as the little dog struggled to release himself from Alex's firm grip.

"Oh, thank goodness!" Felicity loosened her grasp on the revolver and stepped forward to take Pip while examining Alex. "You're not hurt, are you?"

"No. I'm fine, but I heard the shots." Alex raised an eyebrow at the gun in Felicity's hand.

"Oh, no," she said. "I found this just now. Here, on the ground. I wouldn't know how to fire it."

Alex's brow crumpled with concern. "Would you mind if I took it from you?"

"Not at all," said Felicity, and she handed over the revolver.

Alex inspected the gun, releasing the cylinder — which still held bullets — before snapping it back into place.

"I'm not an expert," he said gravely, "but I would say this is exactly the type of weapon we heard." He pocketed the revolver. "I found Pip on top of a rather high wall. Not sure how he got up there. He couldn't get down by himself."

"It's my fault," said Felicity, a deep sense of shame engulfing her. "I put you both in danger. Oh, I'm so glad you're all right. You really can't imagine. I'm so grateful you found Pip, and I already owed you so much."

Alex shook his head dismissively and looked around, but there was nothing to see in the fog. "I'd quite like to know what exactly is going on here."

Despite Alex's lack of concern for his own safety, Felicity made a silent promise to never put him at risk again. She would also give serious consideration to bringing Pip along with her in the future. It was her responsibility to keep the little dog safe, and if anything were to happen to either Pip or Alex, Felicity would simply not be able to live with herself.

"We should go back inside," said Alex.

Felicity had become completely disorientated. Thankfully, Alex was a confident navigator.

As their footsteps tapped across the sandstone paving, there came another sound. A scuffling, as though something were being dragged over the stone tiles. Alex stopped and held a hand out, gesturing to Felicity to be still. With his other hand, he withdrew the revolver from his pocket and snapped the hammer back.

"H-help... Me..."

Felicity didn't recognise the voice, but before she could urge caution, Alex disappeared into the fog. Felicity gripped Pip tightly, but it wasn't long before two figures, one supporting the other, reappeared.

Alex was helping another man who appeared to be injured, a hand held to his face.

The injured man was Derek.

"Someone wants me dead, Coop." His voice wobbled. "That bullet was meant to kill me."

"Easy, old boy." Alex spoke soothingly as he supported Derek under his shoulder, steadying him.

"Dear me," said Felicity with genuine concern. "Is he all right?"

Alex gave Felicity a sharp nod. "Let's get you inside," he said to Derek.

Felicity followed the two men until they arrived at the side of the house. They were no longer aligned with the drawing room and entered the building via a small door that connected with a short, plain vestibule normally used by servants. Both Felicity and Pip sighed with relief to be back inside. Despite his gaudy golfing attire, the sight of Derek leaning against the whitewashed wall was nevertheless troubling. He was shaking, and his face was ghostly pale.

Alex took Derek's hand and lowered it from his cheek. There was a neat, red scrape across his cheekbone.

"It's a scratch, old thing," said Alex calmly. "Nothing more. We'll need to get it cleaned up, but I can assure you, you'll live."

"I only stepped outside for a breath of air," said Derek, his voice trembling. He swallowed. "Another inch, and I'd be dead, wouldn't I?"

If Derek's wound had been caused by a bullet, then he'd indeed had a brush with death. But what sense did killing Derek Langton make? Especially as he was yet to inherit anything from Lord Langton.

"Who could want you dead?" asked Felicity.

Derek looked aghast at her. Even Alex lowered his brow in her direction.

Felicity wholeheartedly regretted the question. Given the circumstances, it was tone-deaf. It wasn't her intention to reveal her doubts about Derek's claims of murderous intent, but she had to know. Whoever had fired the shots into the fog had endangered Alex and Pip's lives as well.

"Who do you think?" Some of the tremble had gone from Derek's voice. "Whoever is to blame for this whole blasted situation, that's who. Whoever it was killed that deuced valet. Whoever it was chased away my father. I don't know who it is. If I knew, I'd have done something about it by now."

Derek's ire was genuine. Was he angry at whoever had injured him? Or was he angry at being challenged about the scenario? The wound on Derek's face was rather superficial. It being self-inflicted wasn't out of the question.

"I sincerely doubt anyone was trying to kill you, old boy." Alex was exceedingly good at providing reassurance. "You'd need to be at point-blank range to take aim in this fog. And as I told you, we've got the gun now. Whoever it was rather clumsily dropped it close to the patio, so there'll be no more shooting for now."

Felicity doubted the revolver she'd found on the ground was the only firearm at Langton Manor, but she desperately wanted to believe there'd indeed be no more shooting.

Alex continued. "But we perhaps want a word with Elodie."

Derek's mouth fell open and rapidly closed. "My Elodie? Why on earth?"

Alex nodded and looked again at the firearm in his hands. "The revolver is Belgian. Elodie's the only person from Belgium I'm aware of at Langton Manor."

Felicity lifted her eyebrows in surprise. She'd presumed Elodie to be French instead of Belgian, but it hardly mattered. Her suspicions were proving correct, and Alex was beginning to see just how dangerous his association with Derek and Elodie really was.

Derek nodded slowly. "I see where this is going. You're going to pin everything on my Elodie, are you?"

"You have to admit it, old boy." Alex chose his words carefully. "She's not the most predictable of characters. If she was out in the fog firing a weapon, then she needs to know—"

"She wasn't outside, she was..." Derek shook his head. "I knew you never liked her, Coop. No one does. No one understands her but me. But I swear to you, she has nothing to do with any of this."

Alex let out a breath. "Are there any other Belgians at Langton Manor?"

"Do you not think any one of us could have brought the thing over from Flanders?"

"I never saw one like this in all my time in the trenches." Alex held the gun flat on his palm. "Did you?"

"Fine." Derek pushed himself off the vestibule wall. "If you don't believe me, I'll have Elodie tell you herself."

He set off for the door leading further into the house.

Alex hesitated, but Felicity saw no need to wait around. With Pip still in her arms, she started after Derek, keen to hear more from Elodie. Behind her, Alex sighed, then followed them deeper into Langton Manor.

Chapter Twenty

Felicity and Pip followed Derek into Langton Manor's grand, lily-scented entrance hall and up the central staircase, with Alex not far behind. Derek was long-legged and moving quickly, taking the steps two at a time. Pip didn't enjoy being bounced up the stairs as Felicity did her best to keep up with Derek, but at least the Yorkie was safely tucked under Felicity's arm. Was Charlotte the Pomeranian safe, too? Clarissa hadn't seemed concerned about the little black dog disappearing into the fog, so Felicity decided she shouldn't be either. Besides, she had other, more pressing matters to think about.

As she passed the portrait of Derek's brother, Alex caught up with Felicity. His scarred brow was creased with concern.

With Derek far ahead of them on the staircase, Felicity spoke in low tones to Alex. "Do you really think the wound on his face is from a bullet?"

Alex glanced at her, perplexed. "Why wouldn't it be?"

"He could have fired the gun himself and injured his own cheek."

"Why the blazes would he do that?"

It worried Felicity that Alex wasn't able to follow her logic. "To throw anyone suspecting Derek of involvement in Lord Langton's disappearance off the scent."

A deep crease formed between Alex's thick eyebrows. "I doubt that very much."

"But if the gun is Elodie's—" Felicity whispered as they reached the first floor landing, Derek having already disappeared along a corridor ahead of them "—isn't it reckless to be at all mixed up with either her or Derek?"

Alex stared squarely at Felicity. "Isn't it reckless to go running around outside on your own in the fog if you believe there to be a murderer on the loose?"

The words stung.

"I wasn't alone. I had two dogs with me. For a short spell, at least."

It was a feeble defence, and Felicity knew it. If she could have turned back the clock, she wouldn't have made the same mistake again, yet she was compelled to defend her actions.

"What I mean to say is," she continued, "I realise your relationship with Derek is somewhat complicated, but you must be open to the idea that Derek and Elodie might be involved in Lord Langton's disappearance. Surely, you must?"

Alex said nothing, his face grim.

They caught up with Derek in a narrow corridor with dark brown wainscotting and pink floral wallpaper. He was knocking on a door. After a brief wait and an anxious glance at Felicity and Alex, he knocked again.

Groaning could be heard in response from within the room.

Slowly, Derek opened the door and went inside.

"What is it?" It was Elodie's voice, but the curtains were drawn, making it too dark to see her. "Derek? Is it you? I told you not to come."

"Elodie, darling. I'm so very sorry to wake you."

Derek crossed the room and eased the curtains open. The thin, grey light revealed a sumptuous bedroom decorated in royal blue with hints of gold. At its centre was a bed with wooden posts carved into twists and a ruched canopy in dark blue damask. Elodie lay in a tangle of white sheets, a dark blue coverlet and several pillows kicked to the floor.

Elodie was still fully clothed in her wispy blue-and-pink dress, but her silver sandals had been flung haphazardly at the side of her bed, and her white-fur wrap had been flung into the corner of the room in a manner rather disrespectful of the poor creatures that had given their lives for the garment.

Elodie pushed herself onto her elbows, blinking as she watched Derek sit on the side of her bed. "Do you have it? Please, darling, say you have it."

Derek smoothed back her jaw-length dark hair where it had become plastered to her cheeks. "I don't, dearest. I'm sorry."

Have what? wondered Felicity, but she couldn't barge into the room and ask any question she liked. They were on the trail of whoever fired the gun in the fog. There weren't grounds for interrogating Elodie on any other point, as much as Felicity would have liked to.

Elodie blinked at Derek. "Darling, what is this?" She lifted a hand to his cheek. Her eyes widened. "You are hurt."

It was an oddly touching scene.

"No, darling, I'm fine," replied Derek, which surprised Felicity, given his earlier insistence that someone had made an attempt on his life. "But I have a question for you."

"A question? You woke me up for a question?" Her voice was groggy and her reactions slow. If Elodie had been out in the fog firing the revolver a short time ago, then she was a fantastic actress. She was also a rather fabulous make-up artist, as the creases from the bed linen pressed into her cheeks were extremely convincing.

But even if Elodie hadn't been out in the fog when the gun was fired, there remained the possibility she was involved in the unsavoury goings-on at Langton Manor.

Elodie turned slowly to look at Felicity, Pip, and Alex, who were stationed at the foot of the bed. Pip remained alert yet calm in Felicity's arms, either because he had tired himself out running in the fog, or because he understood the gravity of the present situation. Perhaps it was a combination of both.

Elodie's face hardened. "What are they doing in here?"

"There's been an incident outside," said Alex. "Someone fired a revolver."

"A gun?" Elodie's eyes widened. She turned back to Derek and touched his injured cheek. "Oh, my darling. Did someone shoot you?"

Derek took Elodie's hand gently by the palm and kissed her knuckles. "I told you, my dearest. I'm absolutely fine. Don't worry yourself."

"Do you recognise it?" Alex stepped forward and held the gun out to Elodie, displaying it in profile.

Elodie looked at the weapon, then at Alex. A small smile touched her lips.

"Belgian gun, Belgian woman," she said. "You think this is mine?"

Alex returned Elodie's stare. "The thought crossed my mind."

"Well." Elodie leaned back. "You are wrong. I have no weapon. I have never in my life seen this gun."

Alex put the revolver back in his pocket.

"What did I tell you, Coop?" said Derek tightly. "But you wouldn't believe me, would you?"

Alex nodded. "Apologies. I wanted to be sure."

Felicity looked from Derek to Alex. Were they really so willing to take Elodie at her word? Felicity wasn't sure anything had been proved.

"Well, now you have your certainty," said Derek. "You can go and make your accusations elsewhere."

"I wasn't making accusations, old thing," said Alex. "I'm sure you want to get to the bottom of this just as much as anyone else."

"The idea that I would hurt my Derek." Elodie stroked Derek's jaw, her eyes full of sadness. "It cannot be possible."

"Who else might be the owner of a Belgian handgun?" Felicity had so many questions, she couldn't keep all of them to herself.

Elodie sank back onto the bed's pillows as if the energy had been sucked out of her. "That gun is not for a peasant like me. That gun was for Belgian army officers, even before the war." She lifted her eyebrows. "Why not ask Miss Blanchard."

Felicity had to think for a moment. "Mrs Ridgeway's companion?"

Elodie nodded languidly.

Alex frowned. "What would Miss Blanchard know about it?"

Elodie shrugged. "I do not know. But like you were already thinking, Belgian woman, Belgian weapon."

It was Felicity's turn to frown. "Miss Blanchard is from Belgium?"

Miss Blanchard had no foreign accent, not that she said much. Indeed, there was nothing foreign about Miss Blanchard at all, although as Elodie said her name — with the *ch* pronounced as *sh* and the *d* going unvoiced at the end — Blanchard was as much a Francophone name as it was an English one.

Elodie nodded, sinking further back into the bed. "Go speak to her. Leave me in peace. Darling, close the curtains, please."

Derek rose and moved towards the window. Felicity saw a chance and took it.

"How did you know the valet, Miss Rossignol?" she said, gripping Pip more tightly. "You knew Mr Greenwood before he came to work for Lord Langton, did you not?"

Alex shot Felicity a disapproving look. Felicity gave him one back. He'd never be able to write up the story without knowing the basic facts.

The question didn't seem to register with Elodie. "Darling, really. I am so tired."

"I know, I know," Derek said soothingly. "We'll leave you in peace. We'll speak with Miss Blanchard, as you suggest."

Derek gave Felicity a hard stare as they withdrew from the bedroom.

Her question about the valet had left both Alex and Derek unimpressed. Felicity usually did her best to remain in everyone's good books, but on this occasion, their disapproval didn't affect her. Revealing the truth was more important than being well-liked, especially with Alex's safety on the line. Felicity might have failed to prompt Elodie into revealing her true nature, but there would be other opportunities to delve deeper into matters. A conversation with Miss Blanchard might be one.

Chapter Twenty-One

The door to Elodie's bedroom clicked gently closed, and Felicity, Pip, Alex, and Derek started along the floral corridor.

"I suppose we'll find Miss Blanchard with Mrs Clarissa Ridgeway," said Felicity, as they headed for the landing. "I last saw Mrs Ridgeway in the drawing room."

Miss Blanchard had certainly been there when Felicity, Clarissa, and Ursula were taking tea together. Had she been in the drawing room when Felicity returned, having lost Pip in the fog? She couldn't quite remember. It had been just before the shots were fired.

Derek interrupted Felicity's train of thought. "You seem rather keen to unravel matters. Planning a glorious write-up for your paper, are you?"

Felicity's thoughts flew to Jasper and his disapproval, but before she could deny any such intention, Alex stepped in.

"Felicity is here to write about your cousin being added to your father's will," he said. "She doesn't report on crime."

"But you do." Derek waggled his eyebrows at Alex. "Or you used to. When was the last time you had anything published, Coop? More a man of leisure these days, aren't you?"

"Enough of that," said Alex shamefacedly as they arrived on the first floor landing.

Felicity wondered what Derek would make of the knowledge Alex had been working undercover the whole time, albeit unsuccessfully. Felicity would never betray Alex's confidences, but her awareness of the situation made it easy for her to notice how awkward Alex now felt about it all.

"I can see the headline now. 'Foreign Terror at Langton Manor'." Derek waved his hands as he spoke, as if printing the words in the air before him. "That's part of why none of you like my Elodie, isn't it? Because she's not one of us?"

Felicity frowned and stroked Pip. "I'm sorry to say that I don't know Elodie well enough to either like her or dislike her." She couldn't allow Derek's claim of persecution to go unchallenged — Elodie's being Belgian or any other nationality had nothing to do with anything, as far as Felicity was concerned — but neither could she lie and say Elodie was someone with whom she hoped to become friends.

Alex flashed an amused smile at Derek. "You do have a knack for drama, old thing. You might want to try writing it up yourself."

"I might," said Derek thoughtfully. "I just might."

As they descended the stairs to the entrance hall, Felicity was keen to change the subject. "Elodie seemed rather weak. Is she sick?"

Derek's face darkened and turned serious. "In a way, yes."

"What ails her?" Felicity asked.

Derek turned sharply towards her. "I don't see why it should concern you. You were accusing her of attempted murder merely moments ago."

Felicity cleared her throat, a little ashamed at how her suspicions about Derek and Elodie had overcome her sensibilities of decorum and good behaviour. Despite Jasper's warnings, Felicity had promised herself she would at least be polite towards Derek. She would need to be more careful going forwards if she wanted people to continue opening up to her.

"I'm sorry I gave you that impression," she said as they reached the bottom of the stairs. "I was quite overcome by the shots fired outside."

"So was I." Derek stopped and turned his injured cheek towards Felicity, his brown eyes no longer warm. "I almost met my end, remember?"

Felicity's mouth fell open, and she closed it. She was unaccustomed to having people upset with her and didn't quite know how to react.

Relief came in the form of the ungainly footman approaching from the other side of the entrance hall.

"There's a telephone call for you, your ladyship."

"For me?" It was unexpected and not at all convenient. "Are you sure?"

"Lord Jasper Quick, Earl of Denbury, your ladyship."

Of course. Felicity could always rely on her brother to make an appearance at the most inopportune moment possible. There were questions Felicity needed to put to Miss Blanchard, and she wouldn't let a telephone call derail her plans.

Turning to Alex and Derek, she said. "Would you be kind enough to wait for me here? I'm certain this won't take at all long."

With a submissive and rather sleepy Pip still tucked under her arm, Felicity followed the footman towards the telephone table, which was tucked in an alcove off the hall.

"Thank you," she said as the footman withdrew.

Taking a seat on an ancient chintz and mahogany chair, Felicity set Pip on her lap and briskly took up the receiver.

"Hello? Cici?" Jasper was already speaking before she'd quite brought the receiver to her ear.

"Yes, Jasper. I'm here."

"Oh, thank goodness you're all right. I had visions of your car in a bally ditch somewhere. I got back from Bristol just in time. This rascally fog has only just made its way to Lower Diddleton. Apparently, it's stretched across half the county."

"It's certainly very thick here." Felicity didn't want the conversation to last any longer than necessary. She wanted to get back to Alex as quickly as possible. She wanted to question Miss Blanchard. "If you were calling to see if I'm all right, then please be reassured that I'm perfectly fine."

"Listen, Cici."

Felicity sighed quietly. The conversation wasn't to be as brief as she would have liked. Pip had already begun snoring, clearly under the impression he would be on Felicity's lap for a while.

Jasper continued. "I heard about some rum doings out there at Langton Manor. Don't ask how I'm aware, because you know very well I won't tell you. A journalist and his sources and all that. Or her sources. Anyway. I'm making arrangements to get you out of there as quickly as possible. Just as soon as this blasted fog's gone. In the meantime, can I ask for your reassurance that you're doing everything possible to stay out of things and remain safe? Listen, I know you're a sensible young woman with your head on straight, and that I'm your over-protective older brother, but when you're working for the paper, you're working for me, and I feel dreadfully responsible for sending you into this situation."

Felicity considered her brother's request carefully.

She didn't know exactly what Jasper knew about 'this situation', and she didn't want to give him any information he didn't already have. Photographing the dead valet hadn't been dangerous, but it could be considered involving oneself in 'rum doings'. However, venturing out into the fog not only the first time when she lost Pip but also the second time, after gunshots had been heard, was rather reckless.

All in all, Felicity had done a pretty poor job of keeping herself out of trouble.

"Alex is here," she blurted. It wasn't entirely clear to her why she'd chosen that piece of information to share with her brother. It was truthful, at least.

"Coop?" Jasper sounded dumbfounded. "What's he doing out there?"

"Investigating a story," said Felicity quickly and succinctly. She didn't want to lie to her brother, but neither did she want to give away too much on Alex's behalf.

"Well, I never. Sly as a fox, that one. Huh. I guess I underestimated him."

Felicity was relieved to hear Alex's presence came as good news to her brother.

"I'm staying close to Alex," she ventured.

"Jolly good, jolly good. Well, as long as Coop's there, and he's on the right track, I'm sure there's nothing I need to worry about. Like I said, as soon as the fog is lifted, I've got someone—" There was a rattling sound on the other end of the line. "Just a minute."

Again, Felicity sighed. Would the telephone call ever end? Pip's snores grew louder as he fell deeper into sleep.

There were muffled sounds. "Felicity? Felicity, dear?" It was Lady Henrietta, Felicity's grandmother. "Are you all right?"

"Yes, Grandmama. I'm absolutely fine."

While Felicity was irked that speaking to her grandmother would extend the call, she was touched by how her family cared so deeply for her.

"Oh, Felicity, dear. You've got Jasper absolutely worried sick about you. He's been pacing up and down, trying to think of ways to get you out of there." A muted voice in the background, presumably Jasper's, made noises of disagreement. "I told him the dead servant was probably due to natural causes, and Lord Langton likely just went for a walk in his gardens and got stuck out in the fog. It's quite clearly all just a dreadful mix up and a coincidence."

Felicity wished for that, too, although Jasper and Lady Henrietta had apparently yet to hear about the gunshots in the fog.

"I'm sure it is, Grandmama," said Felicity, ushering the conversation to a close.

"Please, do stay out of this terrible fog, Felicity. It can play havoc with one's airways. Why, I remember one particularly sinister fog we had in 1873. Or was it '74? No, I believe it was 1875—"

Felicity usually had all the time in the world for her grandmother's remembrances, but this occasion was different. "I'm awfully sorry, Grandmama, but there are people waiting for me."

"Oh, my dear. I'm the one who should apologise. Please. Don't let me keep you on the telephone. Wonderful contraption, isn't it? You know, I was quite against it at the beginning, but now I only wonder where we'd be without it."

"Goodbye, Grandmama," said Felicity brightly and winced as she replaced the receiver. It was painful to put the telephone down on her beloved grandmother so abruptly, but Felicity couldn't waste anymore time.

Tucking a barely awake Pip under her arm, Felicity dived out of the telephone alcove and hurried across the entrance hall, but her pace slowed as the only person waiting for her was the young footman.

Felicity's chest tightened with concern. After what she'd just told her brother, it wasn't an opportune moment to become separated from Alex. "Is no one waiting for me?"

"They were waiting for you, your ladyship. They've moved on into the drawing room. Lord Derek is having his wound seen to by Mrs Ridgeway's attendant."

Felicity took a deep, calming breath as she moved towards the drawing room. Her conversation with Jasper had further highlighted just how potentially dangerous the situation at Langton Manor was, both for herself and for Alex. And Felicity had remembered something.

Miss Blanchard hadn't been in the drawing room when the gun went off.

Chapter Twenty-Two

Approaching the drawing room with a docile Pip still tucked safely under her arm, Felicity found reassurance in the voices on the other side of the door, which were speaking in perfectly normal conversational tones.

Upon entering the room with its fern-inspired wallpaper, she felt immediately relieved to be reunited with Alex. He was standing behind a dark green sofa on which sat an oddly docile Derek, his elbows resting on the knees of his plus-fours and his cheek offered towards Miss Blanchard, who was seated beside him.

Miss Blanchard's sombre face was taut with concentration as she cleaned Derek's wound with a ball of cotton and a small basin balanced on her knees. If she had fired the revolver, she was doing a splendid job playing the innocent while tending to Derek, who winced as she applied the cleaning solution to his cheek.

But perhaps Derek had not been the intended victim? Or it hadn't been Miss Blanchard who fired the gun? Derek certainly didn't seem concerned about her doing him any further harm.

On a nearby chair, upholstered in the same dark green velvet as the sofa, sat Clarissa, watching Derek and Miss Blanchard, concern on her powder-caked brow. Felicity was relieved to see Charlotte the

Pomeranian at rest in Clarissa's lap. The two little dogs perked up as they caught one another's scents, their tails wagging hard, but there was no chance whatever Felicity would allow Pip out of her grasp to run around.

Ursula was in the chair opposite Clarissa's, her handsome blonde head propped on her fist. There was a valise at her side, indicating her resolve to leave Langton Manor as soon as was possible. The fog at the windows, however, was no thinner, and Felicity rather suspected the police, once they arrived, wouldn't allow anyone to leave ahead of being questioned.

Felicity looked over at Alex. She attempted to enquire with her eyes whether he'd asked Miss Blanchard about the revolver yet, but the message was too complicated to be communicated via a glance, and Alex's attention was mainly on Miss Blanchard's treatment of Derek. Given the calmness of the room's atmosphere, the subject of the revolver had likely not yet been broached.

"Lady Felicity, how lovely that you've joined us." Clarissa's unwavering conviviality was in equal parts unnerving and admirable. "Please, do sit down. I've asked for afternoon tea to be brought up. I simply cannot believe how long this fog is hanging on."

"Neither can I." Ursula was glaring out of the window, her mood darker than it had been earlier.

Felicity smiled politely as she took a seat on an unoccupied chair, placing an excitable Pip on her lap. "Thank you, Mrs Ridgeway. How thoughtful," she said, although the last thing on Felicity's mind was food.

"Isn't it absolutely dreadful what happened to poor Derek?" Clarissa's tone was more suited to talk of an accident rather than a murder attempt, and perhaps rightly. What exactly had taken place outside in the fog remained unclear. "Miss Blanchard is simply wonderful," continued Clarissa. "She's been with me for years, and there's almost nothing she can't do. Everyone should have a Miss Blanchard."

Clarissa beamed at her companion, but Miss Blanchard remained concentrated on the task at hand. She dabbed carefully at Derek's wound, but there was still something hard about her manner. It wasn't difficult to imagine Miss Blanchard wielding a deadly weapon if it was necessary.

Yet something was missing. When Felicity had drawn up the three-columned list in her notebook, adding Miss Blanchard to the matrix hadn't been a priority, for she obviously belonged in the *Neutral* column, neither benefiting nor losing from the change to Lord Langton's will. How could she benefit from anything happening to Lord Langton or Derek?

"How does one come across 'a Miss Blanchard'?" asked Felicity innocently, putting a little pressure on Pip's back to make it clear to him he would be staying on her lap.

"Oh," said Clarissa cagily. "It's not my story to tell, is it, Miss Blanchard?"

Miss Blanchard shot a stony look at her mistress.

"Suffice to say," continued Clarissa, "you'll know when you've found someone like Miss Blanchard. They don't come along very often."

Ursula raised her eyebrows. "Yet some of us manage extremely well in putting on our own clothes and shoes and brushing our own hair."

Clarissa tutted good-naturedly, her hand adjusting on her walking cane. "When you get to my age, Ursula, dear, I'm sure it will be quite a different story."

Again, Felicity looked at Alex. She was becoming impatient to learn more about the revolver. Doing her best not to be too obvious to anyone else in the room, she stared at the jacket pocket where Alex had stashed the weapon and then glanced at Miss Blanchard, but by the time she returned her gaze to Alex, his attention had shifted towards the door, which was opening.

"So this is where you're all hiding," said Oswald as he entered the drawing room. His cheeks were pink, and he dropped wearily into the chair next to Felicity's.

Clarissa frowned. "No one's 'hiding'. We're trying to get on with things as best we can. What else would you have us do?"

Oswald peered at Derek. "I say. What happened to you?"

Derek didn't move. He stared at his cousin from under a lowered brow. "Why should you care?"

"Boys," huffed Clarissa. "Really, now."

Felicity took advantage of Oswald's entry into the drawing room to lean forward and speak softly to Miss Blanchard. "Miss Blanchard, my question might come out of the blue, but do you, by any chance, have connections in Belgium?"

Miss Blanchard turned her dark grey eyes on Felicity. Her tightly pulled-back hair made her heart-shaped face hard and angular.

Alex flicked his attention towards Felicity.

"Why do you ask?" Miss Blanchard spoke slowly and didn't use a syllable more than was necessary, but there was still no trace of a foreign accent.

"Come now, Miss Blanchard," said Clarissa, who rarely missed much. "There's nothing to be ashamed of. There's nothing at all wrong with being Belgian. It's not your fault what happened to your poor little country."

Miss Blanchard's eyes widened with surprise at her mistress, and a slight flush of colour rose to her pale cheeks.

Elodie hadn't been lying.

"It's just that we found something," coaxed Felicity, "and we were hoping you might help us identify it."

Felicity thought carefully before speaking. She wouldn't make the same mistake as she'd made with Derek and Elodie. It was always far better to be on a person's good side. They were more likely to share things with you that way.

Felicity nodded at Alex, who was already reaching into his pocket. She, Derek, and Miss Blanchard watched as he withdrew the revolver.

Miss Blanchard's mouth opened with surprise, as did Oswald's. Ursula stiffened in her chair, and Clarissa adjusted her grip on her cane. Derek leaned back on the sofa and folded his arms over his chest, as though preparing to enjoy a spectacle.

Challenging Elodie in the bedroom upstairs had been one thing.

Their actions before the audience in the drawing room took Felicity and Alex's interest in the 'rum doings' at Langton Manor to another level. Still, as long as the revolver remained in Alex's possession, Felicity didn't feel afraid. What was important was to find out who had fired the gun in the fog and put Alex and Pip in such danger.

"Wait a minute." Oswald sat forward, suddenly energised. "You found that revolver? Where?"

"I suppose it's the one we heard going off in the fog earlier, is it?" Clarissa glanced at the weapon in Alex's hands in a rather laid-back manner.

Ursula shifted backwards in her chair, as though keen to get as far away from the gun as possible.

"Going off?" Oswald's cheeks had gone from pink to red. "You mean to say there have been gunshots, and no one thought to inform me?"

"Did you not hear them?" Clarissa sounded doubtful of Oswald's claim. "Well, your suite is on the other side of the house, and between poor James crying and dear Frida having one of her turns, I don't suppose there's much you can hear."

Oswald stood up. "We've a man dead upstairs, Lord Langton is still missing, and now we have someone firing a weapon in the fog?"

The butler entered, accompanied by the footman carrying a large tray of tea with a small selection of cakes and sandwiches. The servants did their best to be unobtrusive, but it was extremely awkward timing.

"Not just firing a weapon, Ossie." It was Derek's turn to rise to his feet. "Firing a weapon at me. What do you think this mark on my face is?" He pointed to his cheek.

"You?" said Oswald in disbelief. "Why would someone try to kill you?"

Oswald had a knack for asking the right questions, and Felicity was silently pleased to hear him challenge Derek on this point. She raised an eyebrow at Alex to bring his attention to the fact that she wasn't alone in finding Derek's story of a murder attempt suspicious, but Alex's focus was on Miss Blanchard, whose eyes were fixed on the gun.

"Really, Oswald," said Clarissa. "You can be quite over the top."

Oswald prodded a finger at his own chest. "I'm over the top? We're in this deuced murder mystery of a situation, and all you seem concerned about is the cancellation of a frivolous party. And you, Mother, are telling me I'm over the top?"

Clarissa tutted and looked away from her son. While Oswald had a point, Felicity saw no need to express it quite so unkindly. Clarissa's party had clearly meant an awful lot to her.

"Someone is trying to frame me." Miss Blanchard's voice was small and careful. "Someone has been in my room. They took the gun, and they're using it to frame me."

Felicity swung her attention to Clarissa's companion. "Frame you?"

Miss Blanchard blinked, her eyes still on the weapon. "The gun was my father's. He was a captain in the Belgian army. I kept it as a memory of him. My only memory of him. But I've never used it."

"We found it out on the gravel." Alex spoke calmly and with no note of accusation. "How did it come to be there?"

"I don't know." Miss Blanchard's voice was barely above a whisper, her pale face now completely white. "In all honesty, I don't know."

"Where were you when the shots were fired?" pressed Alex.

Felicity would have loved to have reached for her notebook, but the balance of everything was so delicate. It would have been a step too far.

The room was hushed as everyone waited for Miss Blanchard's answer.

"I was fetching something from Mrs Ridgeway's room."

"I can confirm this." Clarissa nodded vigorously. "I was in need of powdered bromides, having begun to feel rather queer."

Miss Blanchard scowled at Alex and Felicity. "How did you know to speak to me about this?"

"Lord Derek's companion, Miss Rossignol," answered Felicity.

Miss Blanchard looked at Derek, then back at Felicity. "Miss Rossignol is a drug addict. You cannot believe everything she says."

Felicity and Alex looked at each other. Was this the missing link? Not just with the syringe in Lord Langton's bathroom, but with the story of drug trafficking Alex had been working on?

Derek's cheeks flushed. "Now, wait just a moment—"

"She will deny it, but it is true," continued Miss Blanchard. "I know this because Miss Rossignol has asked me for drugs. She's addicted to opiates."

Ursula sat forward, her eyes narrowed as she looked from Miss Blanchard to Derek.

"Opiates?" said Clarissa. "What are opiates?"

Derek shook his head gravely. "You have absolutely no idea what you're talking about, Blanchard."

Yet Felicity could believe it. To her knowledge, she hadn't met a drug addict before, but she'd read enough newspaper and magazine articles about the phenomenon. It explained Elodie's mood changes, and the exchange between her and Derek.

Do you have it?

I don't, dearest. I'm sorry.

"When she's in London, there is no problem finding what she needs," continued Miss Blanchard. "But here in Devon, in the countryside, it's more difficult. Miss Rossignol tried to be my friend. She pretended to be kind, but when I told her I could not give her what she wanted, she got angry with me."

"How dare you make such accusations," thundered Derek. "The gun is yours. You admitted it yourself. You're the guilty party here. Leave my Elodie out of it."

"I admitted the gun is mine because I have nothing to hide." Miss Blanchard's stare at Derek was hard but not aggressive. "What do I gain from harming the family that gave me work and a home after my people were killed and my home destroyed?"

Oswald was quiet, deep in thought.

Clarissa's eyes were wide with disbelief as she looked between

Miss Blanchard and Derek. "Why didn't you tell me about Miss Rossignol before?" She sounded hurt.

"I am discreet. I don't meddle in the affairs of others." Miss Blanchard paused. "Except Miss Rossignol needs help. That is why I say this."

Felicity's mind worked quickly, but there were so many questions, so many open ends. It was difficult to know where to start.

Alex was faster off the mark. He'd replaced the revolver in his pocket and was leaning with both hands on the back of the sofa upon which Miss Blanchard was still sitting.

"Has Miss Rossignol ever been successful in procuring drugs in Devon?"

Derek clapped a hand on his forehead. "Not you, too, Coop. Surely not? You don't believe all this nonsense, do you?"

Alex fixed Derek with a stare. "You've not exactly been completely honest with me about Elodie's ailments, have you?"

Derek flinched, wounded by Alex's comment.

"Do you suppose this is what it's all about?" Clarissa clutched the top of her walking cane, her other hand rapidly stroking the Pomeranian on her lap, the dog's pink tongue lolling. "Do you think Edward's disappearance has something to do with... With illegal drugs?"

Derek shook his head, his face flushing with anger. "I'll not have this. I'll not have Elodie's name dragged through the mud by people who... Who... Who know nothing about anything, dash it."

"Miss Rossignol doesn't have a steady supplier in Devon." Miss Blanchard addressed Alex. "That's her problem. But I know that awful party man can sometimes give her what she needs." Miss Blanchard spoke as though the man's name filled her with too much disgust to utter it.

Ursula's handsome face was aghast.

Felicity steadied Pip on her lap as she edged forward in her chair. "Who do you mean, Miss Blanchard?" But she felt she already knew.

Just because Alex hadn't been able to find any trace of his old pal's drug dealing, it didn't mean Derek wasn't involved. And as far as motivation went, Derek was still the only member of the household who firmly stood to gain from Lord Langton's new will not being signed.

Miss Blanchard's response was firm. "Him."

Felicity followed Miss Blanchard's gaze to where the drawing room door had just opened.

"I mean him," confirmed Miss Blanchard, her steel-grey gaze fixed on a surprised-looking Sebastian.

Chapter Twenty-Three

A ripple of confusion passed over Sebastian's tanned face as the drawing room door closed behind him. His arresting blue eyes twinkled, and he smiled as though amused.

"Oh dear. What am I supposed to have done now?"

Miss Blanchard said nothing. She stared coldly at Sebastian, unwilling to repeat her accusation.

Clarissa huffed and adjusted herself in her seat, squeezing Charlotte as she did so, which made the black Pomeranian squeak.

"Really, Miss Blanchard. This is quite ridiculous. I'm ashamed to say I expected better of you. Really, I did." Clarissa sighed, the beads on her dress sparkling as her chest heaved. "Sebastian, darling. Miss Blanchard has suggested to the room that you are somehow involved in the provision of illicit drugs. I mean, there can't be an ounce of truth to it, can there? It's not even worthy of your response. Oh, Miss Blanchard. Words cannot express how you've disappointed me."

Sebastian moved slowly and confidently into the drawing room and stood beside Alex, behind the sofa where Miss Blanchard was still sitting. He nodded his head and raised his eyebrows, mulling things over. True or not, Sebastian was unruffled by Miss Blanchard's claim.

"It's an absolutely ghastly thing to accuse someone of." Ursula was sitting up straight, her gaze nervously skipping between Sebastian and Miss Blanchard.

"I'm not offended," said Sebastian reassuringly. "I'm not offended in the slightest. It's exactly the thing one expects from a person trying to worm their way into someone else's will. A deflection technique, if you will."

Miss Blanchard scowled deeply. "I don't know what you're talking about."

"You do, my dear," said Sebastian, leaning lightly on the back of the sofa as he addressed Miss Blanchard in her seat. "You may have mistaken Clarissa for a weak and confused older woman, but I assure you she's anything but."

Felicity's head was spinning with the revelations. If all the claims were to be believed, then Elodie was a secret drug addict, Sebastian was a supplier of drugs, and Miss Blanchard was after a chunk of Clarissa's inheritance.

Felicity looked at Alex. He widened his eyes, which told Felicity they were on the same rather surprising page.

Which of these accusations were true? And how did it all fit together?

"I'll not suffer any more of this." Clarissa dragged herself to her feet, her beaded necklaces clacking and her walking cane indenting heavily in the indigo rug. Charlotte disappeared under yards of gauzy black fabric as Clarissa tucked the Pomeranian under her arm. "Miss Blanchard," she said commandingly, though there was a wobble of emotion in her voice. "For the first time, you've disappointed me. I can guarantee you've also fallen in the estimations of everyone in this room."

Miss Blanchard looked squarely up at Clarissa. There was remorse but also defiance on her serious face. She said nothing to defend herself.

"And I am sick to death of talk of wills." Clarissa looked around the room as she spoke. "Everyone is in my will who ought to be, and that's the end of it. As soon as Edward's back—" the emotion broke in her voice "—he'll sign his new will, and this whole dreadful thing will be over. We'll all go back to normal."

Miss Blanchard rose and went to Clarissa's side, but Clarissa turned away from her, refusing her companion's offer of a handkerchief.

After a brief pause, Ursula cleared her throat. "Opiates may now be less available to the public, but as I understand it, there's no difference between what's prescribed by a doctor and what's available via illegal means. And the need for pain relievers has, of course, become exponential since the Great War."

"Yes, yes," said Oswald with a dismissive wave of his hand. He'd begun pacing the length of the drawing room's carpet. "We've all heard quite enough about your research, Ursula. But do you not think we're losing sight of what's actually important here?" Oswald stopped pacing and looked from Ursula to the rest of the room. "I mean, do none of you care about what's happened to Lord Langton?"

Politeness dictated that Felicity should express concern for Lord Langton's whereabouts, but on balance, it was best to remain quiet. After all, she'd yet to even meet the man.

A sniff from Clarissa broke the silence. "I would say Edward knows how to look after himself. So long as Mollie's with him, he'll do just fine."

Oswald shook his head in disbelief. "A mastiff can't stop bullets, though, can it?"

Derek approached Oswald. "I'm the one that got hit by a bullet, Ossie. Why is no one taking this seriously? They're trying to kill me." He pointed at his injured cheek. "Me."

Oswald frowned at Derek. "Who's they?"

"I don't know," said Derek. "Maybe it was you."

"Me? Why would I try to kill you? What could I possibly gain from that? Your father already wants to leave his business interests to me. And let me tell you something, Derek—" Oswald moved closer to Derek "—if I wanted to do away with you, I'd be organised enough to get the bally job actually done."

Sebastian had difficulty suppressing a chuckle.

"Boys!" Clarissa roared. "You're no longer in the nursery together." She nodded towards Felicity and Alex. "And we have guests. Had we all stayed in the ballroom, as per my directions, then no one would be hurt, and we'd all still be friends. Now, I suggest we all sit back down and enjoy a slice of my birthday cake. Crowther?"

"Yes, ma'am," replied the butler, who, along with the footman, had been doing his best to be invisible in the corner of the room.

Oswald exhaled slowly. "As much as I admire your calm under pressure, Mother, I cannot agree to your plan. Remaining composed and sticking together was for when we had just a dead body and a missing man to deal with. Now, we have someone willing to take up a revolver and shoot..." He gestured limply towards Derek, as though reluctant to admit there'd been an attempt on his cousin's life. "It's time for action. Uncle Edward could be lying injured somewhere, in need of our help. I'm going to the gun room to arm myself, and I'm going to look for him." Oswald was doing his best to speak calmly, but his cheeks had turned crimson. "Perhaps I'm the only person who gives a deuce about Uncle Edward's welfare, but I'd rather take a risk in doing the honourable thing than do nothing at all."

Oswald started for the door.

Felicity looked around the room. She wasn't the only one shocked by Oswald's bold decision. Ursula looked horrified, and for the first time that day, Clarissa looked genuinely worried.

"You can't go charging about with loaded weapons in this fog," said Ursula, moving to the edge of her seat. "It's madness. And who do you think is out there?"

"But Oswald, dearest," said Clarissa. "What about your son? What about Frida? If anything were to happen to you, James would be fatherless. Your wife would be a widow. You survived the war. Why take such a risk?"

Oswald paused before the drawing room door. He turned but didn't look at his mother. "Who's with me?"

Sebastian stepped out from behind the sofa. "Why not?" he said with a shrug. "Lord Langton's only ever been kind to me. And I don't think anyone left in the house wants to play cards with me again."

Derek was next. "Of course I'm coming," he said, tugging down his gaudy golf jumper. "That's my father you're talking about."

Oswald nodded solemnly. "I'll fetch Mr Cherry. We can't really ask the solicitor, but I'm sure the butler and the footman will join us."

The two servants nodded obligingly, but what choice did they have? Felicity's assessment of the proposal aligned with Ursula's and Clarissa's concerns, but it wasn't her place to comment. She was simply glad Alex hadn't volunteered himself.

"As long as we're armed and we stick together," said Oswald as the group mustered by the drawing room door, "I'm sure we'll be able to handle things. We all saw a lot worse in the trenches."

Derek turned. "Are you coming to look for Father, Coop?"

Felicity twisted to Alex with alarm. He hesitated, and she scoured her thoughts for some convincing way of excusing him. She needed his help with her photography equipment. She required his assistance in taking Pip onto the patio to tend to his business. She felt suddenly queer and would collapse into Alex's arms in front of everyone.

Alas, she couldn't think quickly enough to save Alex from his compulsion to come to people's aid.

With an apologetic look in Felicity's direction, he answered Derek's invitation with: "Of course, old thing."

Felicity's heart sank.

Ursula looked deeply concerned. "Really, though. Is this at all wise? What's the point of taking weapons into the mist when you can't see what you'll be shooting at? Someone could easily get hurt."

Ursula expressed Felicity's worries exactly. Yet had it not been completely out of the question because of her sex, Felicity would have volunteered as well and done everything in her power to protect Alex, having failed him at least once that day already.

And Ursula's concerns weren't all Felicity was worried about. Whoever was behind this mysterious mess at Langton Manor would most probably be lurking in the fog, possibly even as a member of the search party.

Normally, Felicity wouldn't meddle in another family's affairs, but on this occasion, she spoke up. "I agree with Ursula. Would you not be putting one another in danger by taking loaded guns into the fog?"

"I'm just glad you're all getting along again," said Clarissa, seemingly unmoved by Ursula's and Felicity's concerns. "It's lovely to see Sebastian, Oswald, and Derek on an adventure together, just like when you were boys." Apparently, any fear Clarissa had felt had been usurped by her delight at seeing her stepson, son, and nephew getting along.

It was Felicity's turn to shake her head in disbelief. She would have to try harder. "But what about whoever is responsible for the valet's death, and for Lord Langton going missing, and for the gunshots earlier? What if that person is hiding somewhere in the fog?"

All eyes were now on Felicity. Her remarks were mostly met with surprise. Her outburst wasn't exactly rude, but neither was it polite. Only Alex looked distinctly displeased, and she knew why. He disapproved of her drawing attention to herself. But she didn't care.

"By venturing outside in the fog, this diabolical person will be able to pick off whoever he pleases," she continued. "Don't you see?"

Oswald scowled. "Now, Lady Felicity. I agree it's dangerous, and I see your point about the fog making everything that much more risky. But the stakes here are very high. We owe it to Lord Langton to attempt to save him. Derek has been injured. What if Lord Langton is lying somewhere with a bullet in his leg, and our dawdling and lack of action ends up causing his demise?"

Felicity looked from Oswald to Alex. He returned her gaze with a disapproving stare.

"Lady Felicity, please," said Clarissa. "The men know what they're doing. Let them go."

Felicity was outnumbered and defeated.

"Well," she said to the would-be search party, although really she was only addressing one of the men. "Please do your best to look after yourselves."

Oswald nodded curtly, and the group filed out into the entrance hall, the drawing room door closing gently behind them, leaving Felicity and Pip alone with Clarissa, Miss Blanchard, and Ursula.

Clarissa lowered herself back onto the green velvet cushion of her seat, untucking Charlotte from the folds of her dress and placing the little dog back on her lap. Miss Blanchard took a seat in a chair nearby, her earlier transgressions swept under the carpet, at least for now. Ursula took a deep breath and leaned back in her chair, but her hands gripped the sides of the seat cushion.

"Please, Lady Felicity," said Clarissa. "Take afternoon tea with us. We're all quite nervous. You might think me too relaxed, but I simply know how to hide it better. That's the only difference between us. But whether or not you show it, there's no point worrying yourself to death. We just have to wait. I'm sure Oswald has everything under control. He always does."

But Felicity didn't want to sit. She didn't want to stop worrying. Alex was in grave danger, and time was running out to prevent disaster.

And as luck would have it, an idea had struck her.

"Thank you, Mrs Ridgeway," said Felicity, gathering Pip to her chest and rising from her chair. "You're being incredibly kind to me. Really, you're a wonderful hostess, but there's something I must do."

Without looking back to see anyone's reaction, Felicity made her way to the drawing room door.

Chapter Twenty-Four

As Felicity hurried across the granite flagstones, Pip firmly under her arm and the scent of lilies taking on something of a sickliness, the men's voices could be heard in a room off the entrance hall as they kitted themselves out.

"I'd prefer a rifle, if you don't mind."

"I'm quite at ease with a handgun, myself."

"Do you suppose we'll need much ammunition?"

"Depends what we come across."

"Best to be prepared for every eventuality."

Time was running out to rescue Alex from the unthinkably dangerous mission into the fog. But while she had a keen idea of what she must do, Felicity didn't know Langton Manor very well and had only a vague idea of where she was going.

It was, therefore, a stroke of rather marvellous luck when Jacob appeared from under the main stairs.

"Aha, Mr Cherry," said Felicity, making a smiling beeline for him, for under no circumstances would she allow him to wriggle away. "You're just the person I need."

"O-oh." Jacob pressed his spectacles up his nose. "I'm not able to join the search, I'm afraid. Not really been able to p-pick up a weapon of any kind since the war."

"That's quite understandable," said Felicity, who found it a wonder that there were any weapons allowed to exist at all in Europe after the horrors endured. "My enquiry is of quite a different nature. I was wondering if you might tell me the way to Lord Langton's study. I understand that's where the solicitor is waiting. Mr Palmer was his name, wasn't it?"

A frown passed over Jacob's brow. "Why, y-yes. What did you want him for? P-perhaps I can assist."

Felicity wasn't a practised liar, for she usually always preferred honesty, but when absolutely necessary, she would call on her abilities to pretend.

"Seeing as we're all stuck here waiting for this awful fog to clear," she said, "I thought I might take advantage of Mr Palmer's expertise and pose a few questions to him related to my situation. Quite unrelated to the goings-on here at Langton Manor, you understand."

That Felicity should choose that precise moment in time to ask the solicitor for personal advice was, of course, absurd. Yet she didn't fear Jacob would find her request strange. At Langton Manor, being completely self-absorbed wasn't anything out of the ordinary.

"W-well, yes. Of course. You can c-come with me. I'm on my way back to Mr Palmer right this moment."

Felicity followed Jacob down another of Langton Manor's labyrinthine corridors, this one panelled with wood right up to a rather low ceiling. Jacob walked quickly, and Felicity had nearly to break into a trot to keep up with him.

"Mr Palmer's actually in m-my office," said Jacob over his shoulder, "which is adjacent to Lord Langton's study."

"I see," said Felicity as she swapped Pip from one arm to another, as he was becoming rather heavy. The little Yorkie fussed only a tiny amount at being disturbed, but on the whole, he was behaving incredibly well.

Jacob stopped abruptly in front of a brass-knobbed door, knocked sharply on it, and entered. Felicity followed him into the room.

Bookcases stuffed with leather-bound tomes in important-looking shades of red, green, and blue covered most of the walls of Jacob's office. At the centre of a herringbone-pattern floor were two oak desks facing one another, each with a simple-yet-elegant swivel chair in front of it, and each upholstered with red leather cushioning and finished with brass studs.

On one of the desks sat a tall black typewriter — much more robust than Felicity's own model at Bradley Court — while on the other desk were pots of ink, papers with handwritten notes, and an untouched tray of tea. A clouded-glass lamp, like a large dinner plate, hung from chains at the centre of the ceiling, providing ample light under which to work. A sleek, modern clock in a jade setting sat atop a cabinet, its delicate tick-tock clearly audible.

The solicitor was stepping back into the room through a set of French doors in the corner. His brown overcoat having been removed, he was in a moss-green tweed suit with a thin grey check running through it. He had a thin moustache and long features. The cool, foggy air that accompanied his entrance into the room made Felicity shiver.

"Just stepped outside to smoke, Mr Cherry." The solicitor closed the French doors behind him, leaving them, to Felicity's dismay, slightly ajar. "Didn't know if you were asthmatic or what have you. I decided not to take any chances."

"That's considerate of you, Mr P-Palmer, but there's no need to step outside on m-my account." Jacob looked at Felicity and the solicitor. "Lady Felicity, this is Mr George Palmer, from Fenwick & Graham, the solicitors' office in Exeter used by his l-lordship. Mr Palmer, may I introduce you to Lady Felicity Quick? Her ladyship was w-wondering if she might have a moment of your time."

"My time?" The solicitor looked somewhat perplexed.

"For advice on a personal matter," clarified Felicity.

"Oh, I see. Why, yes. Certainly. It's not as though I have anything else to do until Lord Langton reappears. Dreadful business, isn't it? Simply dreadful." The solicitor wore a sorrowful expression and shook his head as he spoke.

"Indeed." Felicity echoed the solicitor's mournful expression, but kept her response as brief as possible, because time was of the essence.

"Please, your ladyship. Take a seat." The solicitor gestured to the swivel chair nearest the typewriter.

"Thank you."

Pip squirmed as Felicity placed him on her lap. A new room always contained fascinating smells, and it was clear the Yorkie wanted to be put on the ground and allowed to sniff about, but Felicity was adamant he should stay on her lap, and she rested a hand on his glossy back.

"Allow me to come straight to the point, Mr Palmer. I'm incredibly curious about what is involved in making one's will."

It was a lie, of course, but neither the solicitor nor Lord Langton's secretary seemed to notice. The solicitor had taken a seat in the matching chair at the other desk, and Jacob stood alongside, their interested gazes fixed on Felicity.

She continued. "Now, granted, I'm not yet of an age at which I need to worry about such things, and I'm also so far unburdened by the concerns of wealth or descendants. Nevertheless, I should like to be prepared. The fact is, I've never seen a legal document such as a will before, and I was wondering if you might have an example I could look at in order to satisfy my curiosity."

As Felicity stroked Pip, she blinked innocently at the solicitor and Jacob. Her head whirred with suspicion fed by the revelations of Elodie's use of drugs, Sebastian's role in their supply, and Miss Blanchard's interest in an inheritance from Clarissa, not to mention the shots in the fog, Derek's injury, the hypodermic syringe found with the dead valet, and Alex's undercover investigation.

But in reality, it didn't matter whether the accusations made in the drawing room were true. All these elements were secondary.

At the heart of the mystery of Lord Langton's disappearance were his wills, new and old. She couldn't come out and say it, but her aim — her hope — was to see them. It was too much of a coincidence that the new will was to be signed on the very day Lord Langton disappeared. Felicity was sure of it.

By accessing his wills, she could determine who was responsible for the 'rum doings' at Langton Manor, get word to Alex, and save him from taking part in the uncommonly dangerous armed search party, among whose members may lurk murderous intentions.

Leaning back in his chair, the solicitor tented his fingers and looked at Felicity through narrow, thoughtful eyes. "I see," he said. "Quite understandable, and very prudent of you, Lady Felicity. Only I'm sorry to disappoint. I don't carry example documents around with me as a matter of course."

"Certainly," said Felicity, feeling she had little to lose and everything to gain. "But you have Lord Langton's testaments, his old one and his new one, do you not?"

The solicitor's high forehead furrowed. "You'll forgive me for pointing out that such a document is confidential, Lady Felicity. It wouldn't be proper for me to show it to anyone without his lordship's permission."

Felicity had expected this. "Oh, but I shan't be as indiscreet as to look at the contents. It's the form I'm interested in. Might I have a peek?"

The solicitor looked at Jacob disapprovingly. Jacob looked rather nervously at Felicity, then back at the solicitor. There was a pause during which the jade clock's tick-tock was the only sound.

"I d-don't see the harm," said the secretary with an awkward shrug.

The solicitor's narrowed eyes went from Jacob to Felicity. "Very well."

Relief washed over Felicity. She never liked to lean upon her status as a member of England's aristocracy, but she sometimes allowed it to work in her favour.

Leaning forward, the solicitor lifted his small brown briefcase from the ground and put it on the desk in front of him, beside the untouched tray of tea. Snapping the metallic clasps open, the solicitor lifted the briefcase's lid in Felicity's direction. From the briefcase, he withdrew two pages full of cramped, typed text, with signatures at the bottom of the second page.

The solicitor handed the sheets to Jacob, who brought the document to Felicity and placed it on the desk in front of her, lying the two pages side by side across the typewriter's keys.

Felicity had expected something grander and more ornate than the two rather plain typed pages. She'd not studied her own father's will in any detail, but she remembered seeing it with Jasper and the Quick family's solicitor, and it had been several pages long.

"Wonderful. Thank you." As Felicity spoke, she began reading the document, but in a way that did not make it obvious she was doing so. Her eyes jumped from page to page, occasionally flashing a glance at the solicitor or Jacob.

It was quickly apparent the document was Lord Langton's old will, which was, as far as anyone knew, still in effect. Written after the demise of Lord Langton's eldest son, the first page named Derek as the primary heir, but there were also significant bequests to Clarissa and Ursula. Oswald received only a small sum of money, much less than what his mother stood to inherit, and there was nothing about him gaining the control of any investments or companies.

"Is there special wording that always must be used?" asked Felicity as cover for her extended perusal of the document.

"Well, yes," said the solicitor, slightly amused. "Otherwise, the likes of myself would be out of a job."

"Of course," said Felicity, also smiling. It had indeed been a silly question. "I suppose it must always start: 'This is the last will and testament of…'" she prompted, hoping to buy herself enough time to take in the second page of the will, which, to Felicity's surprise, featured many names.

But the solicitor wasn't particularly loquacious. "That's correct," he said.

As quickly as she could, the tick-tock of the jade clock underlining the rapid passage of time, Felicity scanned the contents of the will's second page.

It was a detailed list of items ranging from vases to paintings to pieces of furniture — presumably antiques of some worth — that were to be inherited by a range of individuals. Recipients included

Frida, Jacob, Sebastian, and Miss Blanchard. Even the butler, Robert Crowther and the deceased valet, John Greenwood, were on the list. There were also names Felicity didn't recognise, like Millicent Davis and Betsy Biggs, although Thomas Clegg was vaguely familiar.

From what Felicity had so far heard about Lord Langton, he didn't seem the type to bequeath antiques to employees and servants, but he was perhaps the sort who didn't like to draw attention to his generosity. Or perhaps the items Lord Langton was leaving weren't worth much.

Felicity yearned to take out her notebook, but so as not to come across as reporting on matters, all she could do was skim the text and hope to have at least some of it committed to memory.

"Hmm," said Jacob.

He'd been peering with interest at the document, but when Felicity looked up at him, he straightened and averted his eyes.

Felicity looked at the solicitor. "Is a will like this typical of the kinds of wills Fenwick & Graham prepares?"

Jacob collected the two sheets of paper together and handed them back to the solicitor.

"Well." The solicitor frowned a little as he replaced the papers in his briefcase. "I've not worked with Messrs Fenwick and Graham for very long, you understand, but I would say so, yes. It's certainly not entirely different from the wills we used to produce at my former place of work."

"Thank you," said Felicity with a tight smile. "That was most educational."

It was difficult to puzzle through what she'd just read while engaging in polite yet deceptive dialogue, but Felicity didn't feel any closer to the truth about Lord Langton's disappearance. Nevertheless, she remained convinced that the answers she needed would be in the wills.

"Would I perhaps be able to look at Lord Langton's new will?" Felicity's own boldness came as a surprise to herself. "To see if anything changed in style in the intervening years?"

Jacob pushed his spectacles up his nose. "The new d-document is ready for Lord Langton to sign when he returns, isn't it Mr Palmer?"

The solicitor hesitated. "I thought the new will was here at Langton Manor, Mr Cherry."

"Here?" Jacob blinked nervously. "W-why would it be here?"

The solicitor frowned. "That's what Mr Graham told me."

"How odd. How deeply odd." Jacob snatched his spectacles off his face and took to cleaning their lenses with his handkerchief. "But why would we have the n-new will here? That's your role as the s-solicitor, isn't it?"

The solicitor narrowed his eyes at Jacob. It was unclear to Felicity who, hierarchically speaking, had supremacy. Was it the solicitor or the peer's private secretary?

A ferocious barking interrupted them.

Pip sat to attention on Felicity's lap, his ears pricking up.

The sound carried in from the fog, through the French doors left ajar. It was brutish — certainly not the bark of Clarissa's Pomeranian — and it caught everyone's attention.

"What the deuce is that?" The solicitor looked fearfully at Felicity and Jacob as the barking continued.

A man's shouting was added to the terrible canine noise. Felicity couldn't quite make out the words.

"It's Lord D-Derek," said Jacob, and he hastened to the French doors.

Was it too late? Was the armed search party — and Alex with it — already outside?

Felicity picked up Pip and followed Jacob as he stepped onto the sandstone terrace, fog rolling around them.

"Blasted dog!" Derek's shouts were now clear. He was somewhere further along the side of the house, though the fog was still too dense for anything besides the vague outlines of treetops to be visible.

The barking of the unseen dog continued. The deep, angry sound matched a large, powerful breed like the mastiff.

"I've always hated the creature!"

Derek's shouting was this time punctuated by a sharp crack that sent a chill down Felicity's spine. The weapons the search party had collected from the gun room had been loaded and readied for action, and Derek was clearly unafraid of using his.

The barking continued unaffected, which was both reassuring and worrying.

"Lord D-Derek is upset." Jacob's eyes flicked between Felicity and the direction of Derek's voice as he wrung his hands. "The search party... Oh, dash it." He began walking through the fog towards Derek's shouting.

Pip struggled under Felicity's arm.

"No, Pip," she said, gripping him tightly. "We're staying together."

Felicity's plan to unravel the secrets held in Lord Langton's wills had failed, but she wasn't ready to give up. If the situation were reversed, Alex wouldn't give up on Felicity.

She set off through the fog after Jacob.

Chapter Twenty-Five

Felicity followed the vague, foggy outline of the fast-walking Jacob as he skimmed the outside of the house, their footsteps tapping across the sandstone terrace.

Pip struggled in her arms, yipping in answer to the surly barking coming from somewhere out in Langton Manor's parkland. Whether the little Yorkie felt brave or scared, Felicity couldn't tell. Assessing her own feelings was difficult enough.

A melee of male voices carried through the mist as the armed search party came into view. The tall windows of the ballroom and the wistful glow of its chandeliers provided a backdrop for the group, Alex among them.

He and Sebastian both held pistols. Oswald, his face crumpled with weariness and frustration, had a rifle on a strap over his shoulder. The butler had a weary-looking shotgun, also on a strap. The footman wasn't armed and looked uneasy.

At the head of the group was Derek. With his back to the house, he had a rifle readied on his shoulder, its muzzle thankfully aimed up into the foggy air.

"Wretched hound!" he cried as he let off another shot, the proximity of which made both Felicity and Pip jump.

Alex had been watching Derek with concern until he noticed

Felicity. From the set of his jaw, she could tell he was not especially pleased she'd joined him, but Felicity didn't care for Alex's mood. It mattered only that he was safe. And to Felicity's relief, he was.

Oswald shook his head. "Derek. Please."

Jacob was as white as the fog swirling around them. "You f-found his lordship's dog, then."

"I'm not going anywhere with that blasted creature on the loose!" *Crack!*

Jacob put his hands over his ears and winced. Again, Oswald shook his head.

It wasn't entirely unexpected that Derek should become agitated, but it was a surprise that his father's dog pushed him over the edge. Her reappearance could, after all, be a clue about Lord Langton's disappearance.

"Is Mollie dangerous?" asked Felicity.

Derek turned to her, his eyes wild, his gun slightly lowered.

Alex took a step towards Derek. "Come now, old thing. There's no need to get so upset."

"Dangerous?" asked Derek, his voice becoming shrill. "The beast could take down a lion if it wanted. Of course it's bally dangerous."

"It's all right, Derek, old chap." The look on Sebastian's face was somewhere between uneasiness and amusement. "It's quite normal the dog's got you rattled. We can't all be brave all the time."

Derek turned sharply to Sebastian. "Brave? I led five charges into battle on the Western Front. What the blazes did you ever do?"

Sebastian held up his hands. "Easy, old chap. I meant nothing by it."

Alex stepped away from Derek as he re-aimed his rifle towards the distant treetops barely visible above the swirling fog. "You can all go looking for Father. I'll settle my score with that blasted hound."

"Don't be ridiculous," said Oswald impatiently. "We can't go anywhere with you firing shots over our heads."

Crack! Derek let another bullet fly.

While Mollie's reappearance might have aided the hunt for Lord

Langton, Felicity was rather relieved at the search party's disintegration.

She cleared her throat. "Should we perhaps return to the police's advice and gather to await their arrival?"

Jacob blinked. Sebastian shrugged. Oswald nodded thoughtfully.

"Shouldn't we go after the dog?" said Alex.

Felicity turned to him in disbelief.

"It might lead us to Lord Langton," continued Alex, addressing the group. "What if he needs our help?"

Felicity recognised the earnestness in his clear blue eyes. Alex could be so focused on doing right for others that he couldn't see the wrong he was doing for himself.

"Shouldn't we leave matters for the police?" Felicity's suggestion was firm. Asking questions to piece together a story was one thing. Playing a proactive role in the story was quite something else.

As the big dog continued to bark in the distance, Pip struggled and yipped in Felicity's arms. Doing her best to ignore him, she looked about the group for support of her suggestion.

Jacob was nodding eagerly. Oswald looked thoughtfully out at the fog.

Sebastian folded his arms in front of his chest, his pistol still in his hand. "With all due respect, Lady Felicity, do you seriously think the local bobbies will swoop in and solve all our problems?"

Felicity didn't miss a beat. "I realise you're a man of the world, Mr Ridgeway, but I'm uncertain how much experience you've had with the Devon County Constabulary. To date, I've been quite impressed by their capabilities."

With a smile, Sebastian raised his eyebrows as if to concede Felicity the point.

Felicity raised her eyebrows back at him. It was out of character, but she was becoming rather fed up with everything. It didn't help that Pip continued to wriggle. She suppressed the urge to hiss *Stop it!* at him, as it might have given the wrong impression. She and Pip were in the habit of addressing one another informally, but it wasn't the moment to explain.

Oswald turned his attention back to the group. "Well, we certainly won't be going anywhere as long as Derek doesn't put his weapon down."

Derek scowled deeply at his cousin and — *crack!* — sent another shot flying into the fog. "I'll not have that wicked creature bounding around, causing mayhem."

"Come now, old chap." Alex approached Derek, a little less patiently this time. "Let's put an end to this."

Alex touched his friend's shoulder, but he'd miscalculated. His touch startled Derek, and he swung his rifle in Alex's direction.

Crack!

Derek's aim was too high to damage anything except the house's masonry, but the whole exchange — which was over in a split second — made Felicity's heart leap into her throat and her arms loosen their grip on Pip.

The little dog saw his chance. One wriggle and he slipped out of Felicity's grasp, bounced onto the ground, and went scrambling over the terrace paving towards the big dog's barking.

"Pip!"

Without hesitation, without even thinking, Felicity went racing after her beloved pet.

Felicity ran as fast as she could, desperate to keep Pip even slightly visible in the fog. She almost lost her footing on the sandstone terrace — her one-strap shoes with their Spanish heel not being at all suitable for running — but the soggy earth of the lawn slowed Felicity's progress dramatically, and Pip disappeared completely from view.

Left with nothing but his yapping to follow, Felicity struggled across the grass as her little dog's bark drew closer to that of the bigger dog.

"Pip!" Felicity's lungs burned from running. "Please, don't do this again. Come back!"

Her cries were no use. Pip wasn't coming back, and all Felicity could do was hope to come across him before the big dog did.

As Felicity's heels continued to sink in the muddy grass, Pip's yapping stopped. The larger dog's barking also ceased.

"Oh, no." Felicity tried hopelessly to increase her speed. "No, no, no." She knew from experience silence was never a good sign with Pip, but she would have given anything to have him safe at Bradley Court chewing on a new pair of shoes.

There was a vague silhouette in the fog.

"Pip!" Felicity rushed forward.

Pip was standing in the wet grass, tail wagging. Above him towered one of the largest dogs Felicity had ever seen. It had a powerful body covered in short fawn fur, a square head with creases between flapped ears, and a black muzzle from which strings of drool hung, threatening to land on Pip's little head.

The creature wore a heavy red collar around its thick neck. On a small brass plate was written *Mollie* in flowing script too elegant for a dog so brutal-looking.

Felicity brought her hands to her mouth in fear.

Pip seemed happy to offer himself as a snack to Lord Langton's dog, but Felicity dared not approach for fear of provoking the mastiff. One bite from its powerful jaws would have been the end for Pip, or even for Felicity herself, was she to get close enough.

She was a terrible pet owner, a terrible sister — her brother would likely never trust her again after this — not to mention a terrible friend. Any manner of mayhem might have broken out on the house's terrace, and she wasn't there to help Alex.

Perhaps Felicity's biggest mistake had been in overestimating herself. She'd imagined she could work with Alex to play a role in reporting on the story while staying out of trouble, but she saw now she'd made a series of silly mistakes. And she and poor, poor Pip would pay the price.

The formidable Mollie took a step forward, squelching a paw bigger than Pip's head down on the wet earth.

“No!” cried Felicity, twisting her hands in fear as Pip’s tail wagged even faster.

Mollie slowly lowered her head, her collar slipping down her gigantic neck. Her black nose twitched as she sniffed the Yorkie, globules of slobber landing on the little dog’s fur.

Poor, innocent Pip lifted his nose towards Mollie’s and sniffed her back.

Tears rose in Felicity’s eyes. “No. Please, Mollie. No.”

The giant dog opened her huge jaws, and lowering her head even further, Mollie gave Pip a huge, slobbering lick, wiping her massive pink tongue across the Yorkie’s face and head. She then gave a powerful bark, her thick tail beating the air, and galloped off into the fog.

Felicity was stunned. “What the...”

Pip turned to her, his fur slicked against his skull with slobber, which made his head look almost comically small. Then he bounded off after the mastiff, and both Pip’s yapping and Mollie’s barking resumed.

“What the...” Felicity said again, wiping a tear from her eye as she blinked into the fog.

She wasn’t quite sure what had just happened, but there wasn’t time to analyse. Once again, Felicity set off after Pip.

Chapter Twenty-Six

Felicity squelched through the grass in her by-now utterly ruined one-strap shoes. With almost nothing visible of Langton Manor's grounds besides fog, Pip's yapping and Mollie's barking pulled her forward. The Yorkie's encounter with the mastiff had left Felicity drained of energy, but she struggled on through the chill of the swirling fog, hoping that Alex was all right and cursing herself for her own stupidity.

Mollie's barking was the first to stop. Then came a series of loud splashes, Pip's yapping continuing all the while. He'd come to a stop and soon the radius of what Felicity could see reached the little Yorkie.

He was standing on the edge of a body of water. Mollie was nowhere to be seen. The rippled expanse of the grey water blended with the fog, making it impossible to say where the water stopped and the fog began. The water lapped gently against the lawn's edge. It had to be Langton Manor's great lake.

Returning to her senses, Felicity quickly scooped Pip into her arms. "Got you." The fur around his legs and belly was soaked, and his little paws were muddy, but Felicity wasn't bothered about ruining her blouse. Her shoes were already done for, so why not the rest of her outfit? Pip was safe now. That was the main thing.

But how would they return to the manor house?

Felicity had lost all sense of where she was in relation to the building. At least there were no more shots being fired from the terrace. Felicity sincerely hoped Alex was all right. It had been very poor form to abandon him.

Pip wouldn't stop yapping, and as Felicity turned to get her bearings, the little dog twisted in her arms to keep watch over the lake.

Something was moving through the water.

Mollie, her head held above the surface, her enormous body submerged under the lake's murky grey surface, appeared through the fog, swimming for the shore.

Felicity sighed deeply. Even in a desperate situation, she couldn't deny her own curious nature. If Mollie was here — and by all accounts, she rarely left her master's side — then where was Lord Langton?

Pip continued to yap as Mollie's paws reached the water's bottom. The great dog pulled herself from the lake and thundered back onto the grass, tail held high. She stopped in proximity to Felicity.

"Oh, no." But it was too late.

Starting at her nose and ending at the tip of her mighty tail, Mollie gave herself a tremendous shake. Though her fur wasn't long, she still shook off a large amount of water, a great deal of which hit both Felicity and Pip, leaving Felicity's curls hanging limply at her cheeks.

The mastiff then resumed barking, her slobbery jowls rippling as her huge jaw snapped shut again and again.

"No, Pip." Felicity held onto Pip extra tightly as he struggled to join Mollie. "No swimming for you. You're staying with me."

Felicity had swung from despair at the situation to exasperation, but she was determined to do at least one thing right: she would keep Pip safe. And despite Mollie's enthusiasm for Pip's presence, keeping the Yorkie safe meant returning to the house, for although Langton

Manor was hardly a haven of security, nothing good could come of loitering in the fog.

Looking around her, Felicity could see the patch of the lawn on which she stood, a limited amount of the lake's surface, and plenty of fog. She tried to silence the barking dogs, to no avail.

Which way was it back to the house? Felicity had no clue.

Deciding that progress had to be made regardless, she turned her back to the water and began striding forwards. Pip twisted in her arms, desperate to keep in contact with Mollie. To Felicity's dismay, the big mastiff bounded forwards and remained at her side as she walked, drool flying as Mollie barked.

"Mollie, please. This really won't do. Go back to your master. Go. Find your master."

The big dog didn't listen. Why should she? Felicity's own dog barely ever did. Counting her blessings, Felicity was at least thankful Mollie wasn't as fearsome as Derek believed her to be. Felicity was considering the potential problems of bringing Mollie up to the house — if that was indeed the direction in which she was heading — when a figure appeared in the mist.

Felicity froze.

With two barking dogs and no idea where in the grounds she was, there was nowhere for Felicity to hide. And whoever was approaching clearly had no fear of Mollie.

But as the figure drew nearer, Felicity recognised the broad shoulders and confident walk.

"Alex!"

Felicity's utterance sounded like a sob of relief. And while she was enormously relieved, she was also deeply ashamed. The man she'd sworn to take care of had yet again come to her rescue.

Alex smiled as he approached, but he stopped a little distance away from Felicity, his smile faltering as his eyes landed on Mollie. The mastiff had stopped barking and was sitting on the ground, her thick fawn tail thumping the grass, her eyes fixed on Alex.

Pip growled, and Felicity gave him a chastising squeeze. It was clear he and Alex would never be friends, but Alex had already saved Pip once that day. There was no need to be ungrateful about it.

Alex frowned with confusion at Mollie. "Here I was, imagining you might be in trouble. Seems you've not only located the fearsome hound. You've also befriended her."

Felicity sighed. "I would say we're less friends, more acquaintances."

Mollie approached Alex. First, she sniffed his shoes. Then she sniffed his leg, leaving spots of slobber on his dark grey trousers as she did so.

"And 'fearsome' I'm not so sure about," added Felicity.

Mollie licked Alex's hand, which was balled into an uneasy fist at his side. When Alex extended his fingers to stroke the velvety creases of Mollie's fawn head, the big dog showed her appreciation by sitting back down on the wet grass and collapsing a heavy shoulder against Alex's thigh.

Felicity raised her eyebrows. "I didn't receive such a warm greeting."

Alex continued to stroke Mollie's broad head. "Growing up, we always had cats. Since moving to Devon, I've noticed it helps if one is also a dog person."

Felicity would leave her observations on the advantages and disadvantages of being a 'dog person' for another time. "What situation did you leave at the house?"

Alex shook his head. "I left soon after you ran after Pip. I took Derek's gun off him first, though. Gave it to Oswald."

Felicity suppressed a smile. Alex could have disarmed Derek at any point, but he chose his battles wisely.

"Derek wasn't too happy, of course," continued Alex, "but Oswald seems like a sensible chap, and Derek's a danger to himself at times."

As he spoke, Alex continued to pet Mollie, who lifted her head so he could rub her under her baggy chin.

Alex quirked an eyebrow at Felicity. "Anyway. Trust you to be out here solving the mystery all by yourself."

Felicity frowned. "Is that what you think I came out here to do?" If Alex hadn't recognised the relief in her voice when she'd greeted him, she was thankful for it.

"Well." Alex looked down at Mollie, who had closed her eyes in some kind of canine bliss as Alex continued to scratch her. "You located Lord Langton's dog. We can't be far from finding the man himself."

Felicity took a steadying breath. Her intention had been to return to the house. "Perhaps."

Mollie's eyes sprang open, and she bounded away from Alex, passed Felicity, and disappeared back into the fog.

"Steady on, old girl." Alex laughed, surprised at the big dog's nimbleness.

Then came the splash. It prompted Pip to yap again.

"The lake?"

Felicity nodded. "My impression is that Mollie wants us to follow her."

Alex raised his eyebrows. "Is that what you propose we do?"

A voice inside Felicity, the voice of a woman much bolder and more adventurous than herself, said, *Of course. What are we even waiting for*?

Aloud, Felicity said, "Well." Then she hesitated.

As curious as she was about Lord Langton's disappearance, Felicity had made rather a mess of things. She'd defied every ounce of advice Jasper had given her and put herself, Alex, and Pip in danger on many occasions.

Following a dog she'd only just met to find a man she didn't even know wasn't in the best interests of the safety of Alex, Pip, or herself. Felicity's earlier attempts at untangling the mystery had also come to nothing.

But what were the alternatives?

Heading back to the manor house wasn't without its risks, as at least one inhabitant was embroiled in a diabolical plot. Waiting around in the fog wasn't much of an option either. Even if Derek was no longer armed, it didn't prevent someone else from becoming active with a weapon.

Yet, aware of the risks, Felicity couldn't ignore her burning desire to know, to find out, to discover, that so often propelled her forwards. It was why she was a journalist. It was how she unravelled things in Lower Diddleton and at Wolborne House. Even if her brother wouldn't let her write about them, she couldn't ignore her desire to know the facts.

Still, she hesitated.

"We should probably go back to the house and wait for the police," she said.

Alex drew back his chin. "That doesn't sound like the Lady Felicity Quick I know."

With a hint of knee-jerk indignation, Felicity tipped her head to the side. "Am I not always careful and thoughtful in the making of decisions?"

Alex smiled. "Always. But add to that a keen desire to know exactly what's going on and a pinch of bravery, then we have the Lady Felicity Quick I know."

Felicity blinked. She'd been called many things before — unthinking, foolhardy, and careless with her own safety, and these were mainly words used by her brother — but never brave.

"Or are you telling me you have no interest in solving the mystery?" pressed Alex. "And no interest in a scoop for the Western Daily News?"

Felicity shook her head adamantly. "Jasper would never allow me to write about any of it." She was certain of that.

Alex started after Mollie, his hands in his pockets. "How about we cross that bridge when we come to it?"

Felicity frowned.

Alex could reach into her frustrations and strike a nerve without batting an eyelid. It was an infuriating quality of his. But despite her doubts about her actions and their potential consequences — particularly as far as her brother was concerned — Felicity had made a promise to herself. For the rest of her time at Langton Manor, she would ensure the safety of Pip and do her utmost to ensure the same for Alex.

With Alex leading the way and Pip still safely tucked under her arm, Felicity headed back into the fog.

Chapter Twenty-Seven

The milky-grey sheen of the lake's surface and the soft pale fog above it were beautiful, in a way. Pip leaned out of Felicity's arms, his little black nose twitching. In the water, Mollie held her wide head and baggy chin aloft as she swam.

As Felicity and Alex approached the water's edge, the mastiff waded to shore.

"Stand back," warned Felicity before Mollie shook herself from nose to tail, water and drool flying.

Alex wiped his cheek. "Thanks," he said flatly, addressing mostly Mollie.

Lord Langton's dog went to Alex and head-butted him gently on the back of his thigh.

"I do believe you're right," he said. "She wants us to follow her."

Felicity's chest was tight with uneasiness and excitement. Following Mollie would be a journey into the unknown, but it would surely bring them closer to the truth behind whatever was going on at Langton Manor.

Alex looked down at Mollie, unfazed by the big wet dog dripping lake water on his already-slobbered-upon trouser leg. "We know what you're saying, old girl. But we can't join you for a swim."

Felicity was glad Alex's sense of adventure had limits.

She squinted through the fog. "What's that?"

Along the lake's shore, at the edge of Felicity's visibility, a large crescent-shaped silhouette bobbed on the water.

Alex turned to look. "How curious."

They started towards it, Pip still in Felicity's arms and Mollie at Alex's side, their footsteps squishing softly through the muddy grass.

The shape grew clearer. It was a boat with a shining black hull curved into ornate gold points at either end. The interior was upholstered in luxurious red velvet, and a long, thin oar lay across the vessel.

"The gondola."

Felicity had never been to Italy, but the Venetian boat was iconic.

It was moored alongside a small wooden jetty, which Mollie ignored as she ran eagerly towards the gondola, her heavy paws splashing in the water at the foreshore.

Alex hopped onto the jetty, put his hands in the pockets of his waistcoat, and let out a whistle. "Must have cost a pretty penny to bring this thing to Devon."

Mollie threw herself back into the lake, her black-and-fawn face serious with concentration as she swam around the boat. Pip shivered in Felicity's arms and yipped as they joined Alex on the jetty. The little Yorkie was eager to join Mollie and frustrated at being held back.

"Pip, please. We spoke about this already. You're staying with me, and that's the end of it."

Alex looked from the boat to Felicity. "Shall we?"

"Is she sea-worthy?"

Clearly, it was, but Felicity bought time for herself as her thoughts raced. Part of her was desperate to move forward, desperate to learn more, but part of her also urged caution and conjured an image of her brother's face, his moustaches sagging with disappointment.

Alex rested a hand on the boat's pointed stern. "Looks it. I've never captained one before, though."

Felicity swallowed. Alex had said she was brave. As long as she, Alex, and Pip were together, they were as safe as they could be, under the circumstances. And Mollie had to be urging them onwards for a reason. As Oswald had said, what if Lord Langton was lying injured somewhere?

"Have you ever been punting?" suggested Felicity. "Out on the Cam?" She was referring to the flat-bottomed boats students of the university at Cambridge would use to amuse themselves in the summer on the river that ran through the city.

Alex scratched his head as he looked at the gondola. "I've been out once or twice, but I'd hardly call myself an experienced punt skipper."

"It can't be that different, can it?"

Alex's thick eyebrows crumpled with confusion, but Felicity had already made up her mind. She climbed into the boat, tugging down her skirt and placing Pip firmly on her lap.

"Mind if I put these here?" Alex reached into the boat with a smart but muddy pair of Oxfords stuffed with plum-coloured socks. He rolled the trousers of his dark grey suit up to his shins. Felicity's chest fluttered with surprise at the sight of Alex's muscular calves. Thank heavens swimming hadn't been an option.

She cleared her throat and refocused her attention on Mollie, who was swimming circles ahead of the gondola's bow.

"Here we go." Alex sprang onto the boat's stern, and the vessel rocked wildly. "Whoa, there. Steady on. Nothing like a punt," he said, having finally got the rocking under control.

Felicity helped pass Alex the long, thin oar, which was much heavier than she expected, and pretended not to hear a whispered oath as Alex wrestled the oar into an arm-like receptacle on the side of the boat. Soon they were moving away from the jetty at an oddly relaxing pace, with Mollie swimming confidently ahead.

Cautiously, Felicity allowed Pip to get off her lap. He positioned himself towards the gondola's bow, a paw raised, his little black nose twitching at the damp, chilly air. With the only sound the gentle lapping of water caressing the vessel's sides, the lake's shore disappeared from view. They were entirely surrounded by grey water and dense fog.

Alex worked the oar in a rhythmic motion. "I think I've got the technique. On a punt, it's a pole that goes into the riverbed. With this oar, you have to sweep the water in a sort of figure eight."

While Felicity had ambitions to explore Europe, she never imagined her first gondola ride would be on a Devon lake in the middle of a murder mystery, although she supposed she could do worse than Alex as her gondolier. He was certainly quick to pick things up.

Felicity wrapped her arms around herself and shivered, again regretting she hadn't kept her top coat with her.

Thwack!

Alex's grey tailored jacket took her by surprise as it landed on the red velvet seat beside her.

Felicity twisted towards Alex, who was now in his waistcoat and shirt sleeves, his bare feet gripping the gondola's polished stern. A portion of his dark blond hair had fallen across his forehead.

"Put that on, if you like."

Felicity turned away from him. "No, thank you."

She could have benefitted from the extra layer Alex's jacket would have offered, but Felicity didn't want to be in a permanent state of being rescued by Alex. She wanted them to be equals, not for her to be constantly in his debt. And, as they had agreed earlier that day, they would work together. They were colleagues.

"What did you learn when you went to play cards?" asked Felicity, her eyes on Pip at the boat's prow.

Alex huffed. "Never to play cards with Sebastian Ridgeway. He's quite the sharp."

Felicity twisted to look at him. "You mean he cheats?"

"I wouldn't go that far, but he certainly knows how to win. His father was apparently also that way."

Felicity squinted out at the water. "Clarissa won't hear of it, but her deceased husband doesn't have an excellent reputation at Langton Manor. And Miss Blanchard accused Sebastian of peddling drugs. Doesn't that connect to the story you were reporting on while undercover?"

"I've all but given up on that line of enquiry. It's beaten me." Alex sounded glum. "But Miss Blanchard herself doesn't come off scot-free, does she? The revolver in my pocket is hers. I suppose it's not entirely right of me to keep it, but it didn't feel entirely right to give it back, under the circumstances. A rather odd idea for a keepsake by which to remember one's father, wouldn't you say?"

Felicity slowly nodded, reassured that Alex was still armed but perplexed at the muddle of accusations and admissions heard that day.

She withdrew her notebook from her pocket.

All she'd written so far was the three-columned list, which remained unfinished. There was Derek under *Loses from the new will,* Oswald under *Gains*, and no one under *Neutral*. Perhaps Jasper was right to keep Felicity off crime reporting. She was doing a pretty poor job of gathering the ingredients for the story so far.

But there was one thing about which she was certain.

"Lord Langton's new will must be the key to it all." She turned to Alex. "It would be too much of a coincidence if it weren't. But I only saw the old will, not the new one."

Alex stopped working the oar. "You saw Lord Langton's will?"

Felicity hesitated, then nodded.

He smiled. "You're as wily as a fox, and certainly much cannier than me. How the blazes did you manage it?"

Felicity sat up straighter. "A combination of quick thinking, strategic planning, and the charms of an aristocratic woman, I suppose."

Alex shook his head with smiling disbelief as he returned to working the oar. "And what's in the old will?"

Felicity sighed, turning again to the front of the boat and sinking into the gondola's velvet cushions. "That's just it. Without the new will to which to compare it, I couldn't draw any useful conclusions. Derek gets pretty much everything, and there are bequests to Clarissa, Ursula, and Oswald. Nothing unpredictable, except Lord Langton splitting his collection of art and antiques across just about everyone in the household. Even the servants get vases and paintings."

"Who knew the old boy had it in him? I've met Lord Langton on a couple of occasions, and he doesn't seem the sentimental type."

"That's also the impression I received from his relatives." Felicity looked back at her notebook and tapped the page with the top of her pencil. "Clarissa mentioned her bequest would be reduced in the new will."

"Do you think she'd do away with her own brother over it?" asked Alex.

Felicity sighed. Clarissa wasn't faultless, but there was a warmth about her that Felicity considered incompatible with harming one's own brother. "From a logical perspective, why admit the reduction in inheritance if it's your motivation for a murder plot?"

"Would-be murderers aren't always the logical type, I suppose. Ursula, then? You say she receives something in the old will. Perhaps she loses out in the new one, just like Clarissa?"

Ursula was cooler and more calculating than her aunt, but Felicity still wasn't sure. "If Ursula wanted to do away with someone, surely it would be done neatly and efficiently using some kind of untraceable poison concocted in her research laboratory at the Sorbonne."

Alex chuckled. "Fair point."

Felicity looked down at the list in her notebook. With the tip of her pencil, she touched Derek's name.

"I wonder what those vases and paintings are all worth," said Alex. "Worth killing for, perhaps?"

There was no point in broaching Derek's motives with Alex. He refused to see his friend's guilt as possible.

Felicity thought back to her discussion with Derek on the staircase, and the vulnerability he'd displayed. Her view of Elodie had also softened in light of her drug addiction, which seemed to affect her like an illness, although Elodie's connection to the dead valet still hadn't been explained. The luck involved in Derek being merely scratched by a bullet and not struck by it was also improbable.

"Without the new will, we can't know for sure." Felicity swapped the tip of her pencil over to Oswald. "Although we can be fairly certain Oswald isn't involved."

"Frida?" suggested Alex.

The thought had crossed Felicity's mind. Frida was ill and unhappy, but was she unhappy enough to take drastic action to stop her husband from inheriting more responsibilities?

The other side of the lake took shape in the fog. Ahead of them, Mollie climbed out of the water and for once completed her nose-to-tail shake without innocent bystanders getting wet.

"I don't see any moorings," said Alex. "I'm going to beach it. Hold on tight."

Felicity snatched Pip back onto her lap as the gondola lurched forward. With a gentle *boom*, the boat came to an abrupt stop, its hull shuddering against the lake's silty shore.

Alex lowered himself into the water with a gentle splash and waded towards the grass. "I would offer to help you down, but I know you'd only refuse me."

"That's right, and please don't look," said Felicity, slipping off her shoes and preparing for an ungainly exit from the gondola. It would leave her stockings sodden, but there was no turning back now. Whether her brother allowed her to write it up was beside the point. Felicity could no longer ignore her desire to unravel the mystery at Langton Manor.

Chapter Twenty-Eight

On the lake's shore, Mollie took up barking again, impatient to bring Felicity, Pip, and Alex wherever she was leading them.

Pip struggled wilfully against Felicity's grip as she lifted him from the boat. "Oh, no you don't," she said as she tucked him under her arm. "I've had quite enough of you darting off into the fog. You're staying with me."

As she joined Alex lacing his Oxfords further up the bank, Felicity shook the water off her stockinged feet as best she could before slipping on her ruined one-strap shoes.

"Mollie, please," she said sternly to the barking mastiff. "We've agreed to follow you. There's no need to behave so uncouthly."

Mollie paid Felicity no mind, the slobber from her enormous jaws flying as she woofed on excitedly.

"I have to agree with Felicity, old girl," said Alex, addressing the big dog as he pulled on his jacket. "There's no need for quite so much noise."

At Alex's words, Mollie stopped barking. A small whine came across as a meek apology.

Felicity raised her eyebrows at Alex. "Didn't I say she liked you?"

The area beside the lake was wooded — mainly silver birch with ghostly white trunks — and far less manicured than the other side of the lake. Mollie led the way, plodding along a rough but well-trodden path winding through the trees. The smell of decomposing leaves rose from the ground, and the occasional rustle of a blackbird or chirrup of a tit were the only sounds besides their footsteps.

Felicity blinked several times. "Are my eyes becoming accustomed to it, or is the fog here less dense?"

Alex scanned around. "We're climbing slightly, so it could be thinner where the ground is higher. Or maybe the fog is finally clearing."

"I'm hoping rather earnestly for the latter."

Alex turned to Felicity. "Would you be satisfied to leave before finding out what's really going on here?"

Felicity drew back her chin. "Well, no. But we shouldn't endanger our lives to do so."

Alex glanced at Lord Langton's mastiff. "You know more about dogs than I do, but does Mollie strike you as the sort to lead us to our doom?" He looked back at Felicity. "Perhaps she brought us all this way to visit a collection of cherished bones she's buried here in the woods."

Mollie's flapped ears twitched at the mention of her name. She stopped and turned to look at Alex, offended by his suggestion.

"Sorry, old girl," he said. "I know you wouldn't do that to us. As you were."

Her reputation restored, Mollie continued along the forest path.

Felicity smiled to herself. Then her nose tickled.

She and Alex looked at each other.

"Wood smoke," he said.

Felicity's stomach squeezed as they pressed forward. What would they find up ahead?

The track through the forest widened, and the fog continued to thin until it was threaded through the trees like gossamer. A small house appeared in the distance.

Again, Felicity and Alex looked at one another.

The dwelling was a rough, stone-built cottage with a slate roof and a squat chimney issuing curls of fragrant wood smoke. Despite the lack of garden and the absence of any decorative flourish, the cottage had a welcoming appearance and was a reassuring sight.

Mollie was first to reach the front door, which was a weathered powder blue that complemented the cool grey of the cottage's stone walls. The mastiff pushed the door with one of her great paws, as though expecting it would open, which it didn't. She sat down, her thick short-haired tail sweeping the forest floor, and let out a powerful bark.

Felicity, with a bright and alert Pip still in her arms, arrived behind Mollie with Alex as the door opened. Alex had one hand in his jacket pocket, likely in contact with the Belgian revolver.

A man in braces with his shirt sleeves rolled up appeared in the doorway. He looked to be around sixty, and his full-headed hair was of the purest white. Lean and sturdy, he was an outdoorsman by Felicity's estimations, but slightly too old and rather too rugged to be Lord Langton.

"Mollie," said the man with both delight and chastisement in his tone. "You've been gone rather a long time." As the big dog barged past the man's legs and went inside, her tail still wagging, the white-haired man looked up at Felicity and Alex. "And you've brought friends with you, I see." As he spoke, he opened the door wider to reveal a shotgun resting over his forearm. "And who might you be, if I may be so bold as to ask?"

The man was well-spoken and polite, with only a slight Devonian twang to his accent. The revelation that he was armed didn't unnerve Felicity, for the gesture had been more defensive than threatening. She therefore didn't hesitate in replying to him, as she knew from experience Alex sometimes lacked subtlety, and Felicity was of the firm opinion that it was always best to meet politeness with politeness.

"I'm Lady Felicity Quick, journalist with the Western Daily News. This is my colleague, Mr Alexander Cooper, a reporter for the same newspaper. I was to interview Lord Langton this morning."

The white-haired man's face was unreadable. He'd not yet heard enough.

Felicity continued. "I suppose it doesn't explain why I'm at the door of your very charming cottage, but it explains why I was at Langton Manor. We crossed the lake and came through the woods because... Well, because Mollie asked us to."

Felicity looked at Alex to confirm her story, which he did with a curt nod.

The white-haired man peered at them both for a moment, taking in their muddy shoes and the Yorkshire Terrier clutched to Felicity's chest. Then he slowly took the shotgun off his arm. "You must consider me deeply rude, your ladyship, and I can only apologise," he said, leaning the firearm beside the door. "His lordship is rather shaken, as I'm sure you can imagine, and I'm under instruction to take no chances."

Felicity flashed a glance at Alex. Lord Langton was still alive.

"His lordship mentioned the interview," continued the white-haired man, "and he's most sorry to have missed the appointment. Please, do come in." The man stood aside and held the door open with the efficiency and grace of a well-trained butler.

"Thank you."

As she and Alex stepped inside, Felicity did her best to hide her glee at an important element of the mystery at Langton Manor untangling itself before her.

The interior of the cottage was as practical as it was homely. A handful of framed photographs and a few hunting trophies, including a rather impressive set of stag's antlers, hung on whitewashed walls. The ceiling was low slung with oak rafters stained dark brown. There was a circular table with an old-fashioned red-and-white floral tablecloth on it and four mismatched but finely made wooden chairs around it. A small kitchen area complete with stove and basin was positioned under a set of windows looking out into the forest.

On the opposite side of the room, there was a smoke-stained granite fireplace with a small fire popping in the grate. Beside it was a single shabby wing chair. In the chair sat a grey-haired man with his head in his hands. At his feet lay Mollie.

"M'lord," said the white-haired man as the newcomers entered the cottage.

The man in the chair looked up. His warm brown eyes were haunted and jumpy, but there was no mistaking the similarity both to Derek and the portrait of Teddy. This was Lord Langton.

"Lady Felicity Quick and Mr Alexander Cooper, m'lord. From the Western Daily News."

"Gracious," said Lord Langton, rising to his feet and revealing a stature reminiscent of Clarissa's and Ursula's statuesque proportions. He had on dark blue trousers and a matching waistcoat with a pale blue shirt underneath, but his jacket was grey tweed and ill-fitting, and he wore no tie at his neck.

"It's a pleasure to meet you, Lady Felicity." Lord Langton approached her and Alex and shook their hands, his face a mix of disbelief and decorum. "And to see you again, Mr Cooper. I only wish it were under different circumstances. How on earth did you find me?"

"We were brought here." Felicity looked down at Mollie. The big dog yawned and stretched out on her side in front of the fire, her work for the day done.

Pip struggled in Felicity's arms, clearly interested in joining Mollie in front of the fire. She pulled him tightly to her and stroked his head.

Lord Langton looked down at the mastiff, his hands on his hips. "It's a sorry state of affairs when one's only genuine friend is one's dog." He looked up and nodded towards the white-haired man. "And Clegg, of course."

"M'lord," responded the faithful Clegg in acknowledgement of being Lord Langton's second-most faithful companion.

The name Clegg wasn't entirely unfamiliar to Felicity. If she was not mistaken, it had been mentioned earlier and featured in Lord Langton's will.

"Worst thing that ever happened to me," continued Lord Langton, addressing no one in particular, "after my wife Marigold's passing and poor Teddy not coming home from that wretched war. Should never have allowed you to leave me, Clegg, old chap, but I couldn't begrudge you your retirement. You'd been so very good to me for all those years."

"Shall I prepare a pot of tea, m'lord?" said Clegg, nudging Lord Langton out of whatever funk he was disappearing into.

"Oh, why, yes. Splendid idea." Lord Langton turned to Felicity and Alex. "Clegg used to be my valet, you see. An absolutely indispensable fellow. Really top notch. So I gave him this cottage when he retired, as I couldn't bear the thought of him being far away from me. And I was right, really, wasn't I? Anyway. Excuse me, where are my manners? Please, take a seat. Ah. Lady Felicity. I see you're a woman after my own heart when it comes to trustworthy companions." This last comment came upon Lord Langton noticing Pip under Felicity's arm.

Felicity looked down at Pip and smiled, all her misgivings about the Yorkie's presence and her own shortcomings as his mistress swept aside for a moment. "I wouldn't be without him."

That there was only one chair by the fire was politely overlooked by the cottage's visitors as Lord Langton retook his position in the wingback, and Alex fetched two wooden chairs from the round table, first for Felicity, then for himself. Clegg brought over a small side table, which he carefully set down next to Mollie before adding the tray of tea to the top of it.

Lord Langton crossed his long legs at the knees and watched the goings-on with a vigilant gaze, thanking Clegg for pouring milk then steaming tea into an elegant albeit chipped china cup. Felicity was fizzing with questions for him. A sobering look from Alex reminded her it was important not to bombard Lord Langton with enquiries. He'd been through a lot, and he had to be allowed to tell his story in his own time.

Having to wait didn't diminish Felicity's excitement, however. Such an interview was precisely what she dreamed about whenever she imagined herself working as a crime reporter. And now here she was.

Lord Langton's hand shook a little as he lifted the cup to his lips. Having taken a sip, he sighed. "I'm terribly sorry to have missed our appointment at the house, Lady Felicity. It's been quite a day, I can assure you."

Felicity nodded with understanding and thanked Clegg for the tea he had set beside her. "Please, don't apologise."

"I'm certain we can't imagine what you've been through today," added Alex.

"'Been through'?" Lord Langton let out a nervous laugh. "I suppose that's one way of putting it. Although I'm not sure it's over yet."

Felicity shifted in her seat. The opportunity was not one she was willing to miss. "Would you be at all offended if I were to make notes, Lord Langton?"

"No, of course not. You're a journalist, aren't you? I wouldn't want to stop you from doing your work."

Felicity slid her pad from the pocket of her skirt and clicked her silver pencil into the ready position, resting the pad on her lap beside Pip. "Would you be willing to explain to us what happened to you today?"

Lord Langton exhaled as he wiped a hand over his grey hair. "Let me start at the beginning."

Chapter Twenty-Nine

Perched on the edge of her wooden seat, Pip on her lap, Felicity took down Lord Langton's words in well-practised Pitman shorthand.

"I'd been out with the dog," he began, shifting uncomfortably in the worn wing chair beside the fire. "Mollie and I walk together every morning. After that, I went to my rooms to get ready for my appointment with you, Lady Felicity. Splendid idea of Frida's, of course, to get Oswald in the papers. It's not every day one's interviewed, but aside from that, there was nothing abnormal about the morning. I was quite relaxed while finishing up at the washbasin. Mollie was at rest on the bathroom floor. She enjoys the coolness of the tiles after a stiff walk. That blasted chap, Greenwood, was in the dressing room. He was supposed to be readying my jacket. Said it had dog hair on it or some such. Naturally, I thought nothing of it. He was my valet, after all. It was when I'd taken up a towel with which to dry my face that it happened, and it all happened in a moment."

Lord Langton still held his tea, but his hands shook so much the cup jumped in its saucer.

Clegg came across from the kitchen area to make a well-timed interruption. "Let me take that for you, m'lord."

"Thank you, Clegg." Lord Langton exhaled deeply and sat up

straighter as Clegg put the tea on the side table. “Mollie barked. That’s what alerted me to it. She’s rather vocal, as you may have noticed, but she’s forbidden from barking indoors, as it quite terrifies some of the younger domestics. Anyway, I turned around—” Lord Langton’s eyes widened, as though he were watching it happen again “—and he was coming for me.”

“Your valet, Greenwood?” asked Felicity.

Lord Langton’s cheek twitched. “Yes. Him. I saw something flash in his hand. I didn’t know what it was at first, but the fact Mollie had alerted me to his approach unnerved the blighter. We locked eyes for a moment, then he lunged for me.”

Felicity raised her eyebrows. It was the stuff of nightmares. The trust one put in one’s servants was immense. Felicity looked upon most of the staff at Bradley Court as a form of family.

Lord Langton continued. “With the element of surprise gone, we were on a more even standing. I was with the army in South Africa, you know. I’ve fought at close quarters. I can disarm a man if it comes down to it.”

Felicity nodded as she continued to write in her brisk shorthand.

“Mollie got stuck in as well, but she only bit through the rascal’s sleeve. Her breed can be a little unruly, so she was trained from a pup to handle people with care. Greenwood clearly knew she wouldn’t hurt a fly. But she did what she could for me, bless her soul.”

Without lifting her head from the ground at his feet, Mollie raised her eyes to her master. Lord Langton looked lovingly down at her. The bond between them was strong.

“What weapon did Greenwood have?” asked Felicity innocently.

“A hypodermic needle.” Lord Langton enunciated each syllable with careful bitterness. “With heaven only knows what in it. I got it off him all right, but the swine wouldn’t give up struggling with me. He’d been so gentle up till then. Meek, even. But with his face twisted and his teeth bared, I hardly recognised the fellow. He clearly wasn’t who he’d pretended to be. He seemed absolutely set on doing me in. That’s when I realised it would be Greenwood or me. So, as soon as I got him on the back foot, I stabbed the needle into his leg and pushed the plunger all the way in. It caused him a great deal of pain. The chap was doubled over, but I couldn't risk waiting to see what would happen next. Mollie and I went out of the dressing room, to the end of the corridor, and down the servants' stairs. I was hardly thinking at all at that stage, as you can probably imagine, but one thing was clear in my mind. Get to Clegg, I kept telling myself. He'll know what to do. I can trust Clegg."

Felicity glanced at the faithful Clegg, who'd returned to the kitchen area. He'd found some pots that needed washing, but his ears must have been positively burning.

"May I ask a question?" Alex looked between Felicity and Lord Langton.

Felicity nodded. Alex's style of questioning could be blunt, but Lord Langton seemed to have no problem being open.

"Be my guest, Mr Cooper," said Lord Langton.

"Why did you not inform some other member of the household about what had happened?"

"How could I?" Lord Langton looked from Alex to Felicity in disbelief. "Don't you see?"

"See what, Lord Langton?" pressed Felicity.

"If I couldn't trust my own valet, who else in the household could I possibly trust?"

"Could you not have trusted Oswald?" asked Felicity, careful to not let her excitement at getting close to the nub of the problem show in her voice. "Or your sister?"

Lord Langton sank back in his chair and shook his head wearily. "That's just it. I can't fathom it. I simply cannot fathom it. I mean, that Greenwood fellow can't have been working on his own, can he? I didn't even know the man before he came to Langton Manor."

"Do you have any thoughts about why someone would want to harm you?" enquired Felicity carefully.

A pained smile flickered across Lord Langton's features. "Oh, there's not a single member of the household I haven't had a run-in with at some point. You see, I've been thinking things through since I got here. Thinking through every single interaction over the years. I arrived here at the cottage in shirtsleeves and in quite a state, I can tell you. Clegg gave me his jacket, but I could hardly speak a word at the beginning. All I could do was run things through my mind, trying to get a grasp on why it had happened. I suppose it was the shock of it all." He dropped his head into his hands again for a moment, then looked up. "Tell me. That Greenwood fellow. Is he... Is he..."

Alex nodded gravely. "I'm afraid so."

Lord Langton leaned back in his chair and wiped his hands over his face. After a spell of silence, he spoke quietly. "It's one thing to kill a man in battle. It's quite another to be forced to do so in one's own bathroom."

As Lord Langton sighed deeply, Felicity shared a concerned look with Alex. Neither of them wanted to pressure their interviewee into speaking further. He was shaken by his ordeal.

After a further silence, Lord Langton smiled sadly. "You know, Marigold would chastise me for my lack of generosity. Since her passing, I don't think I've been a very kind person at all. I've not honoured her memory particularly well. She used to say I was hard on Derek. Since Teddy's passing, I suppose that's only got worse."

Again, the finger of suspicion swung towards Derek. Felicity raised a subtle eyebrow at Alex. He narrowed his eyes at her, as if to refute this.

There was only one way to find out.

Felicity spoke gently. "Do you suppose the change in your will is related to the attempt on your life? You say it could be anyone, but the timing is quite a coincidence."

Lord Langton looked up and blinked. "Derek, you mean?"

"Well." Felicity became flustered. Had she been too blunt? "I didn't quite mean that."

Lord Langton shook his head. "Marigold would have berated me for even thinking this, let alone saying it, but Derek simply wouldn't be capable. He's not tactical enough. He lives by the day. By the hour, even. That's the whole problem with him." The peer shook his head again. "No. Not Derek."

"Did anyone else stand to lose out from the new will?" pressed Felicity, still writing everything down.

"Not really. Ursula's inheritance was unchanged. I reduced Clarissa's bequest rather considerably, but increased the cash going to her son Oswald, which is where it would have all ended up, anyway. Clarissa's older than me, and neither of us are spring chickens anymore, as I hope you can appreciate. I calculated that Oswald, now he has his own family to worry about, could make better use of the funds."

"Could Clarissa have—"

"Oh, poppycock," said Lord Langton with a wave of his hand to emphasise how ridiculous he found Felicity's proposal before she'd even finished making it. "My own sister, try to kill me?"

Felicity smiled uncomfortably, as if making light of the suggestion she hadn't been allowed to complete. But even if Clarissa hadn't done anything about the reduction in her bequest, that didn't mean the over-protective Miss Blanchard wouldn't.

"You have no suspicions about your family members, then?"

"No," said Lord Langton rather firmly, folding his arms across his chest. "Out of the question."

Felicity glanced at Alex. It seemed he'd been waiting for her signal.

Alex leaned forward in his chair. "But you said you couldn't trust anyone?"

Lord Langton lowered his eyebrows. "None of them are independent from those closest to them. Although Frida is a dear. When she's feeling all right, that is."

Alex nodded. "Then who, beyond your immediate family, stood to gain from the old will remaining in place?"

There was a pause. Lord Langton frowned. "No one."

Felicity continued writing in her notebook as Alex went on. "Then how can you rule out your family from the list of suspects?"

Again, Lord Langton waited before speaking. "I know my family. I know what they're capable of. And what they're not."

There was a pause before Alex spoke again. "Derek recommended the valet Greenwood to you, did he not?"

It surprised Felicity to hear Alex presenting his supposedly good friend as a potential suspect. Had Alex changed his mind?

Lord Langton narrowed his eyes. "You've already been doing your research, I see."

"Were you aware," continued Alex, "that it was Derek's companion, the singer Miss Elodie Rossignol, who recommended to Derek that Greenwood be put forward to you?"

Lord Langton's stare was hard. "No, I was not aware."

"Is there a reason Miss Rossignol might have wanted to harm you?"

"Your guess, Mr Cooper, is as good as mine."

The atmosphere was becoming stony.

Felicity switched to an apologetic tone. "We're awfully sorry about putting all these questions to you, Lord Langton."

"Not at all," said Lord Langton brusquely. "You're journalists, aren't you? It's your job to ferret out the truth. Unlike many members of the peerage these days — your brother being an exception, Lady Felicity — I happen to be a businessman. In order to make the right decisions for my business interests, I rely on good information. Where do you think I'd be if it weren't for the daily newspapers? It'd be hypocritical of me to object to you simply fulfilling your role in society."

Felicity nodded. Although she wasn't a proud person, to be reminded of the importance of the journalist's role made her sit up straighter.

Then she remembered something.

"I understand that in your current will, you're to leave some antiques and pieces of art to a variety of people. Is that set to change in your new will?"

"Who told you..." Lord Langton's forehead creased towards his grey hair. "Pieces of art?"

Felicity swallowed. She didn't particularly want to admit to having looked at Lord Langton's will. "Art and antiques. To several people in your household, including servants."

"Art and..." Lord Langton trailed off. "I'm sorry, Lady Felicity, but I'm sure I haven't the foggiest idea what you're talking about. The house and its contents go to Derek, in both my old will and my new one."

"Oh," said Felicity. She'd only read the old will quickly. The list of paintings, vases, and so on had certainly been in the document, as well as the names of the people Felicity had assumed the items would go to. Perhaps she'd misunderstood the list's meaning? It seemed unlikely Lord Langton, an astute businessman, would forget about the details of his own will.

Lord Langton sighed heavily. "In any case, I'm going to have another look at that old will and perhaps reassess the new one. Now that this fog's clearing up, I'm going to have Clegg and Mollie escort me down to North Exridge. They've had one of those newfangled telephone boxes installed on the village green. I shall telephone my solicitor at Fenwick & Graham and tell him to meet me at the cottage. That will be after I've telephoned the police, of course, although I imagine they've already been informed of the situation at the manor."

Felicity nodded. "Oswald telephoned to the police not long after my arrival."

"And your solicitor arrived after the fog settled," added Alex.

Lord Langton tipped his head to the side. "He did? Well, I never. I'd simply assumed he wouldn't have been able to make it through the fog. Mr Graham's getting on in years and his vision's rather bad at the best of times, but there's no one else I trust with matters of legacy."

"Oh, it's not Mr Graham," said Felicity. "It's a Mr George Palmer. A man in his forties, I'd say."

She turned to Alex for confirmation, and he nodded.

Lord Langton frowned. "Never heard of the chap. How very odd that they'd send someone else. In any case, I'm certain we'll get to the bottom of things soon enough. You're most welcome to wait here with us. The fog seems to be clearing, but it'll still be thick down in the village. It's in a valley, you see, and after what happened to me this morning, I'm not venturing out again till I have full visibility. I'm sure Clegg wouldn't mind preparing another pot of tea for you."

"That's awfully kind, Lord Langton," said Felicity. "But I would quite like to head back to the manor."

Alex turned to Felicity with mild disbelief.

Felicity stroked Pip. "I've my motor there, you see." It wasn't a lie, but neither was it the whole truth behind her motivation for wanting to return to the big house.

Alex narrowed his eyes at Felicity, but she ignored him.

Lord Langton sighed. "Very well. I suppose it's not you they were trying to do away with. I'd still advise caution, however. I could be wrong, but it seems unlikely that blighter Greenwood was working alone. Could we perhaps offer you a firearm of some sort to take with you, in case you come across some ne'er-do-well lurking in what remains of the fog? Clegg's quite the marksman, as his trophies attest."

Felicity turned to Alex. There was puzzlement in his dark blue eyes. For once, he didn't know what she was thinking, but Felicity's thoughts were clear. She had a plan.

Chapter Thirty

There was a route back to Langton Manor that didn't involve crossing the lake. Clegg had explained well, so it was easy for Felicity and Alex to follow, although he'd neglected to mention it involved navigating through vast patches of overgrown rhododendrons.

To their right, the lake was visible through the trees, the vague outline of Langton Manor on the other side of the water. Finches chattered in the branches, and above, the sun was a dull milky-yellow ball. Everything was pointing to the fog lifting. They needed to hurry if Felicity's plan was to work.

Alex, who was leading the expedition back to the house, manhandled yet another waxy-leaved branch from a monster-like rhododendron off the path.

"I may be wrong," he said, "but I feel we're returning to the house to do more than simply collect your motor."

Alex had set off with Felicity from the cottage without questioning her intentions. While it was true Felicity wanted to do more than simply collect her motor, she had no plan to get into any trouble.

She'd made the extremely difficult decision to leave Pip behind at the cottage. The diligent Clegg and loyal Mollie could be trusted to take care of Felicity's beloved canine companion, and she had no intention of dallying at Langton Manor. She would return to collect Pip as soon as possible, but it was safer for the Yorkie not to accompany her on this occasion. Just in case.

"And it's my feeling," said Felicity, moving as quickly as she could over the rough forest path behind Alex, "that you already know what the reason is. Otherwise, you wouldn't have agreed to go with me."

Alex glanced back at Felicity, narrow-eyed and smiling. "Something to do with Lord Langton's old will, isn't it?"

She nodded. "I suspect there's something not quite right about it."

Alex lifted his brow. "And the solicitor?"

"The same."

"On whose orders is he?"

Felicity climbed over a fallen tree trunk. "I've yet to work that out. But by my estimation, with the fog cleared, and perhaps even before news reaches Langton Manor that Lord Langton is very much still alive, there's a strong chance the solicitor and the will shall both disappear."

Alex frowned a little as he held another rhododendron branch aside. "And what if they've already disappeared by the time we've arrived back at the house?"

Felicity had considered all her options. Inaction wasn't one of them. If her assessment of the situation was correct, she was the only person who knew enough to make a difference.

"That might be the case," she said, "but we'll at least have tried."

"Tried to do what? You still haven't told me."

"The will I saw. I'm going to take it."

Alex turned again to Felicity, his face serious. "What if it turns out to be the genuine article?"

"Then I'll explain myself to Lord Langton. I'm sure he'll understand. He's a believer in the power of the press and has a healthy respect for our profession. But I'm rather convinced it's a fake."

"While I'm pleased to hear Lord Langton helped you regain your faith in journalism, I'm not sure what pinching a piece of evidence has to do with being a reporter."

Felicity took a deep breath. She was coming to terms with the idea that Jasper wouldn't allow her to continue with her career at the Western Daily News. She'd disobeyed him far too much. Perhaps she'd find work on another paper? The matter wasn't yet resolved in her mind, but Felicity was certain of one thing: being a good journalist meant seeking the truth.

"I'd hand it over to the police, of course, but if nothing's done, there's a good chance of the will being destroyed. Without it, the probability of the mystery being solved decreases. Then the full details of the story might never be known."

And whoever endangered your life by firing those shots in the fog would also go unpunished, she thought, but she didn't say it. It was too sentimental.

Alex ducked under the branch of a crooked birch. "And how do you propose we go about this?"

Felicity smiled to herself, not insensitive to Alex's use of *we*.

"We need the secretary's office to be emptied. It's likely Mr Cherry and the supposed solicitor will still be in there. Once they're gone, one of us can sneak into the room and take the will out of the solicitor's briefcase. Then we'll meet at my motor at the front of the house, and as soon as the fog has cleared enough to drive, we'll speed away."

Felicity longed to be back in the familiar seat of her cream-coloured Alvis saloon. Her run out to Langton Manor that morning felt like a hundred years ago.

Alex peered over his shoulder at Felicity. "May I ask where the air pistol fits into this plan?"

Before leaving the cottage, Felicity had given careful consideration to Lord Langton's offer of a weapon. She'd hardly ever used a gun. There was only the occasional illicit try on her brother's air rifle as a young girl. Alex still had the Belgian revolver, but Felicity turned down the offer of one of Clegg's rifles as it wouldn't have made for a subtle re-entrance into the manor house.

On the other hand, even though she didn't expect to use it, it seemed unwise to turn down the option of a concealed weapon, just in case. Thus, the Webley air pistol with its wooden handle, which Clegg said he used for ratting, swung in the pocket of Felicity's skirt.

"The air pistol doesn't fit into the plan," she said. "It's only for if there's an emergency. Not that I expect it to do much damage, and not that I expect an emergency."

"It can do enough harm." Alex glanced back at her, his face still serious. "Are you prepared to pull the trigger?"

"I don't expect to," said Felicity dismissively. It wasn't a situation she cared to consider in any great detail. "But for my plan to work, we'll need to split up."

As they approached the edge of the lake, the path widened, and they could walk side-by-side as they approached the great house, its large shadow looming in the thinning fog. They reached a sandy path edged with neatly clipped box, just as Clegg said they would.

Alex crumpled his scarred brow as he considered the prospect of splitting up. Without his support, Felicity's plan would come to nothing.

"Very well. We'll split up. But on one condition."

"What's that?"

"Either we persuade Jasper to allow us to share a byline for the story," said Alex with a shrewd smile, "or he'll get no scoop at all."

Felicity was getting a tour of Langton Manor's formal gardens, although not in the way she would have liked. Careful not to be seen from the house, she and Alex passed parterres full of nodding purple verbena, yellow-petaled rudbeckias, and clouds of white and pink asters, all swathed in strands of mist.

Upon reaching a dense yew hedge twice Felicity's height, through which an arched doorway had been formed, they paused.

"What will you say to draw them away?"

Alex nodded decisively. "Leave it to me. I'll think of something."

Felicity nodded in reply. "Good luck."

"You, too," said Alex, and he disappeared through the yew arch.

Felicity was now alone, separated from Alex and from Pip. Her stomach squeezed. She took a calming breath.

Yes, there were dangers, but they had taken precautions, and her plan avoided direct confrontation with anyone. What Jasper would think was far from Felicity's mind. Action had to be taken — both she and Alex were aligned on that point — and if their efforts weren't to be for nought, she needed to hurry.

Felicity peered through the yew arch.

Langton Manor's impressive facade with its regular, unfussy windows and even rhythm of chimneys across its roof gave the impression of calm and order. The chandeliers of the ballroom glowed dimly through the thinning fog. Felicity didn't want to risk being seen, so she moved towards another break in the yew, coming to a paved path lined with lilac Michaelmas daisies spilling from stone urns. Happily, the path was not well overlooked by the house.

Felicity hurried past the lilac daisies, crossed the sandstone terrace — doing so on tiptoes so as not to make a sound with the heels of her mud-stained shoes — and arrived at Langton Manor's facade. She then edged along the side of the house, ducking to avoid being seen through windows, until the clouded-glass hanging lamp and bookcases of Jacob's office came into view.

She stopped a small distance from the office's French doors, which were ajar. The voices of the two men within the room were muffled to begin with, then one of the voices began approaching the French doors.

"—step outside to smoke." It was the man claiming to be the solicitor.

Felicity's heart jumped into her throat. There was nowhere for her to hide. How would she explain herself?

Before Felicity could fathom a plan, a loud knocking came from within the office, followed by more muffled voices.

"Well, yes," said the solicitor. "Of course. Right away."

And to Felicity's relief, his footsteps receded.

She heard a door close, then waited until there were no further sounds from within the room.

Slowly, she peeked through the window. The study was empty. Alex had fulfilled his part of the plan rather splendidly, and Felicity slipped into the office.

The solicitor's small, brown leather briefcase was still on the herringbone floor next to his desk. She lifted the bag onto the desk, undid its fastenings, and opened the flap. There were only two sheets of paper in the briefcase, and they were the two pages of Lord Langton's supposed will that Felicity had seen earlier. Besides the will, there was nothing else in the briefcase.

Her heart rate quickened. This was certainly not the briefcase of a real solicitor.

She slipped the pages out of their leather pocket. She needed to work quickly, but she couldn't resist running her eyes over the text. Her recollections of what she'd seen hadn't been wrong. Besides the bequests to direct family members, many presumably valuable items — paintings, vases, even tables and chairs — were being left to a long list of people. The butler, the footman, and both valets were mentioned, as were Jacob, Sebastian, Elodie, Frida, and Miss Blanchard.

But why?

Felicity froze. There were footsteps in the corridor, which stopped just outside the office door. The brass doorknob slowly turned.

It was too late for Felicity to run, so she straightened her back and steeled herself, ready to face whoever would come through the door.

Chapter Thirty-One

Only a slight flicker in Sebastian's tanned face and a momentary pause in his movements betrayed his surprise at finding Felicity, will in hand, in the secretary's office.

Felicity swallowed and lowered the document to the desk in front of her to prevent any tremble in her hand from being noticed.

Sebastian closed the door behind him, his eyes on Felicity. "Well, well, well."

"Mr Ridgeway," she said as politely as possible, but it was abundantly clear they were beyond the boundaries of polite behaviour. Sebastian's elegant, confident movements were no longer charming and suave. They were calculated and snake-like.

Felicity hadn't noticed the coldness of his gaze upon meeting him, and she chastised herself for this. There was no time to try to fathom Sebastian's motive. Felicity's plan had hit a snag, and in the worst possible way, but she wouldn't give up. She couldn't. Alex had delivered on his part of the plan, and she would deliver on hers.

A charming yet frustrated smile played on Sebastian's lips as he crept closer, his footsteps tapping on the waxed wooden floor. Felicity was eminently thankful there were two large desks separating her from Sebastian. The thought crossed her mind to make a dash for the French doors, but two considerations kept her feet glued to the spot.

She should under no circumstances turn her back on a viper like Sebastian — who, she remembered, had taken a pistol for the ill-fated armed search party — and now, more than ever, she definitely wanted the will.

Sebastian ceased his approach and put his hands into his elegantly tailored trouser pockets. He glanced at the will, the corner of which was still in Felicity's grasp.

"I see we came here for the same thing." An oily smile spread over his leathery face. "I knew you were onto something, but I'll be honest. I hadn't realised you'd figured things out this far. My little jaunt in the park with your dog and Blanchard's gun should have put you off, but apparently, you're a more ruthless reporter than I thought."

Felicity took a steadying breath and kept her gaze fixed on Sebastian. She didn't want to give into her nerves, and her brain was firing on full power as the pieces of the puzzle shifted. When Alex had gone into the fog to rescue Pip, he'd found the little dog on a high wall. Had Sebastian put him there? And were the shots fired intended not for Derek but to scare Felicity? Had Derek's injury indeed been an accident?

"And it seems you have that Cooper fellow wrapped around your little finger, doing your bidding."

The mention of Alex tied Felicity's stomach in a knot. Had he been found out as well? Was he in danger? Felicity did her best not to allow her alarm to show on her face.

Sebastian shook his head as though thoroughly amused. "What can I say? As a charmer myself, I must offer you my admiration. I've been an absolute fool, though. If I'd worked you out earlier, I might have had a better chance of getting away with things more neatly. As it is, we're going to have to make rather a mess, aren't we?"

Felicity didn't quite know what Sebastian was getting at, but she knew she could be brave. And so she would be.

She nodded thoughtfully, looking down at the will. "Well." She returned her gaze to Sebastian with a slightly irritated-sounding sigh.

She tapped a finger on the will. "In all my time working undercover, I've seen nothing quite like this."

Sebastian's suave expression gave way momentarily to a confused frown. "Undercover?"

Delighted at having so easily ruffled her adversary and feeling not an ounce of guilt at telling lies to someone so duplicitous, Felicity continued. "Oh, yes. Women are too often underestimated, overlooked, and ignored. Or, in some cases — yours in particular, I believe, Mr Ridgeway — exploited and misused."

Sebastian grimaced, clearly uncomfortable with Felicity turning the tables on him. "What are you getting at? Undercover for what?"

Felicity had perhaps gone too far. She didn't want to anger Sebastian to the point of taking action. Her target was to buy time until either she thought of a method for extracting herself and the will from the situation unharmed, or for someone else to discover the bind she was in.

She adjusted her approach.

"I came here to interview Lord Langton about the transition of power to your step-brother, Mr Oswald Ridgeway. I would have carried out the interview had I been able to, but surely you've realised by now that wasn't the real reason I came to Langton Manor."

Something of a smile had returned to Sebastian's face as he recovered from his initial surprise. "What, pray tell, was the real reason you came here, Lady Felicity? Was it so your spoiled little lap dog could play with that pampered rat of Clarissa's?"

It disgusted Felicity to hear what Sebastian really thought of Clarissa and Charlotte, but she didn't allow it to distract her. "I came here for another story altogether. A story about—"

She stopped. Again, there were footsteps in the corridor. More than one person this time, and none of them attempting to conceal their approach. Sebastian must have worked with the dead valet and the fake solicitor. How many other accomplices did he have? Was there any chance of reinforcements arriving to support Felicity?

"A story about...?" Sebastian lifted his eyebrows condescendingly. The return of his swagger showed he was unafraid of the approaching footsteps. Felicity might soon be outnumbered. She would have to think fast.

There was a hard rap at the office door and no waiting before it swung open. The man in the long coat and trilby standing in the doorway wasn't a member of the household or one of the guests, yet Felicity recognised him.

"Lady Felicity," said Chief Inspector Luscombe of the Devon County Constabulary. "You're just whom I was hoping to see."

Behind the chief inspector was Alex. A weight lifted from Felicity's chest at seeing him safe and unharmed.

"I thought we might find Lady Felicity in..." Alex's voice trailed off.

Sebastian had used the distraction at the office door to remove a semi-automatic pistol from his pocket, and he was pointing it at Alex and Chief Inspector Luscombe.

Somehow, Felicity kept her cool. There was no point in panicking. She had to think.

"Now, now," said the policeman as he slowly raised his hands. "Let's not do anything silly, Mr Ridgeway."

"Silly?" said Sebastian. "Oh, I'm not that type."

"We've got your pal," continued Chief Inspector Luscombe. "The man claiming to be Lord Langton's solicitor. Been after him for a while, as a matter of fact."

"Oh, I couldn't give a fig about that," said Sebastian coolly. "You can keep him." He swung his gun towards Felicity. "I have other plans."

Remaining as calm as possible, Felicity began raising her hands, but she'd not completed the gesture when Alex stormed forward.

"You scoundrel!"

Sebastian turned his head, but it was too late. Alex tackled him, pressing his arm so that the gun was aimed away from Felicity and towards the windows.

"How dare you!"

Felicity could no longer remain calm. She couldn't just stand by and watch.

Chief Inspector Luscombe stepped into the corridor. "Hopkins, Piper. In here. Quick."

Crash!

The crack of the air pistol going off in Felicity's hands disappeared into the sound of the glass ceiling lamp shattering into a million pieces. It was a dreadful and beautiful sight as glass shards flew like the sparkle of fireworks.

For the briefest of moments, Alex and Sebastian paused their scuffle. Alex's gaze went straight to Felicity, as if to check she was unhurt. Sebastian, Alex's grip on him loosened, took the opportunity. He dashed past Felicity, barged through the French doors, and flew outside, his long legs carrying him at a rapid pace across the terrace through the thinning fog.

"After him," ordered Chief Inspector Luscombe as two uniformed officers went charging through the study, their boots crunching over broken glass, the chief inspector following them out onto the terrace.

Felicity half-expected Alex to go along with the chase, but he didn't. He remained fixed in position on the other side of the desks, breathing hard, looking at Felicity.

The air pistol slipped from her hand and fell with a *thwack* onto the herringbone floor. It had likely dented the woodwork, but Felicity hadn't been able to prevent it.

"You gave him quite a shock." Alex bent over a little and rested his hands above his knees, his dark blond hair fallen onto his forehead. "Me too, if I'm honest."

Felicity tried to take a step towards the oak swivel chair in front of the desk before her, but she ended up staggering backwards. "I gave myself rather a fright as well," she said, feeling increasingly light-headed as the seriousness of what just happened landed upon her.

She thought she might slump to the ground before she could make it to the chair, but Alex joined her on the other side of the desk and moved the chair towards her, making it easy for her to sit down.

Felicity sighed with intense relief as the swivel chair took her weight. "I still don't understand it. Do you really think Sebastian would have had Lord Langton killed for a painting and a couple of vases?"

Alex leaned against the desk and gestured towards the will. "Do you mind if I take a look?"

Felicity pushed it across the desk towards him. "By all means."

Alex picked up the two sheets of paper, his serious dark-blue eyes scanning the lines of text.

He shook his head and replaced the document on the desk. "It seems that way, doesn't it?" He looked towards the open French doors. "I suppose we might have a chance of finding out more if the police are quick enough to catch him."

"I half expected you to chase after Sebastian," admitted Felicity.

Alex lowered his eyebrows. "What, and leave you on your own? I'll not make that mistake again."

"Can I not be trusted to be by myself?" said Felicity, more amused than offended. "You're beginning to sound rather like my brother."

"Jasper's not that bad, is he?"

Felicity pressed her lips together. "Well," she began, but before she could muse over what Jasper would have to say about everything, there was an awful noise from outside, like the smashing of glass and the thudding of wood and the crunching of metal all rolled into one.

Felicity and Alex looked at one another.

Chapter Thirty-Two

Sunshine streamed into the ballroom. The tall mirrors amplified the glitter of the gold leaf on the plaster mouldings, the crystal pendants on the chandeliers glowed, and the sun sparkled on the lake outside. Beyond the water, trees danced lightly in the breeze, their leaves edging towards autumnal shades of orange and yellow.

It had become a gloriously bright afternoon. In her seat by the fireplace, Felicity basked in it. The sun's warmth was, however, at odds with the mood of some of those gathered.

Clarissa, with Miss Blanchard and Charlotte, Oswald and Frida, with James and his nursemaid, and Derek and Elodie were once again assembled in the ballroom. This time, though, there was a uniformed policeman standing by the door, there was no game of mah jong, the butler and the footman were collaborating on the removal of the large floral arrangements that Clarissa had ordered be taken down, and a handful of people were absent. Alex was in the billiard room giving his statement to the police, Jacob was in his office attending to urgent business, and Sebastian was, of course, also elsewhere.

After fleeing with the police in pursuit, Sebastian made it to the front of Langton Manor, where he jumped into Felicity's beloved two-seater Alvis and attempted to use it as a getaway vehicle. His escape came undone when Sebastian swerved to avoid colliding with a police van and crashed Felicity's motor into one of the mighty beeches lining Langton Manor's drive.

Having reduced Felicity's cherished Alvis to a crumple of cream coachwork and tan leather, Sebastian attempted to escape on foot but was quickly surrounded by police officers. Both Sebastian and the fake solicitor were now on their way to the police headquarters in Exeter.

Because of her motor's tragic accident, Felicity had to request that the Quick family's driver, Finnegan, collect her. Jasper had taken the telephone call. He didn't sound very pleased, but beyond reassuring her that the family's Rolls would be sent to collect her and that her own car would be repaired or replaced, he'd not said much else. His full judgement was yet to come.

While Felicity had already given her statement to the police and was free to leave Langton Manor, she needed to wait not only for Finnegan but for Pip, who was being fetched along with Lord Langton from Clegg's cottage by the police.

Felicity looked forward to returning to the familiar surroundings of Bradley Court, where she would ask for hot buttered crumpets and a large mug of cocoa to be sent to her room. On the other hand, returning home meant an audience with Jasper, and that was something she was happy to delay. It was also fascinating to bear witness to the reactions of the household to the unravelling of the mystery, which was now just about solved.

"What an awfully terrible mix-up."

Clarissa sat on one of the ballroom's pale grey-green sofas, cooling herself enthusiastically with a black lace fan. With her other hand, she compressed Charlotte into her lap with repeated caresses. On one side of her rested her walking cane, and on the other side sat the ever-sombre Miss Blanchard, who had once again taken up a piece of needlework upon which to concentrate her hard, grey gaze.

"My poor Sebastian," continued Clarissa.

Felicity was seated on the sofa opposite Clarissa, sipping from a cup of tea. Next to Felicity sat Ursula, whose expression was grim.

"Now, now, Mother," said Oswald, who was in a straight-backed chair close to his mother and held a content-looking James on his knee. "Sebastian's not the victim in this situation, remember."

Clarissa paid her son no heed. "The poor boy must have been in a state of utter confusion when he attempted to drive away in Lady Felicity's motor. And that police van that ran poor Sebastian off the road must have been going so very fast." Clarissa's fan fluttered harder. "Someone could have been killed. The police ought to be more careful. Really, they ought."

Ursula rested an elbow on the arm of the sofa and put her fingertips to her blonde temple. "Auntie, please."

From a chair opposite, Derek frowned at Oswald in disapproval of Clarissa's comments. It was refreshing to see the cousins in agreement. Even Elodie, who was slouched in a chair near to Derek, had a peaceful smile on her face, and Frida, standing with an elbow delicately resting on the mantelpiece, watched the scene with serene alertness.

Felicity calmly took a sip of tea. She was doing her best not to be upset about her motor, a trifling matter in the grand scheme of things, and she didn't find Clarissa's denial of Sebastian's wrongdoing offensive. Clarissa would come round to the truth in time. And even if she didn't, there was nothing Clarissa could do to stop her beloved stepson from facing justice for his crimes.

Oswald handed his son to the nursemaid. She took the gurgling baby to his mother to receive a kiss on his plump cheek before walking with him across the ballroom to look out of the windows at the fog-free gardens.

"I don't believe we can blame the police for anything that's happened here today," said Oswald with a sigh. "We should be thankful they arrived when they did."

"And we should be thankful to Lady Felicity, really, shouldn't we?" Frida took her arm off the mantelpiece and approached Oswald's chair. "Without Lady Felicity's intervention, we might never have got to the bottom of things."

Felicity smiled politely but did nothing to further encourage discussion of her actions.

Clarissa frowned at Frida.

Oswald looked up at his red-headed wife as she perched on the arm of his chair. "You're quite right, dear. We owe Lady Felicity our thanks. And Derek an apology."

Derek waved his hand. "Water under the old bridge, Ossie. You've apologised to me ten times already. Can't we forget you ever said those things?"

"I must agree with Frida," added Ursula, perking up. "I hate to admit to underestimating a fellow female, but Lady Felicity's bravery has been inspirational."

Felicity continued to smile, wrinkling her nose.

Except for the destruction of her motor and her brother's impending judgement, Felicity was supremely pleased that her plan to seize the will had gone as well as it did. But she couldn't take full credit for Sebastian's arrest — nor the fake solicitor's — and she wasn't remotely interested in recognition for her actions.

She cleared her throat. "I believe we should be grateful to Mr Cooper. It's thanks to him a tragedy was avoided. And as Mr Ridgeway rightly says, had the police not arrived when they did, who knows what might have happened? I'm certain we can trust in the Devon County Constabulary to sort everything out as it should be."

Clarissa sighed abruptly and folded away her fan. "I'm terribly sorry, Lady Felicity, but I'm not at all in the right mood for socialising. Do forgive me. Miss Blanchard—" she turned to her companion "—I'm going to retire to my room." Pushing herself to her feet, Clarissa tucked Charlotte under her arm, and with her hand shaking on her walking cane, she began towards the policeman at the ballroom door.

Miss Blanchard folded away her needlework and rose dutifully. "So that you know, I would have let nothing happen to Mrs Ridgeway. And as long as I live, I will not."

Oswald lifted an eyebrow, as did Ursula. Speaking without first being addressed, Miss Blanchard had taken everyone aback.

"Miss Blanchard." Clarissa called to her companion, and she went willingly to the ballroom door.

Derek leaned back in his chair, his long legs in their plus fours crossed at the knee. "Thank goodness for Miss Blanchard. I'm not sure Auntie realises quite how lucky she is."

Oswald watched his mother and her companion leave the ballroom. "No, I don't suppose she does." He turned back to Frida. "I'm happy those two rascals were caught, but I'm not sure we can claim to have quite got to the bottom of things."

Elodie's face creased with confusion. "Why is Clarissa lucky? Her sweet Sebastian sits now in jail."

Derek turned to his companion. "Don't you see, darling? If Sebastian was willing to bribe a servant to do away with Father, there's no telling what kind of danger Aunt Clarissa was in. The man was a snake." Derek turned sharply to his cousin. "I'm sorry, Ossie. I do realise he's your half-brother."

Oswald shook his jowls decisively. "You call the scoundrel whatever you like. I'll not be offended, that's for certain. People used to say our father was a bad egg, but he was a gentle soul compared to what Sebastian is clearly capable of."

"But I still don't understand it," said Frida. "Sebastian was only to inherit a vase or two upon Lord Langton's demise." She looked from Oswald to Felicity. "Did he really try to arrange a murder just for that?"

Felicity gave a polite little shrug. She had her theories, of course, but it wasn't appropriate to speculate before the police had carried out their investigation.

"What do you think, Lady Felicity?" urged Oswald. "You saw the faked will, didn't you?"

Ursula and Derek were also looking at Felicity. This time, there was no Alex to save her from the spotlight, and no Pip to stroke for comfort. With the family looking for answers, it could be considered rude not to oblige.

Felicity placed her teacup carefully on its saucer. "Despite the seemingly small bequest to Sebastian in the false will, I do believe money was at the heart of it."

"I should have known it," muttered Oswald.

"The antiques," continued Felicity, "although small in the grand scheme of things, weren't worthless, and they would have been immediately available. It's possible Sebastian needed direct access to cash."

Derek huffed. "He certainly did a number on me during that card game. Insisted I pay up on the spot, as well."

Felicity nodded. "Then, I'm sorry to say, there is also the matter of the Honourable Mrs Clarissa Ridgeway's will to consider. During my time here at Langton Manor, I heard her say two things in this regard, namely that Sebastian was mentioned in her will, and that her bequest from Lord Langton would be reduced in his new will. It was possible, as I believe Miss Blanchard was somehow aware, that Sebastian had Mrs Ridgeway in his sights as his next victim."

Ursula looked pale, as if she'd just received a shock. She took a deep breath. "I feel awful about it, but Sebastian asked me for money. On more than one occasion. And I gave it to him. I didn't see the harm, but I wish now that I'd told someone."

Derek leaned forward. "We were all duped by him, Sis. In one way or another."

"The valet, Greenwood." Oswald was frowning with concentration. "What was his motive to get involved?"

"Money," said Elodie. "I am certain of this. He had debts. I did not know him well, but I felt sorry for him. He worked in a nightclub, but it did not pay enough. That is why I named him for this job." She turned to Derek, her face twisted with sadness. "But I regret it. I really do."

Derek extended his hand to Elodie, which she eagerly took. "Darling, how could you know? It's not your fault. You were simply trying to do an unfortunate fellow a good turn. You mustn't blame yourself."

"If Greenwood was bribed," said Oswald, "where does the scoundrel posing as the solicitor come into it?"

Felicity nodded thoughtfully. "It's a good question. Whoever he was, he was already known to the police. That might lead one to suspect Sebastian had ties to wider criminal activities, but I suppose we shan't know for sure until the police are further with their investigations."

Felicity distinctly remembered the accusation Miss Blanchard had made about Sebastian supplying drugs to Elodie, but it didn't feel right to bring that issue up in case it upset the peace between Derek and Elodie and the rest of the household. The police would do whatever work needed to be done in that regard.

"Sebastian asked me for drugs, you know." A tear rolled down Ursula's cheek as she spoke. "From my laboratory. Said he had a war wound keeping him awake at night. I gave them to him, but then he asked for more. More than he would have needed just for himself. But I refused to see it." She took a handkerchief from her pocket, dabbed at her eyes, and turned to Felicity. "I kept all his letters, you know. He even spoke to me about marriage. It was our little secret. Oh, he had me right where he wanted me, didn't he? I've been played for an absolute fool."

Felicity took Ursula's hand and squeezed it. Ursula had seemed so strong and self-assured. Her vulnerability didn't diminish Felicity's respect for her, but Ursula's admissions were further proof of Sebastian's diabolical skills as a manipulator.

"He deceived everyone," said Felicity soothingly. "You mustn't blame yourself."

Oswald took Frida's hand and briefly kissed her knuckles. "I'm just glad he didn't do more damage to our family."

The butler entered the room and approached Felicity. "Your driver's here, your ladyship."

"Thank you. Would you please tell him to wait? I can't leave until my dog has been returned to me." While Felicity wasn't enjoying being separated from her Yorkshire Terrier, she was glad Pip hadn't been with her for the events in the secretary's office.

As the butler and footman worked in tandem to refresh everyone's tea, Felicity considered how a newspaper story might do justice to the crimes that had occurred while respecting the private lives of Ursula, Derek, Oswald, and the rest of the household.

Not that it would be Felicity's call.

She'd written on delicate topics before, but there was no chance Jasper would allow her to write up the affair at Langton Manor. She'd be lucky to keep her position at the newspaper. She only hoped that whoever wrote the article would be sensitive to the needs of the family. The Langtons and the Ridgeways needed time to recover from what they'd been through.

"Will you be writing this up for the newspaper?" Although still red-eyed, Ursula seemed calmer with a fresh cup of tea in her hands. She also seemed to know what Felicity had been thinking. "I realise you were meant to interview Father, but I suppose this whole debacle will make the front page."

Ursula was right. It was a huge story, and Felicity wanted to be the one to write it. Desperately so. But the idea was nothing more than a fantasy.

Felicity shook her head. "I'm not a crime reporter, but my colleague, Mr Cooper, is. He will likely be the one to write it up."

Ursula gave Felicity a little smile. "Sometimes women have to fight twice as hard for the recognition we deserve."

With a hint of sadness, Felicity returned the smile. "You have a point," she said, but it was her status as Jasper's little sister more than her status as a woman reporter that held her back most.

Jacob entered the ballroom. "I'm s-sorry to interrupt," he said, approaching Ursula. "I've been on the telephone to the travel agent, Miss Langton. They've changed your booking on the b-boat train for Sunday, but should you wish to stay longer, they'd be happy to move the booking again."

Ursula sighed shakily. "Thank you, Mr Cherry. I expect Father will need some extra support over the coming days, and I want to be here for him."

"You're m-most welcome, Miss Langton." Jacob looked at Ursula with devotion beyond that of a faithful household secretary. "Is there anything else I c-can do to be of assistance?"

Ursula declined the offer, and Jacob withdrew but didn't go far, finding a place for himself beside the grand marble fireplace.

Felicity raised an eyebrow at Ursula.

"What?" Realising what Felicity was alluding to, Ursula swatted a hand at her. "Oh, it's not like that," she said in low tones.

"Isn't it?"

"You can talk."

Felicity blinked innocently. "What?"

"Please. Us women are clever creatures, but that doesn't always prevent us from being blind to what's in front of us."

Before Felicity could make sense of what Ursula was saying, there was a familiar scrambling of paws at the ballroom door, and Pip burst into the room, launching himself at Felicity and yapping with a mixture of distress at having been separated from his mistress and delight at finding her again.

Felicity scooped the little Yorkie onto her lap. He whimpered and licked her face.

"Steady on there," she said, astounded by the outpouring of emotion, which wasn't usually Pip's style. "Although I must admit, I'm very happy to see you, too."

Hot on Pip's heels, Mollie came bounding into the room, her thick tail wagging hard. She went to Ursula and then to Oswald and Frida for copious head scratches, but she kept her distance from Derek and Elodie. The lack of affection was clearly mutual, but while Derek was watchful as the mastiff made her rounds of greeting, he at least remained calm at the big dog's return.

"Father." Ursula rose from her seat.

Lord Langton had entered the ballroom with Clegg at his side. The tweed jacket he'd borrowed from his former valet had been replaced by his suit jacket, and he cut an imposing figure, tall and stiff, his hair steel-grey, his face stony.

With a click of Lord Langton's fingers, Mollie went to her master and sat to attention next to his feet.

"That's right," said Lord Langton, sounding more than a trifle displeased. "I'm back."

Chapter Thirty-Three

An awkward silence descended on the ballroom, broken only by the sound of Pip still scrambling around on Felicity's lap, trying to lick her face.

While Clegg's expression was inscrutable — Mollie's, too — Lord Langton scowled as he surveyed the gathered family members.

Oswald got to his feet. "Uncle Edward—"

"Father," Ursula moved forward.

Lord Langton held up a hand. "Do give me a moment. I have something to say to you all."

His eyes fell on Derek, who had remained seated and now bristled under his father's gaze.

Felicity did her best to calm Pip and have him sit quietly. She'd naively assumed Lord Langton's return would be a moment heart-warming enough to set right all wrongs, but the unease was as fascinating as it was painful.

The nursemaid brought James to Frida, and the red-headed woman cuddled the gurgling baby to her shoulder. "I suppose you'll be signing the new will now." There was a quiver in her voice.

Lord Langton's dark brown eyes were tinged with sadness as he looked at his daughter-in-law. "Not quite."

Clegg and Mollie remained motionless as Lord Langton moved forward, stopping in front of his son.

Derek's face was hard, his arms folded over his chest. Elodie looked up drowsily from under heavy lashes.

Lord Langton towered over his still-seated son. "Derek," he said solemnly.

"Father." Derek's reply was icy.

"I owe you an apology," said Lord Langton.

Derek's face softened for the briefest of moments, but he met his father's admission with silence.

"Sitting in Clegg's cottage gave me time to think. Almost meeting one's maker forces one to look at things somewhat differently. I've not been the best of fathers to you. Certainly not since Teddy died, and perhaps not even before that. I believe your mother would be ashamed of my behaviour towards you, were my darling Marigold still here."

Derek's eyes widened, and he swallowed. He was doing his best not to show it, but his father's words made him emotional.

"Things are going to change." Lord Langton looked over his shoulder at Oswald, who appeared surprised but not desperately so. "Not to anyone's detriment." He looked at Ursula. "But I'm going to be a better father to my children. That's a promise I've made to myself."

Derek remained silent, though his bottom lip trembled. Elodie reached out and clasped his hand.

Satisfied with his son's silent reaction, Lord Langton mussed the pale red hair of baby James and, just as Alex arrived in the ballroom accompanied by Chief Inspector Luscombe, turned to face Felicity.

"Lady Felicity, I'm forever in your debt."

Felicity met Alex's gaze, and he raised his eyebrows at her as she struggled to her feet, Pip wriggling in her arms.

"I'm incredibly touched," Felicity told Lord Langton. "But whatever for?"

"I heard the lengths to which you went to get hold of the will. It'll be easier to secure convictions with evidence like that in our hands. Your efforts shan't be forgotten."

"I must insist that Mr Cooper—"

Alex cut her off. "Lady Felicity's plan was thoroughly clever," he said, stepping forward. "And perfectly executed. I'm privileged to have had a role."

Ursula nodded.

Having opened her mouth to disagree, Felicity closed it again. "Thank you," she said, both to Lord Langton and Alex, who smiled proudly at her. "But we really mustn't forget the efforts of the Devon County Constabulary," she added, with a nod in Chief Inspector Luscombe's direction.

"All in a day's work," said the chief inspector unsentimentally. "Are you ready to speak to us, your lordship?"

Lord Langton looked at his children and his nephew. Then he nodded. "I'll come along if I can bring Clegg and Mollie with me. I'll not be without these two at my side for a long while yet, I can assure you. Thankfully, Clegg's agreed to return to my service, at least until I can find a new valet. And I'll be looking much more carefully this time."

Clegg nodded his white head dutifully. He didn't look unhappy about being called out of retirement. Then again, he didn't look happy about it, either.

"You may do it however you like, your lordship," said the chief inspector, and he accompanied Lord Langton, Clegg, and Mollie out of the ballroom.

Gazing down at Pip and with a small sigh of reluctance, Felicity said, "I suppose we best be leaving."

"You're welcome to stay with us as long as you like, Lady Felicity," said Oswald. "I'm certain Uncle Edward would have no objection to that."

Frida approached, bouncing the happy little James in her arms. "Please, do stay on a little longer."

Derek was out of his seat and approaching Alex. "What do you say we go into town when the police are done with us? Blow off a little steam?"

Felicity shook her head at Oswald and Frida. "I really ought to return to Bradley Court. My grandmother and brother will be eager to see me." And there was no point delaying the inevitable. She would have to face Jasper's judgement.

"That doesn't sound like an absolutely terrible idea, Derek, old chap," said Alex. "But I was hoping I might have a word with Lady Felicity before she leaves." He stepped towards her. "May I escort you outside?"

Ursula raised an eyebrow, which Felicity found misplaced. She and Alex had agreed to work together. They had a story to discuss.

"That would be splendid, Mr Cooper," she said. "Thank you."

The late afternoon sun lit the front steps of Langton Manor with warm golden light and urged the honey-like scent of buddleja to release into the air. In the distance, the gentle contours of the moors had reappeared. The fog had cleared completely.

Alex placed Felicity's white leather photography case on the top step. "Oh, dear," he said. "Probably best if you don't look."

"Don't look at—" It was too late. "Oh."

Drawn up on the gravel at the bottom of the steps was the familiar and reassuring sight of the Quick family's shining dark blue Rolls-Royce, its driver, Finnegan, stepping out from the driver's seat. But beyond the gravel, tyre tracks carved in deep red mud over bright green grass led to Felicity's beloved two-seater saloon.

If it weren't for the tan leather of the upholstery and the cream-coloured carriage work, the motor would have been unrecognisable. It was crumpled against one of the tall, old beeches lining Langton Manor's driveway. In a stroke of luck for any birds living in its branches, the tree had come out on top. Miraculously, Sebastian had walked away from the wreckage.

Alex winced at the destroyed vehicle. "I'm sure they'll fix it up for you."

Felicity nodded. "Jasper said the same." There was a hint of self-pity in her voice.

But while it was crushing to have one's first motor so thoroughly desecrated, Felicity was aware the outcome could have been much worse. Lord Langton had been found safe, and the perpetrators of the crimes against him would face justice or, in the dead valet's case, the worst form of punishment had already been served. The destruction of her cherished Alvis had helped prevent Sebastian's escape. Knowing that helped enormously.

Alex put his hands in his waistcoat pocket. "Is that all Jasper said?"

Felicity had been trying to put her brother out of her mind, but she wouldn't be able to do so for much longer. "Just about. Why?"

Alex paused. He looked down at his Oxfords, which, although still a little muddy, had survived their adventure intact. "Well, none of my business, really, but he's rather protective of you, isn't he?"

Earlier in the day, Felicity had been fully committed to keeping herself out of harm's way. Now, she was pleased and — if she was completely honest — even slightly proud of the role she'd played in unravelling the mystery at Langton Manor.

"He can be." Felicity also looked down. The mud had been removed, but the soft grey leather of her one-straps was stained an unfortunate and irreparable shade of reddish brown. "Apart from my shoes, I'd say I came away unscathed. I'm feeling quite tired, though."

"At least you don't have to drive yourself home." Alex nodded to Finnegan, who touched his hat to Felicity as he ascended the steps to collect Felicity's white leather camera case.

"Good afternoon, my lady. Mr Cooper."

A cool breeze blew, making the leaves of the beech trees hiss and the rudbeckias in the borders nod their yellow heads. Although reunited with her dove-grey top coat and matching musketeer hat, a shiver of goosebumps spread across Felicity's skin. She pulled Pip tightly to her chest. He yielded to her embrace, almost asleep.

Then something occurred to her. She was being extremely rude. "Do you intend to return to Exeter?" she asked Alex. "Shall we run you over there in the Rolls?"

"Not yet." Alex glanced over his shoulder towards the manor's interior. "I intend to keep things smooth with Derek. Plus—" he tapped the breast of his jacket, where he kept his reporter's notebook in the inside pocket "—I have a little more investigating to do."

Felicity smiled weakly, thinking of her own rather empty notebook. She had known from the start that this would be Alex's story. "I suppose you'll get the front page."

Alex frowned. "We'll get the front page, you mean?"

He was just playing with her, but Felicity wished it were true. They didn't agree on everything, but apparently that wasn't necessary to work well together.

"Did you discover anything about the fake solicitor?" Even if Jasper wouldn't let her report on it, Felicity was still keen to understand the crimes that had taken place.

There was a twinkle of self-satisfaction in Alex's gaze. "The chief inspector wasn't keen to talk, but I came across a detective I met in Lower Diddleton. The solicitor was indeed a wanted man, known to the police as Mr Johnny Francis."

Felicity stroked Pip's head. "Should I recognise the name?"

"I'd not come across it before, but apparently, Francis was being sought in connection with some rather serious offences. Offences related to the trafficking of illegal drugs, in fact."

Felicity's eyes widened. "Your story. The one you went undercover for."

Alex nodded, his excitement obvious in his barely suppressed smile.

"What connects Sebastian with Mr Francis?"

"Francis says Sebastian owed him money. A significant sum. They knew each other from time spent in Ireland during the war. It was a popular spot for men avoiding conscription. Neither of them served in the trenches."

So Sebastian had lied about that as well.

Alex continued. "Sebastian had sold him a scheme that hadn't quite come through. Related to the supply of drugs, no doubt, although I didn't hear that from the police."

"You might want to speak to Ursula," suggested Felicity, "but please, be gentle with her."

"Thanks," said Alex, his excitement replaced with seriousness. "I will do."

Felicity turned things over in her mind. "I suppose the artworks and antiques in the fake will were some kind of payment to Mr Francis, something they could get their hands on immediately."

"I was thinking the same. Some of those antiques are worth a pretty penny. And all the other names were to throw everyone off Sebastian's scent, so he could escape with the bounty and sell them on before suspicions were raised. Who would have questioned the distribution of all those items had the plan worked and Lord Langton died?"

A quiver passed down Felicity's spine. "I suppose if the value of the vases and paintings bequeathed to Sebastian weren't enough to keep our fake solicitor happy, then there was always Clarissa's will. We know from Clarissa herself that Sebastian was mentioned."

"Thank goodness we'll never know how things would have played out." Alex smiled. "And Lord Langton is right. That's mostly thanks to you."

"Oh." Much to her displeasure, a blush rose to Felicity's cheeks. "I'm really not sure about that."

She started down the steps towards the Rolls rather abruptly, gripping Pip to her chest and going a little faster than her Spanish heels could comfortably carry her.

"I really must be getting along," she called back to Alex. "I look forward to reading your story in the paper tomorrow." It would have perhaps been polite to ask Alex when she might see him again, but any such idea was now abandoned in favour of departing for Bradley Court as soon as possible.

Alex frowned in a combination of amusement and confusion as Finnegan held the passenger door open for Felicity.

"Cheerio, then," he called out, half smiling though still rather confused.

Felicity smiled and nodded politely in Alex's direction before placing Pip on the Rolls' seat and climbing in after him. She let out a deep sigh of relief as Finnegan took his position behind the steering wheel.

"Very sorry about what happened to your Alvis, m'lady," said Finnegan. "And you're such a careful driver, if you don't mind me saying so."

"How kind of you, Finnegan. Yes, it is rather a shame, isn't it?"

The driver's observation tickled Felicity, and as the Rolls drew away from the bottom of the steps, she smiled in Alex's direction. He smiled back and lifted a hesitant hand in a gesture of farewell, then he was gone, the sweep of the beech-lined driveway stretching out before them, the Rolls' wheels crunching over the gravel, the gates of Langton Manor visible in the distance.

On a green and red tartan blanket laid out especially for him, Pip was already curled up and snoring. Despite her exhaustion, there were so many thoughts whizzing around Felicity's head. Too many thoughts, in fact.

She fished her notepad and pencil out of her pocket and began scribbling furiously, getting down absolutely everything she could remember about the day's events, as well as her thoughts and even feelings concerning all that had happened.

She kept writing as the hedgerows, hills, and villages of East Devon flashed past the window, page upon page filling with rows of dense shorthand, until the dark blue Rolls drew up outside the arched windows and whitewashed crenellations of Bradley Court.

Jasper was waiting on the front steps.

Chapter Thirty-Four

OFFICES OF THE WESTERN DAILY NEWS, EXETER, EAST DEVON, TWO WEEKS LATER

Felicity perused that day's headlines to the soothing clickety-clack of a dozen typewriters at the Western Daily News' cramped Exeter headquarters. In a comfortable, low-slung chair outside her brother's office, Felicity sat with Pip on the lap of her rose-coloured woollen dress, the chill of autumn having settled upon the county. While Felicity did her best to hold the newspaper above the Yorkie's head, Pip's ears batted every time she turned a page.

Developments concerning the affair at Langton Manor continued to emerge, and Felicity read every column inch. Alex was doing a splendid job of reporting on it all.

Charges had been brought against the fake solicitor, Johnny Francis. Prior to his involvement at Langton Manor, he had been wanted concerning the trafficking of illicit substances. The liquid in the syringe had been tested and an autopsy carried out on the dead valet. A large dose of morphine was discovered.

Alex had connected the dots with the investigation that had led him to Langton Manor in the first place, and he even achieved acceptance from Jasper for having gone undercover without telling him. It helped that Alex secured permission from the police to publish the crime scene photos he and Felicity had taken. It was the scoop of the decade.

While nothing pertaining to drugs could yet be pinned on Sebastian, that day's newspaper explained that the Italian police had shown interest in the case. Sebastian was suspected of involvement in several cases of fraud concerning art and antiques in Tuscany and in Rome, and several Carabinieri were travelling from Italy to question him on that matter.

Felicity looked up from her paper. Alex was never at the newspaper's offices. At least, never when Felicity was.

She had questions for him about the case at Langton Manor, because there were always things journalists knew but couldn't put in print. However, if their last interaction was anything to go by — she hadn't seen him since they parted on the front steps of Langton Manor — she risked becoming inexplicably tongue-tied in his presence.

It wasn't that Felicity was intimidated by Alex. He was an outstanding journalist, but he wasn't the only writer to have sold thousands of extra newspapers through their reporting on the Langton affair.

Before Felicity arrived home at Bradley Court on that fateful day, Lord Langton had telephoned Jasper and expressed his desire to speak exclusively to Felicity about his brush with death, the treachery of his sister's stepson, and several other matters he felt it important to get out into the open.

Upon arriving home, Felicity found Jasper in a state of impotent dissatisfaction, as he was forced to make the decision any business-minded editor-in-chief would make.

He allowed Felicity to return to Langton Manor the next day to conduct an in-depth interview with Lord Langton, as well as interviews with Oswald, Derek, and Ursula. The interviews had been serialised across several editions of the Western Daily News over the past two weeks, much to the delight of the reading public and the chagrin of rival titles, who were already struggling to keep up with Alex's intimate understanding and access to matters concerning the criminal prosecution of the case.

Besides detailed eyewitness accounts of the wrongdoings at

Langton Manor, Felicity's interviewees provided personal insight that rounded the whole affair off with something of a happy ending, which had readers forming queues to buy the Western Daily News.

In response to an apology from his father, Derek had agreed to work on the Langton family business investments with Oswald, who was looking forward to spending more time with his wife and young son. Derek and Elodie had become engaged. Even Clarissa was slowly accepting that she had been duped by Sebastian. To help ease her pain, Lord Langton had allocated a rather generous budget for the redecoration of the old Victorian drawing room, which would be covered in the newspaper's society pages.

The interviews were now all published, and Lord Langton and his family had departed for a well-needed getaway on the French riviera. Felicity had already received a postcard from Ursula. She'd been trying some gentle experimental cures on Elodie to help with her drug addiction and was so far pleased with the effects. Ursula also seemed rather happy Jacob had been invited to join the family holiday.

But as pleased as Felicity was about the promising developments for the Langton-Ridgeways, there was a knot of tension in her chest. It was time for Jasper to step aside from his role as editor-in-chief and Felicity's boss and to deliver his verdict on her actions at Langton Manor as her older brother.

At least, that's what Felicity presumed Jasper had in store for her at that day's meeting. She expected sanctions, perhaps even punishment for her dangerous disobedience, yet she felt oddly calm as she perused that day's paper. She'd made her own decisions at Langton Manor and was ready to face the consequences for them. If it meant finding employment at another newspaper, then so be it. Leaving her family's title would be painful, but the Western Daily News wasn't the only paper in the southwest of England. She wouldn't be bullish about it, but she refused to give up on her career simply because her brother didn't have the stomach for it.

"Lady Felicity?"

The voice rose only faintly above the constant clacking of typewriters. Felicity looked up.

A neat young woman in a white blouse and a navy blue skirt was standing over Felicity, delicate silver-rimmed spectacles balanced on the end of her nose.

Felicity folded her newspaper away. "Miss Pearce, isn't it?" she said, rising and tucking Pip under her arm.

The woman's dark eyes sparkled. "That's right, your ladyship. I hope you don't mind my bothering you. Please, don't stand up on my account. It's just I saw you waiting, your ladyship, and I wanted to tell you how impressed I was with how you and Mr Cooper resolved matters at Langton Manor. How impressed we all were, in fact."

Felicity cast a glance across the office. A few female eyes looked up from typewriters and piles of papers. Two typists even smiled at her, though most only glanced at Felicity, too shy to hold her eye. The male journalists and clerks, meanwhile, were mostly oblivious to Felicity's presence.

"That's extremely kind of you to say, Miss Pearce," said Felicity, "but I hardly resolved anything. We were all extremely lucky that the police arrived just in time."

"We were all very impressed with your daring," continued Miss Pearce, undeterred. "And your articles about Lord Langton and his family have been simply superb. Really some of the best writing we've had on the paper in years. You understand the emotional side of things so well. There's not a lot of reporters that can do that."

Felicity lifted her eyebrows. She hoped Jasper wouldn't hear Miss Pearce calling her daring, and the compliments about her writing sounded almost too extravagant to be sincere, but Miss Pearce's honest eyes shone with what could only be described as awe.

"Miss Pearce." Jasper stood in the doorway to his office in a dark grey suit with subtle pinstripes, his chestnut moustache twitching. His voice carried an undertone of polite warning.

"Sorry, sir," said Miss Pearce without a hint of remorse and returned briskly to her desk.

Jasper stepped aside, freeing the doorway of his office. "We're ready for you now, Cici."

We?

Clearly, it wasn't to be a discussion between brother and sister. Whatever it was, she was ready for it. She had to be.

Offering a smiling glance of farewell in Miss Pearce's direction, Felicity proceeded towards Jasper's office. Her heart received a little jolt when she saw who was joining their meeting.

"Hello, Felicity." Alex stood up from his chair and smiled somewhat bashfully. He was wearing a suit in a buttery brown. It was a colour she hadn't seen him in before, but it suited him incredibly well. "It's good to see you. I'm sorry I haven't been in touch."

"I quite understand," said Felicity, as she and Alex positioned themselves in the seats before Jasper's desk. "You've been busy. So have I." Her words came out a little more haughtily than she would have liked, but as she positioned Pip on her lap — the little Yorkie insisting on balancing his paws on her knees, so that he could sit up to attention — she was pleased with how she'd responded. There was nothing of the tongue-tied about it.

What she could expect from the meeting, however, was entirely unclear.

Jasper lowered himself into his chair. "Cici, Coop," he said, leaning his elbows and wrists on the red leather inlay of his desk. "I'll come right to it."

Felicity and Alex glanced at one another. Having already met with Jasper, Alex should have had a stronger idea of where the meeting was going, but his face said he had as little a clue as Felicity.

"You're two of my best reporters. The very best, in fact."

Jasper's compliment was of the highest order, particularly for Felicity, who was relatively inexperienced compared to former Fleet Street newspaperman Alex.

Yet Jasper's delivery implied he wasn't thrilled about it. His eyebrows were drawn low, and he made no effort to reach for a pipe. "You're also two of the least tameable staff members working for the

Western Daily News," he continued. "And with the rabble I have working for me, that's really saying something."

Felicity blinked. "Tameable?"

Alex smiled, perplexed. "You make us sound like wild animals, Jasp."

Jasper glared at Alex. "You, my good friend, go undercover without even telling me first. And you, my dear sister—" he switched his stare to Felicity "—seem rather incapable of following even the most basic of instructions concerning your own safety."

Alex's smile disappeared.

Felicity had prepared herself for this. "I did what I saw as necessary at the time. Would you rather the fake will had been destroyed? That the criminals escaped justice?"

Jasper closed his eyes and drew in a slow breath. Felicity was accustomed to an amount of parent-like overbearingness from her brother, especially since their father's passing, but it wasn't Jasper's place to use techniques like exasperation and disappointment with Alex.

"I didn't call this meeting to rake over old concerns." Jasper eyed his sister with grudging patience. "We're here to find a way forward."

Alex shifted in his seat, but remained quiet. A quirked eyebrow implied he was curious to find out where this was going.

Felicity admired Alex's composure but sadly couldn't match it. "You mentioned you'd get right to the point, dear brother. Would you be kind enough to do so?"

Jasper leaned back in his chair, his eyes narrowed, his fingertips touching. "I've made a decision, and it's my final offer to you both."

Felicity's stomach sank. Were they being demoted? Was Alex in trouble because of her?

"From now on," said Jasper, "the two of you are to work together."

"Together?" Overtaken by a mixture of relief and shock, Felicity had been powerless to prevent the word from flying rather rudely out of her mouth.

Alex glanced at Felicity, then frowned. "And how do you propose that to work?"

"That's for the two of you to figure out." Jasper tapped his fingertips together. He looked pleased with himself, as though his announcement was already having the desired effect. "As you can imagine, I considered all possibilities. The fact is, no matter how much chagrin your behaviour brings me on a personal level, you're both too valuable to let go of. But it seems neither of you can be trusted when left to your own devices."

"But how would we... I mean, how do you suppose..." Alex's composure was gone. He sounded less than pleased with the new direction.

Having passed her initial surprise, Felicity came to a striking conclusion. "Is the ban lifted, then?" She did her best not to sound too eager. "Am I allowed to report on crime?"

Jasper's face again grew serious. "I will allow it on the condition that you do so with Coop."

To prevent herself leaping from her chair and shouting hurray, Felicity squeezed her elbows to her sides. She hadn't wanted to leave her family's newspaper, and while her short and so far rather intense association with Alex had not always gone smoothly, they had the potential to work well together. He was an extremely talented and experienced journalist from whom Felicity had much to learn.

Picking up on his mistress's excitement, Pip wagged his tail enthusiastically.

Alex appeared less impressed. His face was crumpled with confusion in a way that took the wind out of Felicity's sails.

He smiled weakly at Felicity, as if aware that his reaction risked causing her offence, but he couldn't hide his disappointment. "All right. Say we find a way to work together. What stories do you have in mind for us?"

"I've a few, don't worry." Jasper smiled under his moustache, clearly quite satisfied with himself. "But seeing as my sister seems to be a magnet for dastardly deeds, ranging from drug trafficking to blackmail to murder and everything in between, I wouldn't be surprised if something didn't pop up by itself."

Felicity's mouth gaped like a fish. "I'm even allowed to report on murder?"

"Not on your own, you're not." Jasper looked at Alex. "And I'm sorry, old chap, but neither are you anymore. Not for the present, at least. I must learn to trust you both again. I'm sure you understand."

Alex looked pensive. "I suppose I ought to have told you about going undercover. But then you'd have only said no, wouldn't you?"

Jasper nodded, a raise of his eyebrows showing he was not without compassion. "Sorry, old chap. Now, are you ready to hear about the first job I have for the pair of you?"

Felicity was on the edge of her seat. She'd come to the meeting expecting to stand her ground to the point of losing her job. Instead, she had earned the right to report on crime and would work with one of the best journalists in the business.

She looked over at Alex. He was deflated, but he smiled at her as though willing to make the best of it. Felicity promised herself she would ensure Alex had no regrets about their partnership.

Pip yapped, caught up in the emotion of the moment.

Felicity nodded decisively at her brother. "Yes, Jasper. We are most certainly ready."

Claim your free Lady Felicity Quick ebook!

Sign up for my email newsletter and you'll get **Murder at Afternoon Tea** absolutely free.

This exclusive story isn't available anywhere else.

As a newsletter subscriber, you'll also receive writing updates, special offers, and peeks behind the scenes...

Use this link to sign up and claim your copy today:
https://BookHip.com/XMGPNZC

Read the next in the series...

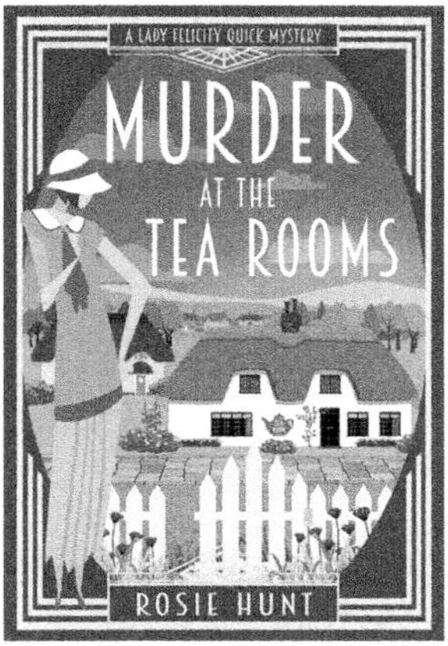

Murder at the Tea Rooms

A Lady Felicity Quick 1920s Cozy Mystery
Book 3

The Green Ginger Tea Rooms have a neatly thatched roof, scones baked to perfection, and under a lace-edged tablecloth ... a corpse!

England, 1921. On the eve of her first official assignment working with the reporter she admires most, journalist Lady Felicity Quick is more than slightly vexed when her grandmother requests a favour she cannot refuse.

Acts of petty sabotage are undermining the success of tea rooms run by a cherished friend of Felicity's grandmother. But on arriving in the village to play the detective, Felicity finds more than spilt food dye and collapsed sponges.

Murder has occurred, and her grandmother's friend is the prime suspect.

Can Felicity use her sleuthing skills to unmask the real killer and still make it in time for her special assignment? Or will Felicity's battle to outwit a deadly foe destroy not only the tea rooms' future — but also her own?

If you love puzzling period mysteries set in the charming English countryside, then you will love this cozy series! For fans of Agatha Christie, Helena Dixon, and Ann Sutton.

The Lady Felicity Quick Mystery Series

Murder at Afternoon Tea

(Novella | Exclusive for Newsletter Subscribers)

Murder on the Village Green

(Book 1 | Available Now)

Murder at a Country House

(Book 2 | Available Now)

Murder at the Tea Rooms

(Book 3 | Available Now)

Murder at the Ball

(Book 4 | Available Now)

Murder on the Coast

(Book 5 | Available Now)

Murder at a Boarding School

(Book 6 | Available Now)

Murder at a Flower Show

(Book 7 | Available Now)

Murder by the Thames

(Book 8 | Coming Soon)

About the Author

Rosie Hunt is a British author of cozy mysteries both puzzling and historical. Her books include the Lady Felicity Quick mystery series set in the green and pleasant countryside of southwest England in the 1920s.

A history addict and former journalist, Rosie grew up immersed in the worlds of Poirot and Miss Marple. This early exposure to baffling murder mysteries rather coloured her outlook on life, and it was only a matter of time before she began writing her own.

Rosie loves clotted cream, knitting, and Golden Age crime fiction, and she'll never miss an opportunity to visit a National Trust property. She lives with her husband and their four-pawed overlord on a river in Northern Europe.

Join Rosie's mailing list:
bookhip.com/XMGPNZC

Follow Rosie on Facebook:
facebook.com/RosieHuntAuthor

Printed in Great Britain
by Amazon

58088208R00148